The Evening After

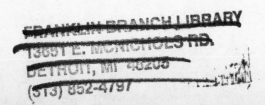
FR

MONICA McKAYHAN

The EVENING After

sepia™

THE EVENING AFTER

ISBN-13: 978-0-373-83037-4
ISBN-10:   0-373-83037-8

www.kimanipress.com

Printed in U.S.A.

For my Granny, Rosa A. Heggie.
You are special in so many ways, and the strongest woman
I know. My life is rich because of you.

Acknowledgment

God is the source of my talent and blessings.

I'm blessed to have an awesome support system—my sons, who've always given me a reason to move forward; my parents, who support everything I do; and my cousin Angel who reads everything I write and is not afraid to give me her true opinion. My family and close friends, who keep me grounded. Linda Kind, LaKashia Wilson, Teresa Barbee, Audbrey McGathy, Rebecca Harmon and Tasha Jones—you are my strong towers.

I have a wonderful editor, Glenda Howard. She has a keen eye for detail and a warm spirit. I'm blessed to know her. Margaret Johnson-Hodge, you are an awesome writer and friend, and I wanna be just like you when I grow up.

The Evening After is dedicated to the women at the Roots Hair Studio—the ones who used to have a standing Thursday-night appointment. You know who you are. Chapter 10 is for you. Antwinette, thanks for making us all look fabulous!

Because of you, Mark...life is brand-new.

CHAPTER 1

Lainey

Saturday Night Live.

That's what I called it when he'd stumble into the family room smelling like a distillery and ask, "Why you just sitting there looking stupid?" Every Saturday night, like clockwork. And if I had to listen to Marvin Gaye's "Inner City Blues" one more time, I was going to scream. But that was the routine.

I was wearing a pair of sweats and a T-shirt, my legs folded underneath my bottom, sipping a cup of hot tea and curled up with a novel that was too hot to put down. I smiled as I read about a woman who was getting more love than I could ever imagine. Books like that did wonders for a woman who hadn't felt the warmth of a man's embrace in longer than she cared to remember.

It had been years since I'd felt Don's touch. After he realized that my womb was barren and I couldn't give him the son he'd dreamed of, his interest in making love to me was long gone. And after twenty-one years of marriage, two failed pregnancies and no hope of ever having children, I learned to change the things I could and to accept the things that I couldn't.

I was a young bride, forced into marriage because I was seventeen years old and pregnant. Despite the fact that Don was a third-year law student and broke, my daddy was from the old school and insisted that we marry. His philosophy was you get a girl pregnant, you marry her. No questions asked. "And what's love got to do with it, anyway?" he'd asked. Needless to say, Don and I were victims of a shotgun wedding, with Daddy holding the gun in a cocked position, ready to pull the trigger if Don even looked like he wanted to run.

Three months after our small courthouse wedding, I had a miscarriage. Thought my world had come to an end.

"Baby, we'll get through this. We'll just try again when the time is right." Don tried to comfort me, but I wasn't convinced that I'd survive the ordeal.

"You want a divorce now?" I asked him in between tears. "I know you only married me because I was pregnant in the first place."

"I didn't marry you because you were pregnant, or because your father held a shotgun to my head." He laughed and then pulled me into his arms. "I married you because I love you."

I smiled, but knew that we needed more than just love to survive. My young husband had taken a part-time position as an intern at a prestigious law firm while he finished school, but the pay of an intern was just barely enough to make ends meet. After graduating law school, he was hired on as a defense attorney with his firm. We were able to move out of the one-bedroom matchbox we'd been calling home, and into our first real home in Alpharetta, with the manicured lawn and a homeowners association that actually enforced its rules. Three bedrooms: one of which would become the nursery for the child that was then growing in my stomach.

Don kissed my stomach and rubbed it with the palm of his hand. He was beside himself with enthusiasm.

"How's my linebacker doing in there?" he asked.

"Girls don't play football." I smiled at my husband whose face was glowing.

"I have a feeling this is a boy," he said, trying to convince himself that the football, baseball glove and toy train he'd invested in wouldn't have to go back to the store.

"What if it's a girl?"

"Then she'll be a great football player."

"I don't think so."

"I don't care what the sex of the baby is. I just pray that he or she is healthy."

He kissed my lips and at that moment I was certain we'd be just like the Cleavers, and live happily ever after.

My world came crashing down the morning I awakened to the sight of blood-stained sheets.

Another miscarriage.

Another disappointment.

Again, depression found me.

Depression found Don, too. Things became different between us. It was as if this time he blamed me for not being able to carry a child to term.

"What do you think the problem is?" he finally managed to ask one morning over breakfast. "Will we ever have a child, Lainey?"

His question begged for an answer that I just didn't have.

Months of testing confirmed that I would never be able to carry a child to term. That's when I almost stopped living, breathing. Depression found me yet again, and I found a sympathetic ear and compassion from a man who belonged to my little Baptist church where I grew up. I'd never had an affair, and I felt as if I was betraying Don by even sharing intimate conversations with Lamar Peters, a man so full of charisma. He was so easy to talk to and began to fill the void that Don left behind as he began to lose himself in his work and started working outrageous hours. I hardly saw him anymore. He started taking on the difficult cases that no one else wanted; cases that demanded a great deal of his time and energy. We lived in the same house and shared the same bed, but were strangers.

As I exchanged giggles of intimacy with Lamar on the telephone, I completely lost track of time. I hadn't even heard my husband walk into the room as I expressed my heartfelt feelings for another man; a man who I'd romanced only on the phone. He'd known all the right things to say, and had known when just to listen. He'd healed my dying soul and mended my empty heart. Was it so wrong to find comfort in such a man? Don lost it, accused me of having an affair, when the truth was I was only guilty of having a conversation…a few conversations that were leading me into the arms of a man whose charms had won my heart. But nothing ever came of it. I ended all communication and vowed to find happiness in my marriage again. Don drifted further away, and so my challenge was to draw him back.

Although Don's salary, which was well into the six figures, afforded us a lifestyle that didn't require me to work, I still needed something to do. I went back to school, finished my degree and became a public relations manager for one of Atlanta's top advertising firms. A career that demanded long hours and soon filled the void of my empty marriage and helped to diminish the depression caused by my barren womb.

I'd lost count of the number of times I'd planned on leaving Don, simply taking my half and moving on; to a place far away from his neglect and verbal abuse. It was a plan that had never materialized, but was merely a discussion that I'd had with myself on many occasions. I'd become too settled; too used to my life just the way it was. Silly me, I'd never given up hope of restoration. I dreamed of a day when I'd find my husband again, in the midst of all the chaos we called life.

I heard the rumble of the garage door ascending; the engine from his Suburban continued to run for longer than necessary. Eventually he turned off the engine, but the music was pumped so loud, I was sure the neighbors would call and complain. But they never did when Don blasted his music. Just smiled and said hello when they caught us pulling in or out of the garage.

Soon the kitchen door slammed and my smile vanished. My peace was shaken.

"He's home," I mumbled to myself, no longer able to focus on my book. I placed the bookmark inside, closed the book and pretended to have fallen asleep. The uneven, slothful patter of his size twelves on the kitchen hardwoods gave me confirmation that he'd been drinking. *Again.* Don had become too acquainted with the bottle, his drinking beginning every Friday night and ending way into the wee hours of the night on Sunday. But by Monday morning he was dressed in one of his tailored Italian suits, clean-shaven, smelling like the men's fragrance counter at Dillard's and ready to save some poor soul from life in prison.

I could hear him stumble over to the stove to check out the pot of chicken chili I'd prepared for dinner that day. The pot rattled as he removed the lid to take a sniff. I could just imagine the frown on his face, nose turned up at the sight of it, and the slam of the top that let me know he wasn't interested in tasting it.

I closed my eyes tighter as his footsteps approached. He appeared in the doorway of the family room, his six-foot-two frame falling against the wall. The smell of alcohol greeted my nose before he even opened his mouth to speak.

"Hey!" he rumbled, and I tried to ignore him. "I know you ain't sleep. And I know you hear me callin' you."

Eventually I looked up at his bloodshot eyes.

"How many times I gotta tell you I don't eat that

mess you got in there on the stove? I'm a meat and potatoes man, Lainey!"

I chose my words carefully, thinking how it's almost impossible to debate with a man who'd undoubtedly found his home in a bottle of Cognac, his drink of choice.

"There's a steak and baked potato in the oven for you, Don," I said calmly.

"And why you just sitting there looking stupid?" His famous phrase. I almost smiled, because I was expecting it.

"I was reading."

"Reading what?" He snatched the book from me. Observed the cover; lost my page. Threw it across the room. "This is stupid."

I stared at the television to keep from looking directly at him. A newscaster was giving the latest on the weather in metro Atlanta.

"Flights at Hartsfield-Jackson Atlanta International Airport are being canceled as an ice storm threatens to sweep through the city tonight. More when we return."

My interest was piqued by the headliner and I couldn't wait for the commercial break to be over to hear more about the storm. I'd heard reports that an ice storm was expected and as a result had stocked the fridge and shelves with food and bottled water that would last us for several days. Atlanta's ice storms were hardly predictable and often left residents without electricity for several days. I needed to be prepared for the worst.

* * *

"You're stupid. That's why you read stupid stuff," Don said, and his words cut through my heart as I stared at the Ford commercial advertising their new Five Hundred sedan, and immediately critiqued the ad to see if it accomplished its goal of making me want to buy a car. In advertising, you often became absorbed in your work; your creative juices consistently flowing, even while simply watching a commercial on television. I missed advertising. Don had convinced me to quit my job, claiming that he made enough money to carry us, and then some. He wanted a wife that would keep his house cleaned and have a piping-hot meal on the table when he came home from work. That is, when he came straight home.

I'd grown accustomed to Don's verbal abuse, and calling me stupid was mild compared to the other descriptive words he often used when he drank. I was afraid of leaving him. Who wants a woman who can't even bear children? "Nobody else will give you the time of day, Lainey," Don often proclaimed. I believed it. Not only that, I wasn't getting any younger.

My non-responsiveness bored him, and I was relieved when he stumbled out of the room. I heard the uneven patter of his feet again, across the kitchen hardwoods and then into the living room. Suddenly the bass from the stereo caused the sofa where I sat to vibrate and I literally felt the throbbing in my chest. I was sure that Marvin Gaye, his artist of choice, certainly had more than one song on that CD. But it was something about that track, "Inner City Blues" that made Don want to play it over and over again.

Just as the newscaster was filling me in on the details of the ice storm, Don appeared in the doorway again.

"By the way, get dressed. We have a party to go to."

"Excuse me?" I asked.

We never went anywhere together and I wasn't up for it tonight.

"My office Christmas party is tonight, and we're going. And I'm not taking no for an answer."

"Don, I'm not in the mood for a party."

"You're never in the mood for anything. All you do is sit around reading books and moping around here complaining about everything I do." He waved his half-empty glass in the air. "I'm not asking you to go. I'm telling you to go get dressed. You are not about to embarrass me by not showing up at this party like you did with the barbeque last summer. I have a reputation with these people, and they're expecting to see both of us."

"Don, I—"

"We don't have to stay long. Just long enough to make an appearance. We'll be home before midnight," he said. "Get dressed! And wear that red dress I brought you back from Honduras."

He was gone again.

When "Inner City Blues" shook the walls in our home for the sixth time, I knew it was useless to try to plead my case. Despite the approaching ice storm, I mentally prepared myself for rubbing elbows with the Who's Who among Atlanta's elite.

I prayed I could still get into my red dress from Honduras.

CHAPTER 2

Nathan

"Coach, did you see that jump shot? It was almost as pretty as mine." Nelson grabbed his third slice of pepperoni and pushed it into his mouth. "I wish we could rewind it and see it in slow motion!"

"That was a nice shot." Edwards smiled, gave Nelson a high five and almost wasted grape soda on my wife's contemporary white sofa.

"Hey, watch the furniture, man," I warned, and suddenly regretted having them in the room that was off limits for any type of human interaction. But because the television in the family room was being serviced, Marva's room was the only room in the house with a television worth watching a college basketball game on.

Marva had spent months working with an interior decorator to design our home. She justified the cost by saying that since she was turning forty, she deserved to treat herself to something nice. Although I was not crazy about the idea of spending that kind of money, I'd agreed to keep her happy. The fact that she was hitting the big 4-0 had become her excuse for everything. "Since I'm turning forty I need a new car. I've had my eye on that new Toyota Camry" and "Since I'm turning forty, I need to work out more, need to lose this stomach, and I need some new exercise equipment." And my all-time favorite, "Since I'm turning forty, I just don't feel like making love that much anymore...I have a headache tonight...I just need to rest for a while...you understand, don't you, Nate?" And I'd just roll over and mumble with disappointment; take a cold shower in the morning.

A lot of thought and energy had gone into this room with white furniture and white carpet that was hardly ever used. Marva always did have caviar taste on a tuna-fish budget. It seemed like a waste of money for a couple who lived on teachers' salaries to be splurging on such nonsense. Money was where most of our disagreements found life. And here we were with a room that was hardly ever used, even to entertain guests. When entertaining, we usually ended up in our kitchen drinking flavored coffee and playing cards until almost dawn. Or we'd hang out in the family room watching rented movies on DVD. It was rare that we entertained at all, though. Often I was too tired from dealing with hormonal teenagers and their issues or coaching the varsity basketball team at the high school where I'd worked for the past seven years. And Marva was often preoccupied with grading the papers of her first-grade class, and before our daughter went away to college, transporting her back and forth to cheerleading practice, debate tournaments, piano lessons or whatever else she had going on.

Tracee had been the center of her mother's life, and once she was gone Marva went into a shell that had me wanting to call somebody for help. She broke Marva's heart when she'd chosen Howard over Spelman or Alabama State, two schools that would've kept her closer to home. Marva must've cried the whole way back to Atlanta. It seemed that Tracee had been her whole world from the time she'd given birth until the day we transported her and her belongings to her college dorm in Washington, D.C.

I was proud that she'd chosen to move away. Spelman was too close to home, as I wanted my daughter to experience life outside of her support system. And Alabama State was completely out of the question, as she detested the mere thought of going there. I remember how often my daughter had appealed to me for help on the subject, one morning in particular when I drove her to school.

"Daddy, please talk to her. Don't make me go to Bama," she'd pleaded. "I'm not trying to go to that country school, in that country town."

"I'll talk to your mother," I'd told her, laughing. "But don't be talking about my hometown like that. I don't appreciate that."

"Now, Daddy." She'd cocked her head to the side, her long brown hair lightly brushing her shoulders. Her smile was mine, but everything else was Marva's; her light brown eyes, golden-brown skin and tall thin frame—all Marva's. "You know Alabama is country."

"Alabama is still my home, and your mother's home," I'd said to her, my finger touching the tip of her nose.

"That's where your grandparents and all your aunts and uncles live. Are you saying they're country?"

"I'm just saying I don't want to go to Alabama State." She'd cleverly avoided my question.

"I'll see what I can do," I'd promised my daughter before she kissed my cheek and hopped out of my Ford pickup.

"Bye. Daddy."

"See you later."

She'd bounced up the stairs of her brick high school building in Riverdale where her best friend, Faye, caught up to her, grabbed onto her arm and started whispering whatever it was that teenage girls whispered in each other's ears. Seemed too early to be talking about anything that was too secretive to say out loud. I watched as they'd both disappeared into the crowd of other students.

It took all I had to convince my wife to at least keep an open mind about Tracee's college choice. When Tracee finally received her acceptance letter from Howard with a full scholarship that she'd earned by having perfect grades and an amazing talent for basketball, Marva watched as Tracee and I did the bump in the middle of the floor to our own music. She tried to be happy for our daughter, but deep inside she could only focus on the empty nest that Tracee would soon leave behind. I realized it was my responsibility to fill that void, and made it my life's goal to win my wife's heart back and to build a new life with her.

It was a difficult task, though, particularly with my track record. She'd long ago labeled me unfaithful after discovering my affair with Jackie, a woman I'd met at an educator's conference in Nashville five years prior. The fling was meaningless and only lasted six months, but it seemed to take a lifetime to regain my wife's trust again. Lucky for me, forgiveness was in her heart and eventually we began to build the life that starting a family and demanding careers had robbed us of. As much as we both loved our daughter, our marriage had suffered for the years during Tracee's rearing. It was so much better after she went away to school. We became best friends again, made a new commitment to one another.

Soon Marva put my commitment to the test, suggesting that we go away for a few days during spring break, take a much-needed vacation and reacquaint ourselves with each other. She knew that spring break was a critical time for my students who had little or no supervision at home. Often they spent time with me during breaks, just as a deterrent from the trouble that awaited most teenagers during times of inactivity. I'd become more than just a teacher and coach, but a father figure to some of them. Over the years as Marva began to absorb herself into the life of our daughter, I absorbed myself into the lives of my students. They depended on me. But so did my wife, who needed me more now that Tracee was gone. She demanded that I make a choice.

"Let's go to Savannah." She'd beamed as I walked through the door. She was flipping through one of her travel magazines, her back rested against one of the oversize pillows on our bed. "Since Tracee has that new job, she's staying in D.C. and working through spring break. We could drive down on a Sunday and stay for seven whole days. Angie has a beach house on Tybee Island and she already said we could use it."

I'd stepped into our closet, hung my blazer, undid my tie and peeled my shirt off of my tired body. Couldn't wait to kick my shoes off and rest my dogs. It felt as if I'd been running up and down that court right along with my basketball team. We'd been up by four points the entire game until the end of the fourth quarter. Anderson High's forward David Carter had stolen our victory with his three-pointer in the last ten seconds of the game. Our foul led him to the free-throw line, where he sealed the deal by making both shots, leading his team to victory. And leading my boys to the locker room with shattered egos, name-calling and finger-pointing.

"Coach, we had 'em, but Collier here kept hogging the ball!" Mitchell was the king of finger-pointing and blame-shifting.

"I wasn't hogging the ball. When I see the opportunity for a shot, I'm taking it," Collier said. "If you wanna blame somebody, blame Jenkins. He the one who fouled David Carter for the third time tonight."

"And what was up with your game tonight, Freeman?" Douglas pulled his shirt over his head and used it to wipe the sweat from his forehead and then his armpits. "Man, that girl got your head all up in her butt. Got you off your game. You need to check yourself." His finger was just inches away from Freeman's face.

"Check myself? You need to check yourself!" Freeman lunged toward Douglas.

"C'mon. What you want?" Douglas braced himself for the confrontation, their faces almost touching.

"You wanna blame somebody, look in the mirror and blame yourselves instead of finger-pointing!" I yelled, slamming my fist against one of the lockers to get their attention. "Look, get into your practice clothes and get out on the court right now! I want fifty suicides from each of you."

"But, Coach, my folks are out there waiting to take me home."

"Well you go out there and tell them that I'll bring you home when you're done."

"Coach, I got homework I need to finish up," Nelson said.

"What are you doing with unfinished homework when you were in my study hall this afternoon, and you knew you had a game tonight?"

"I finished as much of it as I could."

"Go home, Nelson. You owe me ten additional suicides tomorrow at practice," I'd said. "And that goes for every one of you. Go home and get a good night's sleep, because tomorrow's practice won't be anything nice."

As I'd stood in the shower that night, I thought of how much I needed a vacation, and how I'd promised Marva we'd take one. I rubbed my eyes and tried to rid my thoughts of my draining day. Couldn't wait to hold Marva and rest my head against her chest.

"Did you have a bad day, baby?" she'd asked, closing her travel magazine once I'd crawled into bed. She pulled me close.

"That's an understatement."

"Well, come here and let me rub your shoulders."

She did just that and I promised myself I'd take a look at that travel brochure and consider her trip to Savannah. But until then, I gave in to my heavy eyelids.

"Quit hogging the ball!" Edwards yelled at the television, this time dropping his can of grape soda on my wife's white carpet.

"Oh my God, I told you to watch the grape soda, man!" All I could do was stare at the stain that seemed to be staring back at me.

"It's all right. I got it, Coach," Edwards said, and rushed into the kitchen for wet towels. "Don't even worry about it."

"That's it, everybody in the kitchen," I said. "We can watch the game in there."

"But, Coach, there's no surround sound in the kitchen," Collier complained.

"And the TV in there is only like nineteen inches," Freeman said before grabbing another slice of pizza.

"Too bad," I said as the phone rang.

I grabbed the cordless from its base as my kids piled into the kitchen around the small television resting on the countertop.

"Hello?"

"Baby, it's me," Marva said. "I'm on my way home."

"What? I thought you were staying until tomorrow afternoon."

She lowered her voice. "I got into it with Toni."

"About what?" I asked, frowning, throwing Edwards a can of stain remover I'd found underneath the kitchen sink.

"She can be so shallow sometimes. I'll tell you about it when I get home," she said. "Besides, I miss you and I want to sleep in my own bed tonight."

Marva had spent the past two days with her sorority sisters who'd flown in from all over the country for a reunion and retreat at Braselton's Chateau Elan resort, just outside of Atlanta. They were supposed to end their trip on Sunday with shopping at the outlet malls near the resort before going back to their respective homes on Sunday night. Marva's cat fight with her girlfriend of twenty years forced her to want to end her trip early, and drive home in the middle of the night, against my wishes and better judgment.

"I miss you, too, baby, but I don't like the thought of you driving home from way up there at this time of night. Not to mention there's an ice storm coming later."

"The ice storm is not due for at least a few hours. I heard about it on the news."

"It's already drizzling out there," I told her, and then walked into the room to see how Edwards was doing with the stain. Wondering how I'd explain it to my wife.

"It won't turn to ice until the wee hours of the night. If I leave now I can be home within an hour and a half, two hours at the latest."

"I'll come and get you," I suggested.

"Nate, it wouldn't make any sense for you to come all the way up here. I'll be fine."

I relented, realizing she had her mind made up.

"Be careful, then," I told her.

"I will."

"And call me when you get on the road."

"Okay."

"Matter of fact, just call and talk to me the whole way."

"I promise."

"You got gas in your car?"

"I have enough to get me into the metro area. I'll stop once I get close to downtown."

"You sure you can't work it out with Toni?"

"I'm through with her," she said. "Stop worrying, sweetie. I'll see you in a bit."

"Yeah!" One of my students' voices rang through the house.

"Who's that?" Marva asked.

"Some of the kids are here. Watching the game."

"They better not be in my room," she said. "I know that TV in the family room is at the shop and..."

"We're in the kitchen, *baby*," I said.

"Good."

"Hey, coach, you're missing the whole fourth quarter!" Collier yelled from the kitchen.

"Go finish your game with the boys, Nate. I'll call you when I get on the road."

"All right," I said, making my way back into the kitchen, cordless phone to my ear. "Love you."

"How much?" she asked, her usual response when I told her I loved her.

"More than you know" was always mine.

CHAPTER 3

Lainey

"I hate these things," I mumbled to myself as I searched for my husband, about ready to take my shoes off and carry them in my hand.

"Hi, Lainey, long time no see." Evelyn took my arm in hers; brushed my cheek with her red lips. "It's so good to see you."

"Good to see you, too, Evelyn. How're the boys?" I asked, not really caring for an answer, but knowing how much she loved bragging about her children.

"Wonderful, girl. Jason is at Georgia Tech, and Edwin Junior is finishing up his last year at Harvard."

Her husband Edwin was one of three partners at Don's law firm.

"That's wonderful." I smiled. "You and Edwin sure did a nice job with them."

"A shame you and Don could never have children." Evelyn could be so tacky sometimes, which is one of the reasons I never cared for her. "I always felt bad about that."

"Things worked out just the way they were supposed

to," I said, and then continued to search for my husband. "Excuse me, Evelyn, I need to find Don."

"Try the patio. I saw him out there with Cheryl Donaldson earlier. It looked serious," she said, her comment meant to reignite a roller coaster of emotions from a long-forgotten rumor that Don and Cheryl Donaldson were having an affair.

Don swore that it was just that, a rumor. And that the only reason it had surfaced was that he and Cheryl had been working on a case that required they spend long hours together. I knew there was always some truth to every rumor, but dismissed it anyhow.

"Thank you," I said, and headed toward the patio.

Don was there, a drink in one hand and a cigar in the other. He was talking loudly with a few of his colleagues from the firm. When he spotted me, he smiled.

"Sweetheart, come here, let me introduce you to Marvin Lewis." He all but yelled. "Messy Marvin is what I call him. He's the snotty-nosed intern who's been assigned to work under me."

Marvin looked embarrassed, but reached for my hand.

"Hi, I'm Elaine Williams," I said, and grabbed the young man's hand.

"Marvin Lewis. Pleased to meet you, Mrs. Williams. I've heard a lot about you."

"Don't believe everything you hear," I teased.

"Mr. Williams has nothing but wonderful things to say about his wife," Marvin said. "I tell him every day how lucky he is."

"Can I get you something to drink, sweetheart?" Don asked, interrupting the exchange between Marvin and me.

"No, honey. I think we should head on home." I tried whispering, but the eyes of Don's colleagues rested upon me. "It's late, and there's an ice storm coming."

"Yeah, the roads are pretty bad out there." Alvin Taylor, our friend of many years, who'd been eavesdropping, offered his two cents, and I was grateful. He smiled as if he was purposely helping me to plead my case. He knew Don well, and knew the troubles we'd experienced in our marriage over the years. "Now's a good time to head on home before it gets really bad out there."

"Who are you, the six o'clock news?" Don rudely asked Alvin.

"No, man, just concerned about your and Lainey's safety."

Don laughed with intoxication.

"He's concerned about me and my wife's safety." He mocked Alvin. "Don't worry about us. We'll be just fine. You need to figure out how to proceed with that murder case that's been collecting dust on your desk for the past week, that's what you need to do."

"Who's working the case, me or you?" Alvin asked.

"You, but I'm not sure you know what you're doing. Maybe I need to take you under my wing like Messy Marvin here," Don said, and smacked Marvin on the back. "You know you could use the expertise of a seasoned professional like myself."

"A seasoned professional." Alvin laughed, and playfully started boxing with Don as if they were in the ring at Caesars Palace.

Although they'd been friends for many years, they'd also been rivals, vying for the same spotlight as emerging young attorneys.

"You don't wanna mess with this, young man," Don teased, and then stumbled.

"Look at you stumbling. No more Cognac for this brother tonight," Alvin said grabbing Don in a headlock. "Lainey, take this fool home."

Alvin had been with the firm just as long as Don. They'd been interns in the same program as law students. Don and I had attended many functions with Alvin and his wife before they finally divorced several years prior. It had been an ugly divorce and gratefully no children were involved. Their divorce is actually what started me to thinking about divorcing Don. Thinking that Glenda had come out ahead of the game by divorcing Alvin and was now seeing a wonderful man who loved the ground she walked on.

"I couldn't be happier, Lainey," she'd confessed to me. She and I still remained best friends long after she and Alvin parted ways. "Alvin never appreciated me. Not like Robert does."

"You look happy," I'd told her.

"Well, frankly, you don't look happy at all, Lainey," she'd told me once. "Is Don really worth all the hell he puts you through?"

"He's all I know," I'd confessed.

And he was. Since my shotgun wedding to him many years before, he'd been the only man I'd ever known.

Glenda was the only one I could ever share my true feelings with about Don. She knew me better than anyone else. She knew Don for who he really was, outside of the perfect picture he attempted to paint for his colleagues.

"I hope you find happiness someday, Lainey," she'd said, and we never talked about it again.

Don handed the young valet parking attendant our ticket and he rushed to retrieve our car.

I could hear the engine from my car purring as he pulled into the circular drive of the Westin Peachtree Hotel.

"Here you go, Mr. Williams," he said, and handed Don our keys. "Drive safe. Roads are slick."

"I'll take those," I said, and tried to pry the keys from my husband's tightened grip.

"No you won't," Don said as he handed the attendant a ten-dollar bill. "I'll drive."

"Don, you've had way too much to drink."

"Who are you to tell me that I've had too much to drink?" The real Don was back. Not the one who'd called me sweetheart in front of his colleagues less than thirty minutes earlier, but the one who caused me to rethink my life on a daily basis.

"Don, I just think it would be best if I drove us home," I said sweetly, trying to make my point without an attitude. "I purposely didn't drink anything tonight so that I could be your designated driver."

"I don't need a designated driver." He opened the door and sank his six-foot-two frame into the driver's seat of my car. "Get in the car, Lainey."

"Don, please." I stood there, my red dress hugging every curve of my body, my heels killing my feet, shivering from the night air. I'd felt a headache coming on at least an hour before, but I still felt the need to take the wheel.

"You can stand there and freeze, or you can get in," he said. "I have no problem leaving you here."

I contemplated letting him drive off alone and asking the bellman of the hotel to call me a taxi. He must've read my thoughts and knew he could never leave me there and still face the people from his firm on Monday morning. How would he explain leaving his wife stranded at a company party and her having to find a ride home? His reputation was at stake.

"Get in this car, Lainey. And I'm not saying it again!" he said through clenched teeth; not loud enough to draw the attention of the other guests leaving the party, but loud enough for me to understand his lack of patience.

The only thing standing between me and a taxicab was the thought that I'd have to contend with him later. Things would be much worse after I made it home, and I wasn't up for a fight, and knowing it was a losing battle anyway. I closed my eyes a second and then walked reluctantly to the passenger's side of the car, got in and shut my door. I pulled my seat belt tightly around me as Don drove slowly out of the hotel's circular drive. He made his way down Peachtree and maneuvered the car onto 85, heading north. Once the rubber from the tires met the pavement on the highway, Don put the car into overdrive. The speedometer soared close to ninety and I held on to my seat. I closed my eyes and held my breath, and my heart pounded. I said a little prayer in my head and hoped God heard me.

When the car hit an ice patch, we slid a few feet and almost into the cement wall. The tires screeched and Don let off the gas, bringing the car's speedometer down to sixty-five, and I exhaled.

"You aren't scared are you?" He looked at me, my body stiff, and smiled that beautiful smile that had charmed me into falling in love with him many years before.

"This weather is nothing to play with, Don. The roads are slippery and I would like very much to make it home safely."

"I'll get you home safely. What're you talking about?" He laughed. "There are two things I'm great at…"

He paused a moment, as if it was my cue to ask what those two things were. But I was speechless. Could think of nothing but making it to our Alpharetta subdivision unharmed.

"I'm a great lawyer and a great driver." He looked over at me as if awaiting my response to his affirmation.

I kept my eyes straight ahead, praying he would brake before hitting the rear bumper of the car in front of us. He swerved into the lane to the right of the car and then accelerated, holding up his middle finger at the driver as we passed.

"Get out of the way, you stupid bastard!" he yelled.

He was well into the nineties range and my heart raced again. I wanted to cry or scream, but held on to my door handle, pressing my bare feet against the glove compartment as if that would make the car stop.

He turned up the volume on the stereo, which was tuned to the jazz station 107.5, Wayman Tisdale hypnotizing me with his horn for a moment. Becoming bored with Wayman, Don started surfing through the stations, keeping the car steady at ninety. Stopped his channel surfing at Atlanta's oldies station as Frankie Beverly's "The Morning After" started blaring through the speakers. He started singing along with Frankie as if he was at a Maze concert. As he got into it, the car began slowing, and I exhaled again.

When he signaled and moved toward the nearing exit, joy rushed over me.

"What are you doing?" I was hesitant about asking, but needed to know if God had heard my prayer.

"Gotta piss like a race horse," he said, and accelerated instead of slowing off the ramp.

I held on to to my seat again and prayed he was able to stop once he reached the red traffic light ahead. He stopped at the light momentarily before dashing out into approaching traffic. I could see the Chevron ahead and wanted to get out and dance at the sight of it.

"You know as long as we've had this car, this is only my second time driving it," he said. "I just wanted to see how well it could handle."

As Don approached the red light ahead, instead of him hitting the brakes, he accelerated. The tires on the car hit a patch of ice, sending us into a whirlwind. My two-seater BMW spun around and into the middle of the intersection. Don lost control of the car. It was as if the brakes were nonexistent as our car slid head-on into the silver Camry that was heading straight toward us at full speed. The two cars collided with an awful gut-wrenching sound that caused my life to flash before my eyes.

CHAPTER 4

Nathan

Beautiful cinnamon-colored skin, eyes shut, hair tousled, light snores creeping from her mouth. I watched. She looked peaceful, as if her world hadn't fallen apart a week before. My heart ached as I watched her sleep, her stomach moving up, down, and up and then down again, in a slow rhythm beneath the covers. I moved across the room, opened the blinds, let Atlanta's daylight creep in and brush across her face. She frowned, as her eyes slowly opened, resting upon me.

I didn't mean to wake her, but I was glad I did. Needed her. Needed to talk to her, to make sure she was all right. Had questions that I longed for her to answer. Wanted to wrap my arms around her and hold her nightmare away; this stranger. Her eyes were sad, and she hadn't spoken in almost a week. Just cried and slept.

"Hi," I whispered softly, and smiled.

Her eyes watched as I poured her a fresh cup of ice water, handed it to her and helped her to drink.

"How you feeling today?" I asked her.

I didn't expect an answer, because she was still in

shock; in shock from the aftereffects of an accident that had left her husband dead and my wife in a comatose state. She was lucky, or should I say blessed, to come out virtually unharmed. Just a few bumps and bruises to her forehead, her ribs had been fractured a bit, but nothing that rehab couldn't fix. The nurse assured me that she would be fine, but I made it my business each day to stop by her room to check on her just to be sure.

The first day had been the hardest, right after the accident. When I got the call. I'd held the receiver to my ear long after the woman on the other end had told me where to find Marva, and that she was still alive, but that she was not conscious. When they described her car and told me they had gone through her belongings and found her driver's license, I knew it was her. I remembered calling her cellular over and over, but she hadn't answered.

The tears had blurred my vision as I drove my truck cautiously over patches of ice in the wee hours of the morning, trying to think of the quickest route to Grady Hospital. Grady Memorial Hospital, frequently referred to as simply "Grady," is the largest hospital in the state of Georgia, and is the public hospital for the city of Atlanta. It is named after Henry W. Grady, an Atlanta Constitution journalist. Grady Hospital opened in 1912 and was for whites only at the time.

Sunday morning before 5:00 a.m., the only thing moving on those slick roads were emergency vehicles. The sabbath; a day of rest. A day that was meant for early morning service at our church, the smell of collards filling our house, and the Falcons football game that would echo through our home in the afternoon. But today there would be no church, no smell of collards and no football. Just a day of anguish.

"It's the husband," I heard someone say as they had tried reviving Marva, hooked her up to machines, tubes coming from her nose and mouth.

Her eyes were closed as if she was sleeping. I tucked my lips in tightly, my eyes wet from the tears as I stood in the corner of the room, staring in disbelief. My heart pounded in my chest—hard, rapidly. I shut my eyes tightly and said a prayer.

"Lord, please, I know I haven't been the best husband. I haven't even been the best Christian, but I need you right now. Marva needs you, Father," I pleaded. "Please let her wake up. What would my life be without her?"

What would my life be without her? It was a question that forced me to look at life and death a little more closely. A question that shook me; a question too difficult to think about. But the most difficult thing in the world to do—more so than pondering how my life would be without Marva—was how to call my daughter Tracee that morning and tell her that her mother had been in an accident and that she was in a coma.

"Oh my God, Daddy! Is she going to wake up?" Her voice was filled with fear. Her tears matched mine.

"I'm praying, baby."

"Can I come home? I need to come home."

"What about classes?"

"I'll talk to my professors. I can make up my work," she said softly. "I wanna be there, Daddy."

"Okay," I said. "Check on some airline tickets and put it on your credit card."

She was home by the end of the week.

I hugged my daughter, placed her bag into the cab of my pickup, swung the door open as she hopped inside and sunk into the leather seat of my pickup. As I slowly pulled away from the curb at Hartsfield-Jackson, I glanced over at her. She gathered her wool coat closer at the neck, and I pumped the heat up a little. She looked worried, and I knew I had to hold it together for her.

"Can we go straight to the hospital?" she asked, the look in her eyes taking me back to when she was five. The same look that had left me wanting to spend the first day of school in her kindergarten class so she wouldn't have to go it alone.

"Aren't you hungry?"

"A little," she said. "Can we just grab something on the way? Like a chili dog from the Varsity?"

"The Varsity?" I frowned, but wasn't surprised by her request. It had been one of her favorite places to eat, and one of Atlanta's oldest restaurants; an old-school Sonic Drive-in.

"I know you hate it." She laughed. "But they have the best chili-cheese dogs in the world!"

"Yeah, if you're looking for a good cleaning out."

"Daddy, that's gross!" My daughter laughed and punched me in the arm.

"But true, right?" I asked with a grin on my face. "Tell me you don't feel like you just took a laxative when you eat at the Varsity."

She laughed again, and then started shifting through the stations on my radio. She wasn't interested in listening to the smooth, relaxing sounds of Boney James blowing his horn on Atlanta's jazz station, but sought out one of her favorite hip-hop stations instead. She flipped through to 103.3, but when an advertisement came blaring through the speakers, she kept scrolling. Momentarily stopped at 104.1, Atlanta's old-school station.

"Right there," I said as Gladys Knight sang about her man leaving on the midnight train to Georgia, and the Pips harmonized in the background. "You wouldn't know anything about that."

"Who is that?" she asked. "She sounds so depressed."

"That's Gladys Knight and the Pips, girl," I said.

"Oh, I know who Gladys Knight is," she said. "I saw her on the BET awards. Plus I think she owns a restaurant here in Atlanta."

"Gladys Knight and Ron Winans Chicken and Waffles."

"Yeah, that's it," she said thoughtfully. "Speaking of restaurants owned by celebrities...I'm supposed to meet some friends at Justin's on Friday night," she said, referring to P. Diddy's place in Atlanta's Buckhead area. "You think I can get the truck?"

"We'll see," I told her, and left it at that.

She accepted the fact that I hadn't given her a solid

no, and continued to scroll through my radio stations, settling on 97.1 where an entire song was being whispered to an upbeat rhythm. It was obviously a song on Tracee's A-list, because she began to bounce in her seat.

"That is my song," she sang.

Before Tracee had gone away to school, I was up on hip-hop music. Could tell you everything you needed to know about Diddy, Beyonce and the rest of them. My daughter had kept me educated on the subject of hip-hop, but once she was gone I didn't see a need to continue with my education. Nevertheless, music had prompted many of our best conversations. I'd made it a point of knowing the things that interested her; it was a way of gaining her trust. And once her trust was gained, she talked to me about everything under the sun: music, her fears, peer pressure, boys, even sex to some degree. However, boys and sex were subjects I preferred to steer clear of. If she remained a virgin the rest of her life, that would be just fine with me. Unfortunately, the odds of that were slim, so I just blocked the thought from my mind and prayed she'd never bring it up.

"Why is the guy in the song whispering?" I asked her.

"It's called the 'Whisper Song,' Daddy," she said. "And wait till you hear the remix! It's off da hook."

"Off the hook, huh?"

"Not 'the hook.'" She corrected my slang. "Off da hook."

"My bad." I smiled at her. "Off da hook."

As I pulled into the Varsity parking lot and talked about music with my daughter, I prayed she wouldn't fall apart once we reached the hospital and she saw her mother in that state for the first time. Nothing I could've said would prepare her for such an event, so I just kept quiet.

Buffed tile floors, soft elevator music and a woman on the intercom system paging Dr. Latimore were the things that greeted us as we entered through the automatic doors at Grady. As we hopped off the elevator arm-in-arm, I spotted my father-in-law pacing the floor outside Marva's room.

"Poppa Joe?" He looked up, and I stared into his tear-filled eyes.

"Hey there, Nathan," he said, struggling to make the tears disappear as he offered me his hand. I took it and then pulled his medium-framed body into an embrace. He nearly collapsed in my arms. "I can't stand to see her like that."

It had been a week since Marva's accident and her eyes were still closed.

I had been by her side each day, morning, noon and night. Had taken a leave of absence from the school, and pretty much camped out in the Intensive Care Unit, leaving only once a day to go home, shower and check the mail. I wanted to be there when her eyes opened; didn't want to miss it for the world.

"I know what you mean," I said, and let him go.

"Who's that supermodel you got there with you, Nate?" Poppa Joe asked, flashing his pearly whites at Tracee.

Poppa Joe's graying sideburns and mustache were the

only indication of his sixty-seven years. His average height and thin frame had been passed on to Marva's older brother, Rick. The girls, Marva and her sister Darlene, had inherited their mother's light brown skin, round hips and long hair; a mane much too thick to tame. Marva was the spitting image of my mother-in-law, Helen.

"Hi, Paw Paw."

"Well, what d'you know, it's my little Poot Butt," he said, calling Tracee by the nickname he'd given her when she was three years old. "Come here and hug your old grandpa."

He hugged her tightly and kissed her cheek.

"Where's Granny?" she asked.

He let Tracee go and pointed toward Marva's room. His eyes became saddened again. Tracee slowly walked toward her mother's room, leaving me behind with Poppa Joe.

"What's been going on Poppa Joe?" I asked him.

"Not a whole lot of nothin', but a little bit of every-thang." His Alabama drawl was the same one my own father possessed. "Saw ya daddy last week. Whipped his behind on the golf course."

"Let him tell it, he let you win."

My father had already given me the lowdown on their weekly round of golf. He and Poppa Joe had been friends since their days at Alabama State. Our families had lived in the same middle-class, black neighborhood for years. Toulminville, a majority white community until around 1975 when it became eighty percent black. My home-town was one that I shared with baseball legend Hank Aaron.

Marva and I grew up on the same block, attended the

same schools. When Marva and I were married, it was as if the two families became one. Holidays with family meant one house, filled with both families as if they were one. Our mothers traveled in the same circles, playing cards and tennis, and they spoke almost daily. My father and Poppa Joe had a standing golf game each week for as long as I could remember. And went fishing nearly every day, weather permitting.

"Henry know he's a liar, and the truth ain't in him," Poppa Joe said matter-of-factly, revealing the subtle wrinkles around his eyes when he laughed. "*He let me win*. Ain't that a trip?"

He shook his head and rubbed his receding hairline. It was hard to tell which of the two men were lying or telling the truth unless you had observed the event for yourself.

"Who all is here?" I asked, changing the subject.

"Helen's in there with Marva. Rick and his wife are driving down later on tonight. I think your mama and daddy are driving down in the morning. And who knows where Darlene is," he said, pulling a package of Pall Mall out of his shirt pocket. He took a cigarette out of its package. "Goin' outside for a smoke."

"Poppa Joe, I thought you quit pumping your lungs with that stuff," I said.

"I just sneak a puff every now and then, son." He tapped me twice on my shoulder, then headed toward the huge silver elevators. "Don't tell Helen or your mama. I don't feel like hearing either one of their mouths."

He stepped onto the elevator, and as the doors shut I made my way down the hall to the beautiful stranger's room. Everyday I would drop by to check on her. Pour her a cup of water, open her blinds and let sunlight in. She'd stare at me, and I'd give her a warm smile. Silently I wondered if she had a family, and if she did, where were they? And why weren't they here loving her troubles away?

CHAPTER 5

Lainey

My heart ached each time I replayed the accident in my head, and when they told me that Don had died on impact in the crash, I was in denial. Couldn't believe what I was hearing. Thought they'd gotten the details mixed up. Don would never leave me. No matter what problems we had, and how unbearable he could be at times, he'd never leave me alone this way. He was all I had; all I'd ever known. He was my husband, and as flawed as he was, I refused to believe that he was really gone. When I questioned the nurses about it, all they offered was a soft smile and sedatives.

As tears crept down my face and blurred my vision, I welcomed the sedatives. At least the drug offered an alternative to facing the truth; a sleep deep enough to erase reality. It eased the pain. Pain from my aching limbs, as well as pain from knowing the truth. So I slept, and when I'd awaken, a handsome stranger would be staring at me in the shadows of the room. Watching me sleep, offering cool water for my burning throat. How did he know I was so alone?

"How you feeling today?" he asked, his smile as warm as the sunshine in mid-July.

I forced a smile this time, as my eyes searched the room. Red and yellow roses everywhere, a philodendron plant and greeting cards filled the windowsill. Silver balloons with bold, colorful letters of well-wishing bounced against the ceiling. He'd opened the blinds again, and had refilled my plastic pitcher with fresh ice water.

"Are you feeling better today?" he asked.

I nodded a yes, and tried to arch my back enough so I could sit up. He saw me struggling and decided to assist me, grabbed my arm gently and pulled me upward in the bed. Placed a pillow behind my back. He poured a cup of ice water and handed it to me, and delicately brushed a piece of hair away from my face with his fingertip as I drank.

"Oh my God, Lainey, we just got word. We were vacationing in Bermuda." My mother stormed into the room, a dozen lilies in a vase. Her beautiful mahogany skin looked tanned, her hair cut in a tapered style. "We caught the first flight out this morning."

She placed the vase on the nightstand next to the bed, leaned over and planted a kiss on my forehead.

"Hello, baby." Daddy was trailing behind Mother, his tall frame towering over her petite, round one. His salt and pepper hair and beard looking more salt than pepper. He'd aged in the six months since I'd seen them last. Since retirement, they'd settled in Phoenix and had been so busy traveling the country and abroad, they'd barely found time to spend five minutes on the phone with me.

Being an only child and having parents who'd found out how wonderful retirement could be, had left me dependent all the more on Don's companionship.

"Hi, Daddy," I whispered, and surprised myself by the sound of my own voice. I hadn't used it in days, mainly because I hadn't wanted to. It was much easier not to speak; somehow it sheltered me from the pain because I didn't want to talk about what happened. But something about seeing Daddy brightened my mood. His lips brushed across my cheek. "How's Daddy's girl?"

I offered the best smile I could manage. He turned to the stranger and offered his hand.

"Garrett Marshall." He introduced himself.

The stranger took Daddy's hand. "I'm Nathan Sullivan."
Nathan, huh?

"I'm Vivian." Mother took Nathan's hand. "You a friend of Lainey's?"

"I'm…my wife….your daughter…" Nathan swallowed. "My wife was in the other car that was hit in the accident."
So…that's why he's been here every day?

"Oh, my," Mother said, covering her mouth with her palm. "Is she all right?"

"She's in a coma." He strained to say it, tears threatening to do more than just fill his light brown eyes. He struggled to hold them back. "She's right down the hall."

"I'm so sorry," Mother said, and rubbed the sleeve of his wool sweater gently. That sunshine of a smile swept across his face again.

"Thank you. I've been praying," he said. "I've just been checking on your daughter to make sure she was pulling through this okay. I noticed she didn't have anyone visiting, and I didn't want her to feel alone."

"We appreciate that, Nathan," Daddy said.

"That's so sweet," Mother said, batting those long eyelashes. "Isn't he sweet, Lainey?" She turned to me and then back to Nathan. "You're a sweet young man, and I'm sure the Good Lord has heard your prayers. I'm sure your wife will be just fine."

Nathan shook his head in agreement. As if, because Mother had said it, it was so.

"Well, if you'll excuse me, I'm gonna get back to my family," he said, pointing in the direction of the door and then stuffing his hands into the pockets of his tan khakis. "It was a pleasure meeting you, Mister and Missus Marshall." That accent was definitely Southern— Georgia or Alabama. "Goodbye, Lainey."

"Goodbye," I whispered, and wondered if he heard me.

He left without another word. Mother started tidying up things around the room.

"I spoke with Don's mother this morning." She shook her head and pursed her lips. "So tragic, baby. I know this is all so horrible for you. They're having a memorial on Saturday. They're waiting for the rest of his family to get in from Chicago and New York. Gloria said she would've come out here to check on you, but she doesn't get around too well these days. Got arthritis in both her knees and…"

Don's mother, Gloria, my mother-in-law, was never one of my greatest fans. She'd written me off long ago because I hadn't been able to produce any grandchildren.

I was the opposite of Don's sister who was popping them out every three years or so. But it was her son who she'd wished could produce her a grandchild. Particularly a son, who would carry on the family name.

I closed my eyes as the pain returned; the pain that the sedatives had only temporarily relieved. Tears streamed down my face.

"Oh, sweetheart, I didn't mean to upset you." Mother grabbed two Kleenex and wiped the tears away. "I know this is all too much for you right now."

"How on earth did Don manage to mangle that BMW like that?" Daddy asked. "Was he drinking again?"

"Garrett, please," Mother said. "Not now."

"I just want to know if he was drinking. I mean, he put both his and Lainey's life in danger." Daddy frowned. "It could've been worse. She could be dead, too."

"But she's not," Mother said. "She's not. She's here, and we should be thankful for that, Garrett."

"She's here. But meanwhile his life was taken, and that poor woman down the hall may never wake up to see the light of day again." Daddy shook his head and left the room.

My mind drifted to Nathan's wife. I remembered seeing her silver Toyota coming straight at us. I'd looked over at Don to see if he had been aware of the oncoming car. Fear had overcome him as he'd pressed on the brake. By that time it was too late. Too late for all of us to turn back the hand of time. Too late for me to erase the pain that had caused him to drink in the first place. Too late for God to open my womb so I could bear him the child he so desperately wanted. It was too late.

When the nurse had shaken me awake, I had softly asked her, "Where's Don?"

"He didn't make it, sweetie. He was dead when the ambulance arrived," she'd answered, my hand in hers. "But you're going to be just fine. Is there someone we can call for you?"

I didn't answer. Couldn't remember if there was someone for her to call.

"A few of your husband's colleagues have been here. Wanted to make sure you were okay. Left all these beautiful flowers for you," the nurse had said. "Your mother-in-law has been calling every day. Your friend Glenda called. Says to tell you she's in Los Angeles, but she'll be here before the end of the week."

I'd listened as the nurse rambled on.

He was dead when the ambulance arrived. It was those words that had stuck with me; had me in a state of shock. Those words that had me yearning to close my eyes in the hope of waking up to find that it had all been a dream.

CHAPTER 6

Nathan

Changing the linen on the beds was quite the challenge. Marva had always been the one to prepare the house for our guests, making sure the sheets and pillowcases smelled of fabric softener; ensuring that the refrigerator and cupboards were stocked with enough food to go around. My job had been to make sure there were enough Budweisers in the fridge, and to keep the men occupied and out of the kitchen. That was easy, but this? Changing sheets and remembering to fluff the pillows was Marva's thing. In that instant I closed my eyes and prayed that she'd be able to continue the tradition.

"You okay, Daddy?" Tracee asked and I opened my eyes at the sound of her voice.

"Just praying for your mother, baby."

"Think she'll ever wake up?" she whispered, on the verge of tears.

"I hope so." I took a seat on the full-size bed, buried my face in my hands. "I should've tried harder to make her stay in the mountains. Should've made her stay until the next morning."

"You can't blame yourself, Daddy," she said. "You know how stubborn Mom is."

"I know, but it just hurts to see her like that."

"Me, too." She sat next to me on the bed, rubbed my back. "But we have to be strong for each other."

"You're right." I grabbed my daughter and tried to hug her and my pain away.

"What's goin' on in here?" My mother walked into the guest bedroom carrying a set of sheets and pillow-cases. "What's with these long faces?"

"Hey, Nana." Tracee jumped up, hugged my mother and planted a kiss on her cheek.

"I thought you and Daddy were driving down in the morning," I said. Standing, I placed a kiss on the opposite cheek.

"I figured you could use a hand getting this house together." She fluffed the pillows that I had just struggled to put pillowcases on. "Me and Helen gettin' ready to fry up some fish."

"You brought fresh fish?" I asked, knowing I hadn't been to the supermarket all week. And anything that re-sembled fish in my refrigerator definitely wasn't fresh.

"Your daddy went fishin' this morning, took advantage of the mild weather we had. Caught a few croppies," she said, a smile flashing across her almond-colored face. Her short salt and pepper fro, flawless skin and toned body made her the envy of middle-aged women everywhere. Had guys my age trying to pick her up. "They're 'bout big as your hand. Should fry up real nice."

My mother wore a gray sweat suit with pink and gray sneakers. Having two athletic sons had forced her to become athletic herself over the years. Playing tennis, golf and pumping free weights at the gym had kept her looking more like forty than the sixty years that she claimed.

"Will you make your homemade hushpuppies, Nana?"

"Only if you give me a hand in the kitchen," Mama said, and winked at me.

"The kitchen, Nana?"

"Yes, the kitchen, young lady," Mama told her. "You got to learn how to cook at some point."

"But tonight?" Tracee frowned.

"As good a time as any," she said.

The only time Tracee visited a kitchen was to load her plate with food and eat like there was no tomorrow. Unfortunately, Marva had never forced our daughter to learn anything domestic. Instead she spoiled her, and did most things for her. It always bothered me, and I told her she was doing our child a disservice, but she never listened. Said that Tracee was her only child and she loved caring for her. Fortunately, whenever Tracee visited with either of her two grandmothers, she got a good lesson in cooking, cleaning and possibly a few other things. And during this visit, she'd get a double dose. And for that, I was pleased.

"First we need to finish changing these bedclothes," Mama said, grabbing Tracee by the hand and leading her down the hallway to the second guest bedroom. "Nate, you need to go on downstairs and entertain your two fathers for a while. Keep them out of the kitchen, please."

"I'll see what I can do." I laughed.

I heard their voices even before I reached the family room.

"If you don't think that girl look good in that short little tennis skirt, then somethin' is wrong with you."

"I didn't say she don't look good, I said it don't take all that to play no tennis," I heard my father's voice rise above the BB King CD that was playing. "You don't see them little white girls running around out there on the court like that."

"That's because them little white girls ain't got all that junk in they trunk like Serena Williams got."

"What on earth are y'all arguing about now?" I said, walking into the room.

"Hey there, boy." My father, who stood at six feet tall, grinned from ear to ear at the sight of his youngest son. "How you holding up?"

"About as well as can be expected," I said, and embraced my father. "What about you?"

"I can't complain, son. Just tryin' to set your father-in-law here straight. He think he's got the skinny on everything that go on in the sports world."

"Tell your son who won out there on the golf course yesterday," Poppa Joe said, reclining in my favorite chair and twisting the cap off of a bottle of Budweiser.

"Now, Joe, you know you only won because I let you win." My father laughed and his entire frame shook from the laughter. "We been playing together for twenty-one years and I can count on one hand the number of times you beat me."

"You let me win?" Poppa Joe asked, then rubbed the receding spot on his head. "We need a rematch is what we need."

"A rematch won't do you a bit of good, Joe." Daddy kept laughing. "But I'll sure give you one."

"Where's the nearest golf course, Nate?" Poppa Joe asked.

"About a mile from here," I told him. "But it's too cold for golf. And I'm sure they're closed at this hour."

"It's never too cold for golf. First thing in the morning, Henry?" Poppa Joe asked. "You got your clubs with you?"

"Take 'em everywhere I go," Daddy said. "And I'll be happy to oblige you in the morning, old man."

It was a handshake that sealed the deal between the two men.

B.B. King was plucking on Lucille and singing about "Paying the Cost to Be the Boss."

"You know that's my song right there." Daddy shook his shot glass half filled with Old Grand Dad and a few ice cubes. The half-empty bottle sat on the coffee table.

"Now that I'll agree with." Poppa Joe stood and started moving his head to the blues.

Daddy closed his eyes and pretended to be plucking on Lucille, his bottom lip turned in as he made a face and shook his bald head from side to side. "Check this out right here." He tapped Poppa Joe on the arm and commenced to pluck on his makeshift Lucille, as if he was making her sing himself.

My father's coffee-brown skin, bald head and six-foot frame matched mine. It was Marva who'd teased that if I ever wanted to know what I'd look like when I turn sixty-five, that I should just look at my father.

"Woo wee!" Poppa Joe yelled. "He sure can make that guitar sang."

"That's why he calls her Lucille," Daddy declared. "B'cause he making love to her just like he would a woman."

When Helen walked into the room carrying the cordless phone, Poppa Joe took her by the hand and started slow dancing with her.

"Phone's for you, baby," Helen said, handing me the phone. "Joe, please. I got to get this fish to frying, now."

"You got a couple of minutes to dance with your old man, girl," he said, and swung her around. She gave in and followed his lead, moving her hips to the music. And I imagined that the two of them could really get down back in their day. Daddy's eyes were closed, still plucking on Lucille.

I took the phone to the kitchen, where Mama was showing Tracee how to make hushpuppies.

"Hello?"

"Mr. Sullivan?"

"Yes."

"This is Amy, your wife's nurse in ICU—"

"Did she wake up?" I was too excited to let the nurse

finish her sentence. Mama and Tracee were both staring at me, awaiting the response to my question.

"No, sir," she said, and my heart seemed to drop down into the pit of my stomach. "We have a little problem, though."

"You tell his ass to gimme the password!" I heard the irate female voice in the background.

"There's a woman here," Amy continued, "who says she's your wife's sister…"

Within a few seconds, the irate voice was in my ear. She'd obviously snatched the phone from the nurse.

"Nate, you tell this heifer that I'm Marva's sister. I just wanted to know how my sister's doing, and she tells me that she can't give me no information without a password. And she won't even let me see my sister!"

"Darlene?"

"Nigga, who you think this is?" Darlene slurred, obviously drunk. "Yeah, this is Darlene."

"I'm on my way down there."

"Good. And you need to get here fast before I go off up in here!" she said.

"Darlene, you need to be cool. They'll have you arrested if you act a fool up in there."

"I don't care if they have me arrested! Arrested for what? I haven't committed a crime. If it's a crime to come and see about my sister, then they need to go on and arrest me now."

"Darlene, please."

"Whatever, Nate. Just hurry up and get here. I caught a ride with somebody all the way here from Toulminville," she said, referring to our hometown, a small suburb in Mobile, Alabama, "and they dropped me off at the hospital and kept on going. So you need to get here fast!"

Darlene handed the nurse the phone before I could respond.

"Mr. Sullivan, I'm sorry, but I'm not allowed to release any information to anyone who hasn't been given the pass code. It's up to you to share that information with your family. We have to protect our patients," she said, her voice trembling. "And visiting hours were over at eight-thirty. But if you say it's okay, I'll let her visit for a few minutes…"

"No need to apologize, Amy. You did what you thought was necessary," I told her. "I'm on my way down there. Don't let her visit until I get there."

She agreed before hanging up.

"You need me or Poppa Joe to go down there with you, Nate?" Helen asked. "Darlene can be a handful when she's been drinking."

"No, I can handle Darlene," I told her, and grabbed my keys off the hook on the wall in the kitchen. I massaged the back of my neck and wondered if I'd get a good night's sleep tonight. For the past week, I'd slept cramped in a chair in Marva's room. But my mother-in-law had convinced me to go home and sleep in the comfort of my own bed. "I'll be back in a little bit."

Darlene sat in the waiting room nursing a styrofoam cup filled with piping-hot coffee. Her long thick hair in a flyaway style, a red tube top barely covering her breasts, a pair of tattered jeans hugging her thirty-two year old figure. A second-hand, gray winter coat was draped across the back of the chair. She blew into her cup to cool her coffee. I took an empty seat next to her.

"What's up with you?" I asked.

"Is my sister gonna die, Nate?" she asked, much calmer than she had been on the phone earlier. The stale alcohol filled my nostrils.

"I don't think so," I said, trying to convince myself more than her. "No, she's not gonna die."

"Because, I got some stuff I need to say to her, you know," she said, "got some things I need to get off my chest."

"Like what?"

She wiped tears from her bloodshot eyes with her palm.

"We had this big fight the other day, and I cussed her out and told her to get out of my life." Her voice trembled. "We fight all the time, Nate...you know that...but I never thought that..."

I grabbed my sister-in-law's hand and held it tightly, her fingers intertwined with mine. She rested her head on my shoulder. It was no secret that Marva and Darlene were constantly at odds with each other. They were as different as night and day. Marva was a scholar, with a Masters degree in Education. Darlene barely had a high school diploma. Marva was a successful elementary school teacher with a successful husband and family, while Darlene barely held down a job for longer than a month at a time and changed men like she changed underwear. Darlene resented her older sister, and because her life hadn't gone quite the way she'd planned it, she drank her troubles away. Kept her parents on edge, wondering if she'd turn up in somebody's gutter, given the lifestyle she'd chosen and the unsavory characters she kept company with.

"I never thought that I wouldn't have a chance to, um…"

"Shh-hh," I said, not wanting her to speak of Marva as if she wouldn't be around anymore. "Come on, let's go in and see her."

I stood and tried pulling Darlene up from her chair.

"Just forget it, man," she said. "I'll just see her another time."

"You sure?" I asked. "The nurse said she'd make an exception even though visiting hours are over."

"Yeah, I'm sure." She stood.

"You came all this way, and caused all this fuss, just to change your mind about seeing her?"

She looked away, stared at an abstract painting on the wall in the waiting room.

"Come on. Let's go see her." I pulled Darlene up from her chair and ushered her into Marva's room.

She just stared at her sister; quietly in the corner of the room, her arms folded over her chest.

"Why you standing way over there?"

"Man, I didn't know it was like this…" She became fidgety, started pacing the floor.

Pretty soon her face was soaked.

"You all right, Dar?"

She kept crying, and rocking and pacing. I grabbed her

around the shoulders and held her. We watched Marva, a feeding tube pumping nutrients into her body.

"You see that, Nate?" Darlene asked, and wiped her face with her wrist.

"See what?"

"Her eyes moved."

"I didn't see that." I said, and dismissed Darlene's claims as alcohol talking.

"I'm telling you her eyes moved, man!" she said, and then I saw it.

My wife's eyes fluttered, and something inside of me wanted to sing or dance or something. I started breathing hard, and watched them flutter again. Darlene took off out of the room.

"Nurse!" she yelled.

I was paralyzed. Didn't want to move, or blink, or miss another flutter.

"Marva," I whispered, and her eyes opened for a moment, looked straight at me. Those beautiful eyes looked right at me. "Hey, baby."

Darlene rushed back into the room, the doctor on call for the night following behind her. After observing Marva, he turned to me with those paper-thin lips and asked, "Mr. Sullivan, does your wife have a living will?"

"No…I…no, we don't have…she doesn't have a living will," I said. He caught me off guard. "She's going to be okay, right? She opened her eyes for the first time in weeks. That's a good thing, right?"

"Let's step out here." His hand on my shoulder, we moved into the hallway. Darlene was on my heels. "Sometimes, following a coma, a person may enter what is known as a vegetative state. Patients in a vegetative state lose all cognitive neurological function but are still able to breathe and may exhibit various spontaneous movements."

"What that mean?" Darlene asked.

"It means your sister may be awake and appear to be normal but the cognitive part of her brain no longer functions. The fluttering of her eyes was just a spontaneous movement."

"So will she ever come out of this vegetative state, or will she stay in it forever?" I had to know the truth. "Give it to me straight."

"Many patients who have gone into this state go on to regain a degree of awareness. Others may remain in a vegetative state for years or even decades."

"So there's a chance she may never recover?" I asked.

"There's also a chance that she will," the doctor said. "Now, if you'll excuse me, I have rounds. Marva's regular doctor will be here in the morning. If you have additional questions, you should come by and speak with him."

"Thank you, Doctor," I said, and then he strolled down the hall.

"Why did he ask about a living will if she's not going to die?" Darlene asked as we stood at the elevators.

"Just in case…"

"I remember all that stuff that went on with that Terri Schiavo case. Remember when that white girl was in a vegetative state and her folks didn't want them to remove her feeding tube? That was messed up, man," she said. "Every person in America rushed out and got a living will. Why didn't you and Marva? Y'all are so responsible and all."

"I guess we just never thought it would happen to us, you know?"

"I know." She said, "Sorry about that stuff with the nurse, man."

"Look, you wanna come and stay at the house? Our mothers are cooking up some fried fish, and I can't wait to get to it."

"Nah, last thing my folks need is to see me like this."

I had to agree as I looked into her bloodshot eyes. How could someone so beautiful be so ugly?

"Your folks love you, Dar."

"Correction. They love Marva." She said sarcastically, "You see where they are, right? Never mind that I had surgery a couple of months ago to remove a cist from my ovary. It was outpatient surgery, but neither of them bothered to show up."

"Marva's unconscious, Dar."

She gathered her thick hair with her hands and then let it fall back to her shoulders. "Yep, you're right. How could my surgery compare with that?"

I was silent for a moment and then decided to change the subject.

"What will you do about sleep tonight?"

"Can you put me up in a hotel for the night, Nate? I'll pay you back. I swear."

"How you gon' pay me back, Darlene? You working now?"

"In between jobs right now," she said, and ran her fingers through her thick mane, "but as soon as I get this settlement from when I was injured...you remember when I fell down on the job and messed up my knee?"

I didn't remember, but nodded a yes anyway.

"I swear I'll pay you back, Nate."

"Tell you what, don't even worry about, girl. I'll put you up for the night, and then first thing in the morning I'm buying you a bus ticket back to Alabama," I said. "You cool with that?"

"I'm cool with that." She tied the arms of her coat around her waist.

"Good."

I wrapped my arm around her neck in a semi-headlock.

"You're my favorite brother-in-law, Nate," she said, "you know that?"

"I'm your only brother-in-law." I laughed as the elevator doors opened and we hopped on.

CHAPTER 7

Lainey

Hiding behind the smoked tint on the windows of the black limousine seemed to shelter me from the world as we pulled into driveway of our Alpharetta traditional home. Mother released my hand, which she'd held all the way from our little Baptist church to the cemetery in Forest Park, where Don had been laid to rest, and then all the way home. My fragile state had them so worried that she and Daddy had canceled their travel plans back to Phoenix.

"We'll stay for as long as you need us, baby," Mother said as she gave my hand a strong squeeze before letting go.

Relieved, I forced a smile. Grateful for the support.

"Thank you," I said softly. "I don't really want to be alone right now."

Daddy opened the door, stepped out of the limo that belonged to the funeral home, and helped Mother out. As she headed toward the house, dressed in a dark gray suit, Glenda swung my front door open. She waved as Daddy reached for me. Barely able to stand on my own, he steadied me. I waved at my dear friend, who'd spent most of the day cooking and preparing the house for guests who had gathered after Don's funeral.

"You got a houseful," she whispered once Daddy and I reached the porch. "Are you up for that?"

"I guess I don't have a choice," I whispered back as Don's two little nieces rushed past me, dressed in ruffled dresses and patent-leather shoes, ribbons in their hair.

"Hi, Auntie Lainey," they both sang.

"Hello, girls," I said. "Stop running before you fall and hurt yourselves."

"They're so full of energy." Brenda, Don's younger sister laughed, her belly swollen from her fourth pregnancy. She planted a kiss on my cheek. "How you holding up, Lainey?"

"Fine."

"We ran out of salad dressing, so I'm gonna run to Publix and grab a couple of bottles." Keys to her husband's Expedition in hand, she asked, "You need anything else?"

"Some herbal tea would be nice," I said, and stepped into the house.

People were gathered in my living room, some of them engaged in conversations about how nice the ceremony was. Others just sat, plates filled with Glenda's fried chicken, macaroni and cheese, and salad. I gave everyone smiles, hugged people I hadn't seen in years. Indulged in casual conversations with a couple of the ladies from our church. Listened to Don's colleagues ramble on about how great a lawyer he was and how much he'd be missed at the firm.

I was exhausted from the emotional day and wanted nothing more than to retreat to my bedroom, bury myself beneath the covers and sleep my troubles away. But I knew that wasn't an option. As I made my way toward the kitchen, Alvin Taylor, Don's colleague and friend, stood with his back against the wall, his tie loosened around his neck.

"Hey, Lainey," he said. "Is there anything I can do for you before I leave?"

"You're leaving so soon?"

"Got some things I need to finish up at the office."

"You sure you're not running away because your ex-wife is here?"

"Who, Glenda?" He chuckled and straightened his tie. "Nah, we've been cordial today. She seems happy with what's-his-name in her life, and I'm happy for her."

Glenda's eyes roamed our way, with a look on her face that asked if we were talking about her.

"Yes, she is happy, Alvin." I smiled at her and then looked at him. "And you could be happy, too, if you'd stop running around here trying to romance every woman in metro Atlanta. You need to settle down, Al. Find a nice young lady and settle down."

"Yeah, you're right, Lainey." He laughed sarcastically, then kissed my cheek. "I'll keep that in mind."

"Good," I said. "Thanks for coming."

"You don't have to thank me, Lainey. You and Don are like family to me. I had to be there today," he said. "To pay my respects."

"You were one of his best friends."

"And he mine." He rubbed his clean-shaven face, shook his head. "I'm gonna miss him."

"I know you will, Alvin." I tried comforting him as tears threatened to fill his hazel eyes. He forced them back.

"If there's anything at all that you need, Lainey, you just let me know."

"I will."

"Promise you will." He pressed; his eyes serious and staring into mine.

"I promise."

"And when you're feeling better, I'll help you gather his things at the office," he offered. "But only when you're feeling better, okay?"

"I appreciate that," I said, and stroked the sleeve of his crisp white shirt. "I'll let you know when I'm up to it."

"Good." He pulled me into an embrace. "I'm gonna get out of here. I'll come by next week to see how you're doing."

"Thank you," I whispered.

He let go, planted a kiss on my forehead, then strolled out the front door.

I pulled the aluminum foil from the kitchen cabinet and started covering dishes of fried chicken and macaroni and cheese. I placed the two-liter bottles of soda into the refrigerator. Brushed crumbs from the kitchen counter with a dishcloth, and dumped them into the trash can. I grabbed the broom from its place in the closet.

"What do you think you're doing?" Glenda stood in

the doorway of the kitchen, placed her hands on her hips and looked at me sideways.

"Just straightening up in here a little."

"If you don't get out of this kitchen and get somewhere and rest your bones…" she said, taking the broom from my hand. "I got this."

"I'm not totally helpless, you know," I told her.

"I know that, but while I'm here, you need to use me as much as possible." She smiled. "I'll be gone in a few days."

"Where you off to next?" I asked.

Glenda's book, *Empowering the Woman Within*, had taken up residence on the *New York Times' Best Sellers List* for the past ten weeks. From the moment it hit the shelves in bookstores across the country, she'd been traveling from city to city promoting it and doing empowerment seminars for women everywhere.

"Philly's next." She said, "Women are hungry for this stuff, Lainey."

"I thought 'Oprah' might be next." I smiled.

"Don't rule it out, girlfriend. Don't rule it out." She placed the aluminum foil back on the shelf, picked up the broom and started sweeping. "Don't be surprised if I wind up being interviewed by that talk show diva herself."

"I wouldn't be surprised," I said. "I look at your life and how you've grown since…"

"Since divorcing Alvin?" She stole the words from me.

"I look at you, and I'm empowered." I smiled at her. "And when I read your book…"

"Lainey, you should've left Don years ago." She interrupted, shifting the conversation to a subject that we'd both avoided for years. "I watched him steal your youth and suck the life from you for years. Now don't get me wrong, I loved Don like a brother, but I hated what he'd become. An alcoholic. Hated to see you so unhappy."

Glenda was never one to hold her tongue; always told it like it was, no matter how painful it was to the person receiving it. Particularly if she thought she was making you a better person by saying her piece. Her bold, no-nonsense approach to life was making her a wealthy woman as she coached women across the country and taught them how to empower themselves. But for years, this had been a conversation we'd avoided.

"Did I really seem that unhappy?"

She looked at me sideways again, a crooked smile on her face. "Did you even read my book? Other than just the part where I gave you a shout out?" She laughed.

"Of course I read your book."

"Well, if you did, you would know that I was talking to you, and women just like you," Glenda said.

"I loved Don." It was the truth.

"I loved Alvin, too." She mused, "Didn't mean I had to put up with all the crap he was dishing out in our marriage."

I silently took a seat at my kitchen table.

"I'm not gonna preach today. I'm sure Pastor Phillips did enough of that this afternoon at the ceremony," she said, and commenced to pulling my shoes from my sore feet. She rubbed the soreness away. "But you know I have to tell it like it is, right?"

"You always do." I smiled.

"What's the plan now?" she asked. Her question was one that I hadn't pondered.

"I don't know, Glenda. I wasn't prepared for this."

"Well whatever you decide, I'm here for you. Okay?"

"Thank you," I whispered.

I closed my eyes and leaned my head back. I was grateful for Glenda's friendship.

After ushering everyone out of the house, Glenda and Mother cleaned the kitchen and put food away. Daddy caught the end of a football game until sleep found him in Don's recliner in the family room. I lay curled in a fetal position in the center of my king-size bed, staring at the television set. The Channel Two news reporter stood shivering in some Atlanta community, her blond hair blowing in the wind as she pulled her winter coat tighter and stared into the camera. I couldn't hear what she was saying because I'd muted the volume on the television, but evidently several Atlanta residents were still without electricity because of the recent ice storm.

My eyes wandered over to Don's closet, where his Italian suits hung, never to be worn by him again. He'd never again slide his feet into the Stacy Adams's shoes that rested on the closet floor, and he'd never loosen one of those silk ties around his neck again. He'd never crawl into bed beside me, his warmth making me feel safe. He'd never come home, ever again.

I shut my eyes until sleep finally captured me and held me until daylight crept across my face the next morning.

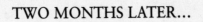

TWO MONTHS LATER...

CHAPTER 8

Nathan

"What are we playing, girls' basketball?"

"Coach, put me in!"

"What, are you scared to play defense?" This time I grabbed Collier by the collar of his jersey. "What's up with you, man?"

"I'm just trying to get the ball down the court, Coach."

"You all look like a bunch of sissies out there!" I yelled.

"Coach, put me in!" Nelson kept pulling on the tail of my corduroy blazer from the bench.

Nelson was the kid you only put in the game when you were up by ten points, and you were at the end of the last quarter. He wanted very much to show his father, who happened to be in the stands, that he really did have game. His father was an advertising executive for a huge company and rarely made it to the games, but he was here tonight, and I felt obligated to give Nelson some playing time. I knew it was the right thing to do, but we were losing by four points, and I needed to get us ahead before I made a decision like that. On the other hand, I was real close to pulling my star player, Collier, out of the game just to prove to him that the world really does not revolve around him. He was a pro at taking the plays we'd practiced all week and turning them into his own personal dramatic performances. And he knew he was working every last nerve of mine tonight.

Collier hit a three-pointer, did a dance down the court until his eyes met mine. His smile was from ear to ear, then faded when he saw that my face was like stone. I stared at him. I was grateful for the three points, but everything in me wanted to grab him by the neck and yank him down the court for not sticking with the plays. His teammates were ready to take him outside and wear his behind out. I rubbed my bald head with the palm of my hand, sighed and took a glance into the stands.

I missed Marva's smile from the bleachers, which usually gave me the encouragement I needed to get me through to the fourth quarter. She knew my frustrations with keeping my cool during a game, and I usually looked to her for a smile, a thumbs-up, or that sensuous wink of the eye that said, *Don't worry, baby, I'll make this up to you later.* I missed her voice and that tight little five-foot-three, one-hundred-and-forty-three-pound body that she complained about daily. I missed the warmth of it snuggled against mine as we slept through the night. I missed the smell of that stuff she used in her hair, and the lotion she bought at Victoria's Secret. I missed the aroma of her Colombian-blend coffee brewing in our kitchen each morning, and the cute little yellow sticky notes she'd leave for me on the refrigerator. I wondered how much longer God intended to let her sleep, and how long the guilt of allowing my wife to drive home in the middle of an ice storm would continue to torment me.

I was so busy staring at the spot where Marva usually sat, that at first I didn't see the woman waving and smiling from the top of the bleachers. She was wearing a short black leather jacket and her soft brown hair fell onto her shoulders. The cinnamon-colored face I recognized immediately. I waved back and couldn't help smiling. What was she doing here?

"Put me in, Coach. I swear I won't let you down." Nelson interrupted whatever moment I was having with the stranger from the hospital.

I turned my attention back to the game, where Collier was shooting a free-throw.

"Go check in," I told Nelson.

"For real, Coach?" he asked.

"Hurry up, before I change my mind," I said. "You're going in for Collier."

As the buzzer sounded, Nelson and Collier switched places.

"What's up, Coach? Why you taking me out?"

"Because you need to sit while you remember the plays we went over in practice."

"But, Coach, if I'm making the points, what difference does it make if I stick to the plays?"

"You sit there for a while, and I'm sure you'll figure

it out." I turned my attention back to the game, my arms folded across my chest.

Nelson placed himself in a position of defense, crouched and followed as one of Landmark High's players tried to get the ball down court. The player tried with everything he had to get around Nelson, but Nelson's eye was steady on the ball; he was relentless. Before I could blink twice, he had stolen the ball and was headed in the other direction, toward our basket. I stood there in awe as he sunk the ball into the goal with a swift jump shot that I didn't even know he owned.

"Lucky shot," Collier, who was slouched on the bench, mumbled, and then turned up a bottle of orange Gatorade.

"That should be Haterade you're drinking, instead of Gatorade." I grinned at Collier, then snuck another peek into the stands.

She was still there.

In the locker room I congratulated the boys on their win. Grabbed Nelson in a headlock and told him how proud I was.

"You keep playing like that, boy, and I'll let you in every game."

"Nelson. Nelson. Nelson," his teammates began to chant. Before long, they'd lifted him and were headed to the showers.

I left them to their fun, anxious to see if she was still in the gymnasium.

"Practice is at four o'clock sharp Monday afternoon. Be on time," I said, then headed for the door.

"That's it, Coach?" Mitchell asked. "Just be on time for practice?"

"Unless you have something else, Mr. Mitchell."

"You going to see Mrs. Sullivan?"

"Yep."

"I hope she wakes up soon." He smiled.

"Yeah, I've been praying for her, Coach," Edwards yelled.

"Me, too," Douglas said.

"I appreciate that, guys," I said, and pulled the door opened. "See you on Monday."

I headed out of the locker room. In the gymnasium, I searched the stands.

No sign of her.

"Coach Sullivan." Nelson's father approached, held his hand out to me.

"Mr. Nelson." I took his hand in a firm handshake. "Good seeing you."

"My boy looked good out there tonight," he said, his face clean-shaven, his nails perfectly manicured, his trench coat opened to display his tailored suit.

"He only plays like that when you're in the stands," I said, hoping he'd take it as an invitation to drop by more often.

"Yeah, I wish I could be around more, but this job of mine has me on the road all the time."

"I understand."

"When Stephan's mother passed away three years ago, she left me to raise him alone, and I…" He shook his head and started telling me things I didn't ask to know.

"I have to tell you, I wasn't equipped for this at all, man."

I had no response. Just listened.

"I'm a good father, Coach," he confessed, as if I'd challenged his ability to be a father. "My kid has everything he could possibly want or need."

"I understand," is what I said again, although I wanted to say, "Your kid has everything except your time, and that's all he really wants or needs. And if he had it, he wouldn't spend so much time at my house thinking I'm his father." But I didn't. Figured that was another conversation for another day.

"Well, I know you've had a long night, Coach. I won't keep you." He smiled. "Good game."

"One of our best."

We shook again before he walked away. I pulled my coat tighter as I braced myself for the brisk night air.

"Mr. Sullivan?" As soon as I heard my name, I figured another parent needed therapy, and I wasn't in the mood for giving it tonight. I needed to get to the hospital, check on Marva, then get home for some much-needed shut-eye. It had been a long week, and Friday-night games always left me worn out and longing for my warm bed.

I turned around and found the most beautiful pair of brown eyes I'd ever seen.

"Hello," I said. "I saw you in the stands."

"Yeah." She smiled. "That was a good game. You must be very proud of your boys."

"I am, but don't tell them that." I said, "When they know I'm proud they get all self-righteous and stuff, and I can't do anything with them."

She laughed. "I won't tell them."

"Good."

"I bet you're wondering why I'm here."

"The thought did sort of cross my mind."

"I never had a chance to thank you for coming by my room in the hospital, and checking on me like you did."

"I was just worried about you," I said truthfully. "Wanted to make sure you were okay."

"And…I wanted to thank you for the floral arrangement you sent to the church for my husband's funeral." Her eyes became sad. "That was very thoughtful."

"It was the least I could do."

"It was the least you could do, but I wanted to thank you personally."

"Well, you're welcome."

"And honestly, it took me a little while to figure out who was having the home-cooked meals delivered to my doorstep." She chuckled. "I accused my parents of being overprotective."

"I don't know what you're talking about," I lied.

"Well, I paid a visit to a little café in my neighborhood. And the waitress there confirmed that one, Nathan Sullivan, was responsible for having dinners delivered to my house at least three times a week for the past three weeks." Her hands on her shapely hips, she said, "But you wouldn't know anything about that, right?"

"I guess I'm busted." I unintentionally flirted with this woman, and guilt rushed over me immediately. Her smile had me mesmerized.

"Yes, you are busted." She giggled at first, then became serious. "Thank you, Mr. Sullivan. I appreciate all your kindness."

"Please call me Nate, Miss…"

"Elaine." She held her hand out to me. "Lainey. Everyone calls me Lainey."

I took her small hand in mine. "Lainey," I said, "you never told me how you found me."

"Are you kidding? I've seen you in the *Atlanta Journal Constitution* many times," she said, referring to Atlanta's newspaper, often called the AJC. "You're a pretty popular coach here in the metro area."

"You read the sports page?"

"You're surprised."

"Yes," I admitted. "You don't look the type."

"Excuse me?" She had that sister-girl tone in her voice. "The type?"

"Have you had dinner?" I asked, and wasn't quite sure where I was going with that question, but wanted to change the subject. I knew I wanted to continue talking to her, but not here, with my kids in the gym and the parents of my kids in the gym.

"No."

"Would you like to go grab something to eat?" I guess I was dying for some adult conversation. That, and I didn't know what else. I knew I was lonely. I jumped in with both feet, and both eyes wide open.

"Okay," she said. Maybe she was lonely, too.

"I know a place not far from here."

CHAPTER 9

Nathan

We both ate like it was our last meal, and sat there so long, the waitress didn't know whether to fill our water glasses or ask us to leave.

"Can I get you a to-go box for those pancakes, ma'am?" Lecretia asked, her IHOP uniform looking a little dusty as it hugged her round figure.

"No, thank you, Lecretia," Lainey said. "But I'll have another cup of coffee."

"Make it two," I said.

She filled our mugs with freshly brewed java.

"Let me know if I can get you anything else." Lecretia smiled, revealing the overbite that braces would've fixed had her parents been able to afford them. The blue contacts were a bit much for a woman her color, but she was pretty in her own way.

"Thanks," we both said in unison, and then she made her way over to another table to take their orders.

We were already past the formalities of "How's your wife?" and "I'm sorry about the loss of your husband" and "How're you getting along in spite of it all?"

It was the unspoken things that drew us closer. After talking to Lainey for less than one hour, I felt closer to her than I did some of my relatives.

"You know some nights I stay awake all night," she said, "wondering what I could've done differently."

"Same here," I confessed. "Even though I'm a true believer that things happen just the way they are supposed to."

"But you still blame yourself for allowing Marva to drive home that night?"

"I just keep thinking that I should've put my foot down and made her stay there."

"Yeah, you could've beat your chest like Tarzan and said 'Woman, I command you to stay in the mountains.'" She laughed.

"Very funny."

This woman had a sense of humor.

"I'm sorry, I don't mean to make light of the situation, but I wanted you to see how ridiculous it is for you to blame yourself."

"Yeah, you're right." I took a sip of coffee. "And the same goes for you. Wasn't much you could've done, either."

"I could've insisted on driving. Despite Don's protests." She stared into her coffee mug, as if the coffee itself had all the answers swimming around in it. Too ashamed to look up. "I could've insisted."

When she lifted her eyes, they were pools of tears.

"Lainey, the way you described your husband—" I took her hand into mine "—it wasn't easy to convince him of anything."

She didn't agree, or disagree, just looked into my eyes. "I'm so sorry, Nathan."

"You don't have anything to be sorry about," I said. "You lost just as much in this, maybe more than I've lost. At least Marva is living, breathing..."

She pulled her hand away, as if the reality of my wife living and breathing made her uncomfortable. Or maybe she took offense to the fact that my wife was alive and her husband was dead. Her vibe changed.

"I'd better get going," she said. "Lecretia probably wants to get this table cleared for someone else."

That was probably true, since people were crowded around the front of the restaurant awaiting the first available table. But I didn't care. Something about Lainey made me want to be around her. I could've sat there at IHOP until morning if it meant talking my pain and loneliness away.

She grabbed the check, with its grease and coffee stains all over it. "I'll take care of this."

"No, I got it."

"Not a chance," she said, and reached into her purse—pulled out a twenty-dollar bill. Held on to the check. "You leave the tip."

"I can handle that," I said, and left Lecretia a ten-dollar bill.

In the parking lot, I watched as Lainey climbed into her Suburban. Drove away. Left me standing there, the brisk Atlanta night air brushing across my face.

* * *

At the hospital, I stepped inside the room, lights dimmed. Helen, my mother-in-law, was uncomfortably dozed in a chair in the corner of the room. The door creaked and woke her.

"Hi, baby." She smiled.

"I didn't mean to wake you." I made my way over to her, kissed her cheek.

"It's okay. I need to get out of this chair before my back gets to aching."

"I didn't know you were here," I said. "Where's Poppa Joe?"

"At home. Rick drove me down." She said, "I knew you had a game tonight. Tried calling your cell phone. Kept getting your recording."

I pulled my cell phone out of my pocket, flipped it open and looked at the dark screen. "I turned it off during the game. Must've forgotten to turn it back on."

"Rick's coming back to drive me home in the morning." She stood; stretched. "I just wanted to come and check on my child. See if there was any change."

"Why don't you stay until Sunday? I'll drive you home then."

"You sure, sweetheart? I know you spend a lot of time with your kids from school on the weekends. And I wouldn't want to impose."

"I'm free this weekend. Besides, I could use the company." That was true. I was tired of crashing in the recliner in the family room, remote in hand. Tired of staring at the walls with nobody to hold an adult conversation with. I had to admit, it was lonely, and getting worse by the day.

"I'll make you some of my homemade biscuits." She smiled and winked.

"Oh my goodness!" I said, grateful, because I couldn't remember the last time I had a home-cooked meal. And Helen's homemade biscuits weren't anything to play with. They were lethal to a lonely man on a Saturday morning. I planted another kiss on my mother-in-law's cheek. "You gon' mess around and be held hostage until next Sunday."

"Oh no, son. I can't stay that long." She laughed and patted my cheek. "Poppa Joe wouldn't know what to do with hisself for a week. But I'll definitely let you hold me hostage for a couple of days. Let's see if I can't fatten you up a little bit."

"Have I lost weight?" I asked, patting my stomach.

"You lookin' a little skinny." She frowned. "You been eating?"

"Not like I should," I confessed.

"Gotta do better than that, Nate. You can't stop living, baby." She said, "You gotta take care of yourself."

"It's hard, Mother."

"I know, sweetheart. But you gotta be strong. Gotta be strong for Marva, for your kids at school, for Tracee. Gotta be strong for you."

"I know." I grabbed Helen in an embrace and felt like I was twelve again. She held me just like my mother would have, and I snuck a peak at Marva. Hoped she wasn't aware that I was crumbling. She rested peacefully, her chest moving up and down underneath the covers.

"Go on over there and talk to your wife. She can hear you. I'm going on down to the cafeteria and find me a sandwich or something." She asked, "You hungry?"

"No." Guilt rushed over me as I thought about IHOP, and my heart pounded. "I grabbed a bite already."

"Good." She smiled; touched the handle of the door. "I'll meet you in the lobby in a little bit."

"Okay." I smiled.

She was gone. I kissed Marva's forehead.

The smell of homemade biscuits swept across my nostrils and I opened my eyes. Stared at the ceiling for a minute, then closed my eyes again. Said a little prayer.

"Dear Lord, thank you for allowing me to see another day. Wish I was the one lying in that hospital bed, God, instead of Marva. I would take her place in a heartbeat." I closed my eyes a little tighter. "But you, Father, have your own special will for our lives. We don't always understand it, but we'll understand it later on, right?"

I opened my eyes and stared at the ceiling again, then made my way into the bathroom. Washed my face and brushed my teeth. Swished a little mouthwash around in my mouth, and then rushed downstairs to see what else besides biscuits was waiting for me. Between my mama and Helen, the two of them could bring a grown man to tears with their cooking.

"Well, good mornin'." Helen smiled and finished loading dishes into the dishwasher. "You finally decided to turn it loose?"

"Yes, ma'am," I said, rubbing my hand across my five o'clock shadow. "Biscuits woke me up."

I grabbed a biscuit and bit into it.

"Get yourself a plate, son," Helen said, and I obeyed.

I loaded my plate with country ham, biscuits, scrambled eggs and seasoned potatoes. Poured a glass of orange juice and plopped down at the kitchen table.

"What you wanna do today?" I asked my mother-in-law.

"Honey, don't feel like you got to run me all over town. I just wanna see my daughter. That's it."

"I thought we'd go out to the hospital, spend some time with Marva. And later on, I wanna take you over to that new Atlantic Station area."

"Oh, I've been reading about that in the newspaper. They have a Dillard's over there."

"Yes, they do. Your daughter has hit them up a couple of times." I chuckled. "Got my Visa bill the other day."

"Did she do much damage?" Helen laughed. We both knew how Marva liked to shop, and could put a hurting on a credit card.

"Nah, not too bad," I confessed with my mouth full of scrambled eggs. "I miss her so much, Mother."

"I know, baby," she said, and grabbed a plate from the shelf. She placed a biscuit, one piece of ham and a few eggs onto it. "But think of it like this. She's resting. You know she was always on the go, and never taking much time to relax, right?"

"Yes. I was glad she decided to do the retreat with her girlfriends," I said. "She never got to do stuff like that when Tracee was home."

"She was so busy trying to be a wife and mother, she forgot that she was a person too." Helen sat across from me at the table. "Not that there's anything wrong with being a wife and mother."

"She just didn't know when to quit."

"She always was a fighter," Helen said. "Hopefully she'll fight her way through this one."

My mother-in-law was a strong praying woman, and her usage of the word *hopefully* disturbed me. Made me wonder if she'd lost her faith.

"You don't seem that sure that she will, Mother."

"What I'm sure of is, God has a plan for each and every one of us. And we have to just put our trust in him." She reached across the table, rested her hand on mine. Her hand identical to Marva's, only a little more aged. Her diamond, the one Poppa Joe had given her more than thirty years ago, glistened under the chandelier above the kitchen table. Tears threatened to fall from my eyes, but I fought them back. If I fell apart, Helen would worry, and then she'd have my mother worried and the two of them would take turns commuting here every weekend. I didn't want that, so I straightened up in my chair, hardened the muscles in my face.

"Thought we'd grab some dinner at this restaurant in Atlantic Station. It's called Copeland's Cheesecake Bistro." I told her.

"Mmm. Anything with cheesecake in its name sounds delicious." She smiled like a child would after being told they're going out for ice cream. "I can't wait."

CHAPTER 10

Lainey

With my back against the foot of my bed, I sat on the floor, legs spread wide. Stretching, I did the exercises that my physical therapist had taught me, to loosen my muscles and regain my motor skills. The television tuned to "Girlfriends," I laughed as I leaned back on my elbows and stretched my legs toward the ceiling. I could smell the well-seasoned piece of Tilapia I had baking in the oven downstairs, my reward for completing my exercises.

Thoughts of Nathan had been invading my mind since the night we'd spent at IHOP, chatting like we were old friends. He had been so easy to talk to; understood my pain. It had been so long since I'd enjoyed being around anyone so much. Not to mention, he was very easy on the eyes. I constantly fought the urge to call him; just to talk. But knew I had no business even thinking about him, let alone calling him up on the phone. He was married. She was unconscious, but deserved more than some woman thinking about her husband in ways that weren't innocent.

I brushed Nathan Sullivan from my thoughts, pulled myself up from the floor and headed downstairs for my reward. My fish, covered in seasoned bread crumbs, was golden brown as I sprinkled fresh sautéed vegetables: broccoli, cauliflower and carrots, onto the plate beside it, along with a splash of garlic-mashed potatoes. I'd spent too much time watching those cooking shows. Especially the one hosted by Emeril, who had me in the aisles of the grocery stores in search of spices that I'd never even heard of. Everything he cooked, I'd tried to recreate in my own kitchen.

Thoughts of Don filled my head. *I'm a meat and potatoes man, Lainey.* He wasn't a big fan of my creative recipes.

Just as I'd popped a piece of broccoli into my mouth, the sound of the phone echoed through my empty house.

"Hello?" I said, glancing at the clock on the microwave. Nine o'clock.

"Girl, I know you are not just now eating dinner," Glenda said. "You'll be big as a house eating this late and then going to bed. What did Emeril have you cooking tonight?"

"Baked Talapia with bread crumbs, garlic-mashed potatoes and fresh veggies on the side." I smiled. She knew me too well.

"Just finished your workout?"

"Gotta have some motivation for doing those awful, painful exercises."

"Those awful, painful exercises will help to rebuild your muscles and regain the motor skills you lost in the accident."

"I know, but I don't have to like them," I said. "Where are you?"

"La Guardia Airport. On my way home," she said. "What's your schedule look like tomorrow?"

"Doctor's appointment in the morning, then I'm headed to the beauty shop—sometime in the afternoon," I told her. "Why?"

"Thought we could do lunch or dinner."

"I'm free for dinner."

"Good. Why don't you call me when you leave the shop?"

"I will."

"Good, I'll make reservations for us at Ray's in the City. Why don't you just meet me downtown?"

"Sounds like a plan."

"Good. Gotta run, they're boarding my flight. But I'll call you tomorrow."

She was gone.

Angela's was crowded as usual, but it was only because she was an expert at making the average woman look like a superstar. There were four of us that had a standing Saturday appointment: Patricia, a veterinarian who not only adored the animals she made well, but had three dogs of her own at home who were just like her children. Patricia always kept us abreast of her adventures with a man she was seeing in Detroit. She'd fly up for the weekend, he'd sweep her off of her feet, she'd come back to Atlanta and grace the rest of us with the details. For some of us, her stories were the only romance we'd received in a long time.

Then there was Deon, who was sort of quiet, but was planning a wedding.

Valerie had been separated from her husband, but they were making plans of reuniting.

When I walked in, Patricia was telling a story of her last weekend adventure with Deangelo, the man who seemed too good to be true. Had the rest of us wondering if he had any brothers.

"...and he met me at the airport with a bouquet of roses," Patricia was saying as I grabbed an *Essence* magazine and took a seat. "Had the whole weekend planned out for us. We visited the museum, went ice skating and then had a picnic by candlelight at a local park at midnight. He fed me chocolate-covered strawberries, y'all!"

"That's so romantic," Deon said.

"He sounds like a keeper," Valerie said as Angela put a relaxer on her hair. "Are y'all getting serious? Talking about marriage?"

"We're just having a good time. Taking it one step at a time. Enjoying the moment."

"Sounds good to me," I chimed in as I flipped through the pages of my magazine.

The voice Ludacris, Angela's artist of choice, rang through the room. Her golden twists freshly done as she bounced to the music and continued to relax Valerie's hair.

"I need to get me one of them," she said, and then bounced over to the shampoo bowl to rinse Deon.

"One of what?" Deon asked.

"A man like Patricia got. The way she talkin', I wonder if he got a brother, cousin or something."

"Amen," Valerie said.

"You burning?" Angela asked Valerie, whose hair was plastered with white chemical relaxer.

"I'm good," she said, and flipped through Oprah's O magazine, and then sent someone a text message from her cell phone. "I'll let you know when I'm burning."

"Lainey, how you doing?" Angela asked. "I'm sorry about Don, and sorry I didn't make it to the funeral. You know if I had been in town I would've been there."

"I got your card in the mail, Angela. And the flowers. Thanks."

"You're welcome," she said, drying the excess water from Deon's hair and then saturating it with a conditioner. "It was the least I could do."

Angela placed a plastic gheri-curl-looking bag onto Deon's head and placed her under the dryer. She motioned for Valerie, whose scalp was burning, to come to the shampoo bowl. She rushed over and sighed as the warm water saturated her burning scalp.

"Are you feeling better?" Patricia asked.

"Much better. Been through therapy for my injuries."

"Did that woman ever die?" Valerie asked. "The woman who was in a coma?"

"No, she's still unconscious."

"Man, that has to be a trip for her husband to see her like that. Must be a trip for you, too, knowing that your husband—" Patricia cut her comment off in midsentence. "Sorry."

"Go ahead say it...must be a trip, knowing that my drunkard husband killed himself and left another person in a coma. Believe me, I think about it every single day. The thought haunts me endlessly. And whenever I talk to Nathan, I'm reminded of his wife's condition."

"Nathan?" Angela asked. "You're on a first-name basis with the husband?"

"How often do you talk to the man?" Patricia asked.

"We've become good friends. Survivors together," I said.

"I see," Patricia said, and pulled the dryer up, feeling her hair to see if it was dry.

"Did you know that there's a twinkle in your eye when you talk about him, Lainey?" Valerie added.

"It's not like that." I tried convincing myself more than them.

"Well, what's it like?" Angela asked, hands on her hips.

"Don't look at me like that," I said.

"You like him, don't you?" Patricia asked.

"We're just friends."

"You can save that friends stuff for some folks who don't know you," Valerie warned. "We know you, girlfriend."

"And we want details," Patricia said, now on the edge of her seat. "What's really going on?"

"I don't know what y'all are talking about," I pleaded.

"Come on over here to this shampoo bowl and maybe your memory will be refreshed after I shampoo your hair."

"It's gon' take a lot of shampooing, Angela, because she really playing the nut role," Valerie said.

I sat in Angela's chair, leaned back as the water cascaded over my head.

"Now give us the details," Angela encouraged, as the other ladies moved to the edge of their seats.

I was trapped. Had to give them something, but didn't know what. It was true, I was falling for Nathan, but knew there was no future. I couldn't share that with the sisters at the beauty shop. It was too intimate, I thought. But then, they were my friends…we'd all shared secrets too intimate for the rest of the world…secrets that could never be repeated outside of the shop. I owed them an explanation.

"Is anybody interested in any CDs? I got Luther and some really nice mix tapes." The CD man saved the day.

CHAPTER 11

Nathan

I held the door for Helen as the sounds of loud conversations and laughter filled the air. A couple sat in a corner booth toasting something special; their half-filled wineglasses clanking in midair. The place was busy and crowded, and I hoped it wasn't too contemporary for my mother-in-law.

"Sir, the wait is about an hour," the host proclaimed. "Would you like for me to place your name on the list?"

I looked at Helen.

"I could have a meal cooked and on the table at home in an hour," she said, pulling her coat tighter to brace the night air again.

"Or we could grab something on the way home," I added.

"Nathan?" The familiar voice from behind stopped me in my tracks as I moved toward the door. It was familiar and soft; not to mention sweet.

I turned to meet the eyes of this voice.

"Hey, Lainey."

"How are you?" she asked, smiling a genuine smile, her soft brown eyes dancing.

"I'm fine," I said. She had me shaken, and I couldn't understand why. Couldn't quite understand why my heart was pounding so rapidly and my palms held this unusual moisture. I rid my hand of its excess moisture by rubbing it against the leg of my pants.

"Hello." Helen jumped in.

"Hello." Lainey, so cool and calm, took Helen's hand in both of hers. "You must be Nathan's mother."

"I'm his mother-in-law."

"Lainey, this is Marva's mother," I said, after regaining my composure. I turned to Helen. "Lainey is the young woman who was injured in the car accident with Marva. Her husband didn't survive."

"Oh, my goodness." Helen rubbed her hand along Lainey's arm. "I'm so sorry, sweetheart."

"I'm sorry about your daughter," Lainey said. "At least I was able to have closure with my husband's death. It must be really hard for you."

"It is, honey. But God is faithful."

"He is that," Lainey said, and we all stood in the midst of a moment of unusual silence. "Are you guys waiting for a table?"

"No, we were headed out. The wait is an hour long."

"Well, I have a table," she said. "It's just me and my girlfriend. Why don't you join us?"

I looked at Helen, who shrugged.

"I am hungry, baby," she said to me. "And my feet are killing me."

"Are you sure we wouldn't be imposing?"

"No, not at all," she said. "Follow me."

We followed Lainey through the dimly lit and crowded restaurant. Past a group of people engaged in what seemed like a birthday celebration. Their laughter rose above the other animated conversations throughout the place.

"We haven't even ordered yet," Lainey said loudly, trying to be heard over the noise. She wore snug jeans and a cashmere sweater. "We were just seated when I had to make a mad dash for the restroom."

At the table, an attractive woman with lavender eye shadow that matched her lavender blouse, smiled up at us. Her face was friendly and familiar.

"Glenda, this is Nathan Sullivan."

She seemed to know me as she held her hand out to me.

"Hello, Nathan." She took my hand in hers.

"And this is his mother-in-law, Miss Helen," she said, and Glenda took Mother's hand, too.

"Hello, Miss Helen."

"Very nice to meet you, honey," Helen said.

"I spotted them on the way from the restroom and asked them to join us," Lainey explained. "The wait is over an hour."

"I know, we waited at least that," Glenda said. "We were supposed to have dinner at Ray's in the City, but someone insisted on this place."

"It's because the food here is wonderful." Lainey smiled. "You don't mind if they join us, do you?"

"Not at all. Please sit down," Glenda said, a smile still genuinely plastered across her face. I wondered how she really felt about the intrusion. She motioned for the waiter. "What are you drinking?"

"Water with lemon for me," Helen said to the waiter as he approached, and then she reached for the menu.

"I need a glass of water, too, please," I said, "and a cup of decaf. Cream. And can you make sure it's freshly brewed?"

"Yes, sir. I'll be right back with your drinks." The tall, lanky server disappeared into the crowd too quickly. If I'd wanted to change my mind, I wouldn't have had time.

As Helen and I flipped through the menu, Glenda struck up a conversation.

"Thank you for checking up on my girlfriend while she was in the hospital. I thought that was really sweet, Nate," she said.

"It wasn't a problem. Her room was right down the hall from my wife's. I wanted to make sure she was all right."

"How's your wife doing?" she asked.

"No change," I said, and then buried my head into the menu again. "She hasn't moved a muscle since that night."

"I'm sorry," Glenda apologized.

"Don't worry about it." I was tired of hearing people saying they were sorry, as if there was something they could've done. What happened was not their fault, so why were they sorry?

The couple seated at the table across from us stood.

The man helped the woman with her coat and then they approached our table.

"Excuse me." The woman's eyeballs met Glenda's. "Are you Glenda Holbrook-Taylor?"

"I am." Glenda smiled.

"Oh, wow! Can I have your autograph?"

"Sure," Glenda said, and the woman began frantically searching her purse for something to write on.

"I told my husband that was you. I kept looking and looking…" she said, pulling a folded envelope out of her purse. A gas or electric bill, no doubt. "I thought that was you."

Glenda asked the woman her name, then scribbled a few words on the paper. Handed it to the woman.

"Thank you so much," she said, and her husband ushered her out the door.

"Can't take her nowhere." Lainey laughed.

"Are you a celebrity?" I asked. Her face was a little familiar, but her fame escaped me.

Lainey and Glenda laughed hard.

"She's a famous author," Lainey offered.

"I wouldn't say famous," Glenda said modestly, "but I am an author."

"What did you write?" Helen asked.

"I wrote a book called *Empowering the Woman Within*," Glenda said, and pulled a copy of the book from her leather bag. Handed it to Helen.

"Oh my goodness." Helen chuckled as she flipped open the front cover. "I didn't know I was seated among greatness."

"What d'you mean? You're around me all the time," I teased.

"I know, sweetie." Helen touched my face and laughed. "And you are a great son-in-law, Nathan."

"I'm just kidding," I said, and closed the menu. I had decided on the crab cakes. "That's really cool that you're an author, Glenda. Is the book doing pretty good?"

"It's been steady on the *New York Times Best Seller List* for the past several weeks. It's been on the *Essence* bestseller list, and it's been featured in *Time*. I'd say it's doing pretty good."

"She travels all over the country doing these empowerment seminars," Lainey said. "She just flew in from New York this morning."

"Oh honey, you must be exhausted," Helen said.

"I'm a little tired."

"It's so good to meet you, though. It's not every day I get to meet a celebrity," Helen said. "Where can I pick up your book?"

"That's your copy in your hand." Glenda smiled. "Let me autograph it for you."

"O-oh, Nate, your mama will be so jealous." Helen playfully punched me in the arm.

"How 'bout I sign a copy for her, too," Glenda said, and pulled another copy from her bag. Signed both of them, and handed them to my star-struck mother-in-law.

"Savannah will be so excited." She said, "Savannah is Nathan's mother. We're very close, almost like sisters. Grew up in the same hometown. Attended the same schools and everything."

"Where are you from?"

"Toulminville, Alabama."

"Is that anywhere near Birmingham?"

"Just a hop, skip and a jump." Helen laughed. "It's about three hundred miles."

"The reason I ask is because I'm doing a seminar in Birmingham next month. Maybe you and Miss Savannah can come out and see me."

"You serious?"

"Yes, ma'am," she said. "I'll make sure you have tickets to the show. You'll be my special guests."

"You're so sweet," Helen said, and the three of them went on and on about the empowerment of women until the food finally arrived. I was grateful, because the woman-talk was driving me crazy.

"It's funny you mentioned Toulminville, Miss Helen," Lainey said. "My father went to Alabama State."

"No kidding," Helen said. "What's your daddy's name, child?"

"Garrett Marshall."

Helen thought for a minute, hoping the name would ring a bell.

"Tall fella...dark brown skin?"

"Yes, ma'am."

"I believe I know your daddy," she said. "Did he play football?"

"Yes, he did," Lainey said.

"My, my, my. It's such a small world," Helen said. "I believe he used to have a crush on my friend Betty. That was long before you was the apple of his eye. He was just a freshmen then."

We all laughed. By the end of dinner, we were all family.

CHAPTER 12

Lainey

Tears burned my cheeks as I packed away Don's things in boxes. Silk ties, shirts, suits, too many pairs of shoes to count.

"What are you doing with all this stuff?"

"Charity."

"You sure? Because you could make a fortune selling this stuff."

"I don't really need the money, Glenda. Or the hassle of trying to sell it."

"There's really no hassle, sweetie. I have a girlfriend who owns a consignment shop in Midtown. Let me give her a call," she said. "These things are too nice to just give away."

"But there are people who really could use it," I told her.

"Up to you, sweetie," she said. "You let me know."

I quietly continued to fold Don's shirts. I had already called a men's shelter downtown, and they'd agreed to pick up Don's things. They profusely thanked me for the donation, and I wasn't about to renege on a promise.

"You like him, don't you?"

"Who?" I asked, completely thrown.

"Nathan."

"No," I lied. "What gave you an idea like that?"

"The way you two were avoiding eye contact last night, the entire restaurant could tell."

"Was it that obvious?"

"No. Just to me, because I know you."

"You think his mother-in-law knew?"

"Probably. Older people know stuff like that." She laughed. "Relax."

"It's not funny."

"Have you two been…you know, together?"

"No. I mean, we had dinner once. But that was it." I confessed, "I am attracted to him. But mainly we're just friends. He's a nice guy."

"Okay."

For some reason I couldn't get Nathan Sullivan out of my head. But just as quickly as thoughts of him appeared, so appeared thoughts of Miss Helen. I imagined her with arms folded across her chest, peering at me with a disappointed look on her face. She was Marva's mother, and I was attracted to her son-in-law. I wondered if she could tell at dinner. Older people did have a way of knowing things like that. Like the first time I became pregnant, my grandmother knew even before I made the announcement.

"That child is pregnant. Can't you see?" she'd said to my mother. I wasn't even showing at the time, but she knew. Grandmothers always knew.

Even though Nathan and I had managed to avoid eye contact all evening, I wondered if Miss Helen could feel the energy. I certainly felt it. His presence shook me. The best thing would be to avoid being around him at all costs. That was what needed to happen.

When my phone rang I was soaking in a tub of hot water, filled with bubbles. I debated on whether or not to answer, but by the third ring, I'd decided that it might be important.

"I hope I didn't catch you at a bad time." His voice was gentle; I detected a little fatigue.

"I was just...no, it's not a bad time." I tried desperately not to let the water splash.

"I just wanted to thank you for dinner," he said. "My mother-in-law enjoyed herself, and so did I. She went home telling my mother all about your friend Glenda, and how we had dinner with a celebrity. They've already planned their trip to Birmingham, probably already decided on what they're wearing."

We both laughed.

"I didn't really want much. Just wanted to tell you that," he said, after the laughter stopped.

"You sound tired."

"I am. We got up at six this morning and I drove Mother home. Spent the whole day going to church, eating a huge meal that she and my mother cooked. Watched the football game with my two fathers."

"Your two fathers?"

"My father and my father-in-law. They argued

through most of the game, so I missed a lot of it." He laughed. "They're inseparable, those two."

"Oh."

"Our families have sort of merged into one big family."

"I bet that gets real interesting during the holidays."

"Actually it's sort of nice, because Marva and I never have to decide whose family we'll visit on holidays. They're always together," he said. "It's been that way for so long, it's like breathing. Marva and I knew each other long before we were married."

"What's she like, Nate?" I needed to make her real in my mind, because if she became real I could stop thinking of him in ways that were un-Christian-like.

"She's funny. A wonderful mother and wife. Very nurturing." He said, "But she's also hardheaded. She's one of those people who have to find things out for themselves. Can't tell her anything."

He was quiet for a moment.

"I tried to tell her to stay in the mountains that night, but she wouldn't listen." He almost spoke in a whisper. "She wouldn't listen."

I didn't know what to say, especially when dead silence rang through the telephone receiver. Then there was this wimpering sound. He was crying.

"Are you okay, Nate?" I asked, sitting straight up in the tub. Wished I could hug his troubles away.

He was silent until he regained his composure. I let him get it all out. Sometimes people just needed a good cry, without interruption.

"I'm okay," he finally said. "Sometimes I just need to talk."

"You can talk to me anytime," I said. "Or not talk. You can just cry if you need to."

"Sometimes I just get lonely for an adult conversation."

"Same here," I said. "If it weren't for Glenda breezing through here in between book engagements, I wouldn't know who to talk to."

"Do you miss him?"

"There were so many times I'd planned on divorcing Don. But then, he'd become like a fixture in my life."

"Did he always drink like that?"

"Mostly on the weekends."

"Was he a good husband?"

"In the beginning he was. He wanted children and when he saw that I couldn't give him any, he pulled away. Went into this shell and never came out," I said. "He became this terrible person who didn't even love himself, let alone me."

"Why did you stay?"

"Because I kept thinking...hoping that he would change. Kept hoping that he would suddenly go back to being the Don that I once loved and married." I chuckled, as sad a thought as it was. "He never did."

There was silence.

"I've forgiven him," Nate said, and I was surprised by his words. "It took me a while, but I finally did. I was very angry with him in the beginning. After the accident, you know."

"I understand, Nate."

"I would've killed him with my bare hands!" His words shook me, almost scared me. "I'm sorry. I shouldn't have said that."

"No, that's how you feel and I totally understand," I said. "You're honest and I respect that."

"Thank you for listening to me ramble on," he said.

He was leaving me; going much too soon. I needed him to stay, wanted him to.

"Call me if you ever need to talk," he said.

"You do the same."

He was gone.

The doors of the elevator sprang open at the eleventh floor. I pushed my way past the crowd, got off and strolled down the hallway to Don's office. The waiting area had beautiful leather furniture, the expensive type found in wealthy people's homes. Van Gogh's oil on canvas, *Quay with Men Unloading Sand Barges,* adorned the wall. Edith sprung from behind her desk.

"Mrs. Williams, it's so good to see you. How are you?" She pulled me into an embrace and wouldn't let go until I responded.

"I'm much better, Edith," I told her. "I received your flowers while I was in the hospital. Thank you so much. They were beautiful."

"I just thought the whole thing was so awful," she said. "It was all over the news, dear."

"So I heard." I was tired of the small talk and just wanted to get to what I came to do...collect Don's things. "Is Alvin here?"

"He is, dear, but he's in a meeting," she said, and then took her place behind her desk again. Her green-and-orange plaid wool suit was one that she'd undoubtedly purchased in the early seventies. Her hair was probably blond at one time, but was rapidly graying now. And her beige skin that was most likely flawless in her younger days, held a million wrinkles. "He asked Marvin to assist you. Let me just call him."

Messy Marvin. I smiled to myself as I thought of the nickname that Don had given his awkward assistant.

"Mrs. Williams is here, dear," she told Marvin on the opposite end of the speakerphone. The way she called everyone dear, made me think that she would've fit right in on the Brady Bunch or in Mayberry with Andy Griffith.

I took a seat on the edge of the leather sofa.

"He'll be right here, dear. Can I get you something to drink?"

"No, I'm fine, Edith. Thank you," I said. "Must be a pretty important meeting Alvin's in."

"I gathered it must be, because he said he didn't want to be disturbed under any circumstances."

"Mmm." I slid to the back of the sofa, crossed my legs.

Marvin appeared, dark gray Armani suit, freshly cut hair. When he held his hand out to me, his nails looked as if they'd just been manicured.

"Mrs. Williams, it's so good to see you again."

"You too, *Messy*...I mean, Marvin." I giggled. "I'm sorry."

"No problem." He had to laugh, too. "Follow me."

I followed him down a corridor that I'd only traveled a few times. Once, early in Don's career when I brought him lunch. We ate in his office, picnic-style, with wine, small sandwiches and soft jazz playing on a boom box. Another time when Don's father had a heart attack, and rather than tell him over the phone, I showed up at his office, a walking telegram bearing the bad news. A third time when my pregnancy test had shown up positive. That was a good visit. He had pulled me close into his strong chest and we danced circles around his office. We were so happy then. That was decades ago.

Marvin stopped in front of Don's door, unlocked it with a silver key.

"We haven't been in here since…" he started. "No one has touched anything."

There was a cold draft inside and the blinds were drawn. Marvin opened them to let daylight creep in.

"Do you need me to stay?"

"No, I'll be okay."

"Holler if you need me." He shut the door behind him.

I made my way across the room to the credenza. Picked up a photo of Don and me. The one we'd taken in Belize so long ago. My hair was shorter, and colored. I was young and beautiful, and so sure of myself then. The beautiful crystal frame had been a wedding gift from one of Don's colleagues and his wife. I placed the photo back on the credenza, ran my finger across it. Memories were a trip. I'd spent a lifetime trying to get back to a fantasy that was no more. I brushed my fingertips across the mahogany credenza that hadn't seen furniture polish in a few months. Wiped the dust onto the leg of my jeans.

I plopped down and sank into Don's huge leather chair, and began straightening things on his desk. Moved the picture of his mother so that it was centered right in front of his blotter and calendar. The tap on the door caused me to look up.

"I brought you some boxes," Messy Marvin said, and placed them near the door.

"Thank you."

He didn't answer, but was gone just as quickly. I strolled across the room and grabbed one of the boxes.

"Okay, let's get this over with," I whispered to myself.

I placed all of Don's personal items from atop his desk into the box. Engraved pens, framed photos of me and his family, office supplies. I opened his middle drawer and emptied those things into the box. I took the small key from the middle drawer and tried opening the huge side drawer with it. It didn't fit. I searched the drawer for other keys, but there was none.

I picked up the phone and called Edith.

"Hi, Edith, it's Mrs. Williams. Do you know where Don kept the key for his desk drawer?"

"No, ma'am, but I'll get Marvin to help you find it."

Before I hung up the phone good, Marvin appeared in the doorway. He came over to the drawer and pulled on it.

"Locked," he proclaimed, as if I hadn't already discovered that fact. "Only other person who has a key is

Kendall, the maintenance guy. He's got a master key to everything. I'll see if I can track him down."

"Don't go to any trouble," I said. "I can always get it later."

"It's no trouble, Mrs. Williams. I would hate for you to have to make a second trip here. I know this is hard for you." He stood in the doorway. "I'll be right back."

In Don's closet hung a couple of blazers and a winter coat. I took them off of their hangers and placed them in a second box. I stood in front of the window and took in the picturesque view of downtown Atlanta. What a view, I thought. Don's philodendron plant on the windowsill hadn't been watered and was near death. I gave it a drink from the wet bar in the corner of the room, and then placed it in the sink and let the water drain. Don was good with plants. It was me who killed them.

Messy Marvin came in, holding a small golden key in the air.

"Here it is," he sang. "Just give it back to me when you're done. I had to pry it away from Kendall."

"I'll make sure I give it back." I smiled, then plopped back down and sank into Don's huge chair again.

As Messy Marvin shut the door behind him, I stuck the little key into the lock of the drawer. The lock clicked and I pulled the drawer open. Inside were three big egg-yoke colored envelopes. The kind you mailed important papers to people in. I pulled them out and placed them on top of the desk. At the bottom of the drawer were several photos. I picked up the first one. It was a photo of me standing in front of the first house Don and I had ever purchased, my arms spread wide and the grin on my face was even wider. It was a ranch-style home, two bedrooms and a small kitchen. Small, but it was ours.

Then there was a photo of Don and a woman I didn't recognize. She was caramel-colored, with sandy hair and a smile that said she was more than a second cousin. In the next photo she straddled his lap, and I wondered who was taking the picture. In several of the other photos, Caramel was in a bathing suit, Don was in trunks and they were on a beach somewhere. I flipped one of the bathing suit photos over and read the letters printed in blue ink… "Me and Ursula, Maui 1985."

I remembered Maui. The trip that nobody was taking their spouses on because there would be no time for fun.

"Business meetings from sunup to sundown," he'd said. "And you'll be complaining the whole time, and I don't wanna hear it. I'll bring you something nice back, though."

He did…bring me something nice back. Diamond earrings and a diamond necklace to match.

There were several other photos with inscriptions on the back: "Me and Ursula in Ft. Lauderdale…Me and Ursula on the slopes in Denver…

So many photos. I decided to get off the train that was taking me down someone else's memory lane so fast that my head was spinning. Decided to open up one of the big yellow envelopes. My heart pounding, I was afraid of what I might find there. The first held a set of mortgage documents which read: Don and Elaine Williams, Alpharetta, Georgia. A mortgage note in the amount of $300,500. A note I protested against, but had lost the battle.

"Why do we need a three-hundred thousand dollar house, Don?"

"Because I can afford it."

End of conversation.

In the second envelope was a second set of mortgage documents; a settlement statement which read, "Don Williams and Ursula Douglas, Westwood, California." A mortgage note in the amount of $750,000. A copy of an appraisal showing a property with four bedrooms, three baths, three thousand square feet. My heart dropped to the floor. I was halfway between laughter and tears.

My hands shook as I opened the third envelope. I pulled out a large photo of the fattest, cutest little baby girl I'd ever seen in my life. Samantha was her name. I knew that because Don had scribbled it on the back of the photo in his terrible penmanship, along with her date of birth. In fact, the inscription read, "Samantha Marie Williams, Born June 3, 1987."

Her birth certificate, which I found in the same envelope listed her proud parents as Ursula Douglas and Don Williams. The same two people on the seven-hundred-and-fifty-thousand-dollar mortgage note. And they certainly looked proud in the photos that were also in the envelope. The proud parents holding their baby girl.

"You bastard," I whispered.

My fingertips went numb. I collapsed into the back of the chair for a moment as I gathered my thoughts. My heart pounded so loudly, I could hear it. Not only had

Don had an affair, but he'd also fathered a child. He had fathered the child that I could never bear for him. I couldn't do it, so he'd found someone who could.

The tears on my cheeks came so suddenly, I couldn't control them. I was hurt. No, I was angry. Hurt and angry. Both emotions overtook me. I cried. Cried hard; the kind of crying that comes from deep within. I wondered if Alvin had known about this. Had he known all these years? I was about to find out! I stormed out of Don's office and made my way past Edith's desk toward Alvin's office. Client or not, I needed some answers and he was going to give them to me. How could he know this information and never tell me? What kind of friend would keep this from me? Hadn't he been my friend, too?

"Are you okay, Mrs. Williams?" Edith stood and followed me.

"I need to see Alvin," I said, and kept moving at record speed toward his office.

"He's not to be disturbed, dear," she said.

"I need to see him right away."

"Mrs. Williams!" she said, still behind me, but she was too slow. "You can't go in there!"

I reached for the handle on his door, turned it and pushed it open. Was just about to give him a piece of my mind...about to ask him about this woman named Ursula, and hers and Don's child they called Samantha. Was about to rip him apart and dared him to deny any part of what I was about to say.

Alvin sat on the corner of his desk, his shirt completely opened, revealing his golden, muscular chest, with chest hairs the color of cinnamon. His pants were wrapped around his ankles, as a young handsome man—couldn't have been more than twenty-one—stroked Alvin's chest with his strong hands. The muscles in his strong cheekbones moved back and forth, as he planted a trail of kisses along Alvin's neck. Alvin leaned back, murmuring with sounds of pleasure. That is, until I burst through the door.

"Lainey?" He looked up at me, his face beet-red. "What are you doing here?"

"I tried to stop her from bursting in," Edith said, un-alarmed at the sight of Alvin and his young lover.

He pushed his young lover away, and pulled his pants up. I took off running toward the elevator.

"Lainey, wait!" Alvin was right behind me. "What's going on?"

He buttoned his shirt and tucked it as he struggled to keep up. I pressed the button to call for the elevator, then turned to face him.

"Why didn't you tell me about Ursula and Samantha?" I asked.

He stood—silent for a moment, not prepared for such a question.

"I wanted to tell you, Lainey," he said. "So many times, I wanted to tell you."

"You mean that in eighteen years…that's how old Don's daughter is, by the way….you couldn't find one single opportunity?"

"I'm sorry, Lainey," he said just as the elevator doors opened. "Glenda never told you?"

"She knew?"

His silence was my answer.

I hopped inside the elevator and pressed the button for the lobby.

CHAPTER 13

Nathan

"You win some, you lose some."

Try telling that to a group of hormonal teenagers, a basketball team, who had just lost one of the biggest games of the season. They would look at you like you're crazy and then swear that you're in support of the other team. But my philosophy had always been that it's not important whether you win or lose, but how you played the game. They still weren't hearing it, but I knew they would understand my philosophy later on.

So I just sat on the bus, my head propped against the back of the seat, my eyes lightly shut. The silence was so thick in the air, you could hear a straight pin fall to the floor. A couple of freshmen on the team actually cried. Most of the guys were so angry, they just sulked or slept as we traveled back to our high school in Riverdale. The smell of sweat and sneakers floated in the air as I propped my feet up on the seat across the aisle.

It was late, quickly approaching midnight when the bus wheels came to a screeching halt in front of the gymnasium door. As Jerome, our bus driver, slowly opened the doors of the bus, my boys began to slowly pile out. They dragged themselves and their gym bags into the locker room, mumbling and grumbling the whole way. Trying to convince each other that if they'd just done this…or just done that, they'd have won that game. Then came the finger-pointing and name-calling.

"I don't see how you missed that shot, man," Edwards said what the rest of the team had wanted to say to Collier all night.

"I know, if you not gon' stick to the plays, you could at least make the shot when you take it," Nelson said.

"You need to stop trying to be a one-man team!" Mitchell added.

Collier was silent, and I was glad, because his teammates might have taken him out had he said one word. He just flung his gym bag across his shoulder and strolled into the gym locker room.

I didn't have a pep talk in store for the boys. I was tired and so were they.

"I'll see you all at practice on Monday," was all I said.

They piled out of the gym as I sat in my office, gathered some papers that needed to be graded and stuffed them into my briefcase. Collier lagged behind.

"Can I talk to you for a minute, Coach?" he asked, standing in the doorway of my office.

"What's up?" I asked.

"I think I wanna drop from the team, try to focus on my grades a little more."

"Is that what you wanna do?"

"It's hard trying to play ball and maintain a decent grade point average. I don't have much time to study, and sometimes after those late night games during the week, I fall asleep in my classes."

"So it's getting to be a little too much for you, huh?"

"No doubt, Coach."

"Well, you know, grades are important," I said. "But are you sure this is not about the guys giving you a hard time tonight?"

He was silent.

"They were right, you know," I said. "You shouldn't have missed that shot."

"I know," he admitted, already having let that reality fester the entire ride home, I was sure.

"And you never stick to the plays," I said, loosening my tie and snapping my briefcase shut.

"And I'm always trying to be a one-man team, right?"

"You're certainly not a team player. Not during the crucial times, when your team needs you to be."

"Coach, it's just that sometimes, the plays that we practice are not necessarily what's best at the moment."

"And you determine that based on what?"

"Just based on my intuition."

"What about your coach's intuition? Don't you believe in what I think? What I know?"

"I just go with what I feel, man," he said. "No offense, but some of your plays are whack."

"How would you know when you've never even carried them out?" I told him.

"I'm used to playing street ball and..."

"Well, see there's your problem. This is not street ball. On the court here, there's structure. The purpose of us practicing the plays is so that we're all on one accord during game time. That's what makes us a team. We're like a machine, and a machine can't operate unless all of its parts function properly. Each part has a role, and the other parts depend on each role being carried out. Without that, the machine doesn't function."

"I understand that, Coach." He said, "But I was always taught to stand out in the midst of my peers. That's the only way you can make your mark in this world."

"At the expense of others, right?" I asked. "Let me tell you something, man. You don't have to force your mark upon people. If you have talent, it will show without you even trying. This is a team, Collier. It's not about you winning or losing, but about the success of the team. What you do affects the entire team. If you make a stupid play, the whole team suffers. Tonight we played one of the biggest games of the season, and against a team that sucks! But we lost to them because you're trying to make your mark in the world. Do you think that was fair to your teammates?"

"You said yourself, you win some and you lose some, Coach," he said. "You said it's not important if we win or lose, but how we play the game."

"Exactly!" I said. "The way you played the game caused us to lose tonight. It's okay to lose when you know that you've given your best. That's all you can do.

I feel like the loser here, because I can't get one of my most valuable players on the team to understand the concept of teamwork."

"I'm your most valuable player on the team?"

"I said *one* of my most valuable players." I corrected him. "Remember when Michael Jordan played for the Bulls?"

"Yeah."

"Why do you think that team was so successful?"

"Because Michael Jordon was on it," he said matter-of-factly.

"True." I said, "But he wasn't the only player on the team. He was a team player. He forced every player on that team to step up their game. He understood the dynamics of teamwork."

"But he was the star of the team, Coach," he said. "People didn't pay to see the Chicago Bulls. They paid to see Jordan do his thing."

"He took the plays that were practiced, carried them out at the game and made them his own. And not only did he take ownership of the plays, but he made sure every one of his teammates did the same." I said, "He was a team player. Go to the library, get you a book about MJ, and let me know what you find."

"I will, Coach."

"Cool," I said, and then headed toward the door, turned off the light. Collier moved out of my way as I brushed past him.

"Can I get a ride home, Coach?" he asked.

"Yeah, man."

* * *

I pulled up in front of Collier's ranch-style home, the porch light beaming and lighting up the entire front yard. Collier sighed.

"What's up?" I asked as he suddenly seemed distressed about getting out.

"My brother's car," he said, referring to the souped-up Chevy Impala parked in front of me. "The basketball star is home."

"So he plays?"

"Averages twenty-eight points a game, starting forward, full athletic scholarship..." he said. "Dean's honor roll."

"Your parents must be proud."

"No doubt," he said. "My mother can't stop talking about him to all of her friends. And my father...man, he's reliving his college days vicariously through my brother."

"Vicariously? That's a big word, brother. I see you've been paying attention in your English class." I laughed. "Your grades aren't bad, Collier."

"Yeah, but I'm not on the honor roll." He said, "And I haven't broken any basketball records."

"So that's what this one-man-team crap is all about? Trying to outdo your brother?"

"I'm not trying to outdo him, I just want my father to recognize my skills for a change." He dropped his head. "I can't even get him to come to one of my games. But he'll drive down to Athens with a quickness, whenever Dre has a big game. Says that when I do something that makes the AJC, he'll come and check me out."

I was at a loss for words. I suddenly wanted to have a conversation with Mr. Collier. Wanted to ask what type of father would treat his son like that, but my experience with teenagers had taught me to believe only half of what you hear. However, the look on Collier's face told me that he had a lot of resentment toward his brother. It was real to him; living in someone's shadow.

"Thanks for the ride, Coach," he said, opening my passenger door and grabbing his gym bag. "I'll see you at school on Monday."

"Don't forget what we talked about."

"I got you," he said as he shut the door and made his way toward his front porch, pants sagging at the rear, and baseball cap turned backward on his head.

I made a mental note to reach out to Mr. Collier real soon.

I stepped into the kitchen, swung the refrigerator door open in search of something cold to drink. Found a bottle of water, and knew I needed to find a supermarket soon. The fridge was empty besides an egg carton with two eggs in it, half of a two-liter bottle of flat Coke, and some leftovers that should've been thrown out days ago. Reminded me of the fridge in my college dorm, which was always empty, with the exception of an occasional pizza box and a couple of beers.

In my bedroom, I kicked the Stacy Adams' off my feet, peeled my tie and shirt off, and fell backward onto the bed. Wanted to shower, but was too tired to make my way into the bathroom. Grabbed the remote from the nightstand and tuned it to CNN to catch the latest news.

The phone rang and I contemplated not answering, but knew that the hospital might call at any time. I grabbed the receiver.

"Hello?"

"How are you?" the familiar voice asked. "It's Lainey."

"I'm fine." For some reason, my voice smiled. "How are you?"

"Not so good," she said. "I need to talk."

"What's up?"

"Can you meet me for a bite to eat?" she asked, and sounded desperate.

I glanced at the digital clock on the nightstand. Twelve-thirty. I was tired, but it seemed important. I managed to sit up.

"IHOP?"

"I'll be there in thirty minutes."

CHAPTER 14

Lainey

Nathan walked through the door and made his way through the crowd. I'd already snagged us a corner booth near the window and was nursing a cup of coffee. He smiled as he slid his tall frame into the booth, a wool sweater hugging his muscular chest.

"Hey," he said.

"Hey."

Before he could pick up his menu, the waitress was there, pen in hand, ready to take his drink order. He ordered a glass of water with lemon and a cup of coffee. She disappeared.

"What's up? Sounded serious on the phone."

"How was your day?" I asked. "You look tired. And now that you're here, I feel horrible for dragging you out. You had a game tonight, right?"

"Yeah, I did. But it's okay." he said, "I got a second wind now."

"I'm sorry still," I said, and really was.

"Don't worry about it, Lainey," he said, and grabbed his menu. "What's going on?"

I took a deep breath.

"I went to my husband's office today...to retrieve his things."

"That must've been hard," he said, peering over the top of his menu, his eyes becoming sad. "Did you go alone?"

"Yes, and it was hard, at first. Packing his things into a cardboard box like that. It broke my heart," I told him. "But what really broke my heart more was what I found when I started digging through his things."

"What'd you find?"

"Pictures of Don with another woman."

He shut the menu and laid it on the table, looked at me tenderly. "I'm sorry, Lainey."

"That's not all I found. I discovered that not only did he have relationship with this woman, but he also owns property with her...in Westwood, California. A seven-hundred-thousand-dollar home."

"What?" He stared at me in amazement, his eyes wide.

"Yeah, a mortgage twice the amount of ours," I told him. "But that's not all."

"There's more?" he asked as the waitress approached carrying his drinks on a tray.

"Are you guys ready to order?" she asked, and set Nathan's water and coffee in front of him.

"I'm just gonna have the steak and eggs, Susan," he said, reading the waitress's name on her name tag.

"How would you like your steak, sir?"

"Medium," he said. "Eggs over easy. Wheat toast."

"And for you, ma'am?" She looked at me.

"I'm just having coffee," I said. My appetite was long gone.

Susan disappeared and Nathan's eyes were steady on me.

"What else?" he asked.

"He has a child with this...this woman, Ursula." I said her name through clinched teeth. Saying her name was somewhat therapeutic, as though saying it made it less painful. "Their child's name is Samantha."

"He left evidence of all of this in his office?"

"Under lock and key, of course."

"Wow," he said, and then grabbed my hands in his. "You did have a bad day."

"How could he do this?" I asked, not really looking for an answer, just needing to pose the question out loud.

"I'm sorry you had to go through that, Lainey. I can't even imagine how you must feel," he said.

"I'm just trying to come to grips with it," I said.

"How old is the child?"

"She's eighteen."

"Eighteen?" He was shocked. "And you had no idea?"

"Not a clue." I took a sip of my coffee. "Turns out my best friend did have a clue, however, but never told me."

"Really?"

"My friend Glenda," I said. "Remember you met her at dinner?"

"I remember," he said. "She knew?"

"If I can't trust my best friend, who can I trust?"

"You can trust me."

"I'm never speaking to her again."

"Have you asked her about it?"

"I won't take her calls," I said, and wrapped my hands around my coffee mug again. "I'm through with her. She's dead to me, like Don."

"You don't mean that, Lainey," he said, and I looked at him cockeyed. "You should at least give her a chance to explain."

I was silent. He changed the subject, and I stared out the window.

"What are you going to do?"

"I have to go there," I said.

"There?"

"California," I said, looking at him for a reaction. "I bought a ticket today."

"You serious?"

"I wanna see this for myself," I said. "This is the woman who stole my life from me. Robbed me of my marriage for eighteen plus years."

Nathan stared at me as if I was speaking Japanese.

"What?" I asked. "I'm curious."

"Curious enough to just hop on a plane and fly out there? What will you do there? What will you say?"

"I'll let her know who I am, and ask for some answers," I said as the waitress appeared with a tray filled with pancakes, steak and eggs.

"Here we are," she said, placing Nathan's plate in front of him. The smell of the sirloin made me wish I'd ordered one, too. He cut into it to make sure it was cooked the way he'd ordered it, juices drizzling all over his plate.

Susan refreshed my coffee. "Give a holler if you need anything else."

She was gone.

"So you're going out there, huh?" Nathan asked, his mouth filled with buttermilk pancakes. "How long will you be gone?"

"Just a few days." I took a walk on the wild side. "Come with me."

There was that look again, as if I'd said something in Japanese.

"Never mind. I was just kidding." I laughed, mostly from embarrassment. I'd overstepped my boundaries.

"Don't play with me like that." He waved his fork at me; smiled. "I almost took you seriously."

"What if I were serious?"

"Were you?"

"Would you say I was crazy?"

"No," he said. "No, I wouldn't say you were crazy."

We left it at that. Nathan finished his steak and eggs, paid the check and walked me to my car.

"Thanks for dinner," he said as he pulled my driver's door open.

"Thank you for coming." He was close enough for me to smell the mint that he'd popped into his mouth.

He straightened the collar of my leather coat. Leaned in. His arms around my neck, he pulled me close. Gave me the strongest hug I'd ever known.

He pulled away, his Acqua di Gio cologne lingering. Flashed his beautiful pearly whites. "Drive safe."

CHAPTER 15

Nathan

In my bedroom, it felt like déjà vu, as I kicked the Stacy Adams' off my feet again and peeled my tie and shirt off. I fell backward onto the bed, grabbed the remote from the nightstand and tuned it to ESPN to catch the latest sports news. My mind drifted to thoughts of Lainey. It was something about her that drew me, and I felt guilty for not only enjoying my time with her, but for spending the entire ride home actually contemplating a trip to California.

"This is crazy, man. You can't even consider this," I'd told myself just moments before in my pickup. "What would you do with your kids...what would you tell the school? And besides, you hardly even know this woman. You're playing with fire. You've been down this road before."

I thought about the woman I'd had a brief roll in the hay with only a few years ago. The one who almost cost me my family. But just as quickly, I was engaged in thoughts of Lainey again.

The other half of me answered. "Mike Holmes could

practice with the kids...get them ready for the next game. They could find a sub for your Algebra class. You have like, four weeks of vacation time built up...not to mention you haven't taken a vacation all year. And it's not like you're cheating. Lainey is a friend. She's a victim of circumstance, just like you. Separate hotel rooms... and no leisure time. Just business. Yep, it would be a business trip."

"What if Marva wakes up? What then?" the responsible part of me asked. "Squash the thought of this trip. It's too risky."

I pulled myself up from our Serta mattress, the one Marva had talked me into just a few months before. She claimed that it would do wonders for my back, and it had.

I found my way to the shower.

The lighting in Marva's room was dimmed as usual. I took my usual place in the orange leather chair in the corner. On Saturday mornings I stayed most of the day, grading papers and reading my students' essays. Sometimes she'd open her eyes. Other times she'd appear to be crying or even laughing. But it wasn't because she was aware that I was there, it was just par for the course.

I decided that after my visit, I would take a drive to Alabama for the weekend. The thought of Mama's sweet potato pie made me drive a little faster to Toulminville. I seemed to have gotten there in half the time, as I walked into my parents' house, Shaquille O'Neal running down the court on their floor model television in the living room. Only nobody was watching. I watched as Shaq dunked the ball. The television, that had been a fixture in my parents' living room since I was seven years old, was muted as an old Al Green tune was playing loudly on Daddy's old stereo. The smell of mustard and turnip greens floating through the air, I followed the aroma as well as the voices that I heard coming from the kitchen.

"Why's the TV on in there, and nobody's watching it?" I asked as all four of my parents yelled in surprise. I hadn't shared that I was coming.

"Lord, Nate, what're you doing here?" Mama asked, springing from her chair at the kitchen table and planting a kiss on my lips. "We weren't expecting you today, baby."

"Thought I'd come and see what y'all got cooking up in this kitchen." I smiled.

"How you doing, son?" Poppa Joe asked, refreshing his plate with fried chicken and the biggest mountain of macaroni and cheese I'd ever seen.

"Doing fine, Poppa Joe," I said, patting my father-in-law on his stomach. "Thought you were watching that diet."

"After today, boy. After today."

"Hush your lies, Joe," Helen said. "You been going on a diet for twenty years now."

"Supposed to quit smoking, too." Mama chimed in. "But we all know he sneaks a puff when nobody's looking."

"Aw, here they go. You see how they team up on me, Nate?" Poppa Joe asked.

"Yep, I see."

"How're you, baby?" Helen asked and hugged me.

"Doin' fine, Mother," I said, reaching on the shelf for a plate. "I'll be doing even better when I get some of this good food in my stomach."

"We see that you came straight for the kitchen and grabbed a plate." My father gave me a strong hug. "How was your drive, son?"

"Enjoyable. I popped in a jazz CD, and it was smooth sailing."

"You sure need to eat, Nate," Mama said. "You looking mighty puny. I don't like you looking like that. Are you eating at all?"

"I'm eating, Mama." I kissed my mother's forehead and pushed past her, reaching for a golden-brown chicken wing.

"Fix me another highball, Joe," Helen said, asking my father-in-law to refresh her glass of Rémy Martin and Coke.

He grabbed her glass and poured her another drink.

"Helen told me about the author lady you all had dinner with, Nate," Mama said. "I can't wait to go to her seminar. I already have my outfit picked out."

"She was a very nice girl, Savannah. You would've liked her," Helen said. "Lainey was pretty nice, too. She seemed sweet enough."

"How's Lainey doing with all that she's been through?"

"She's getting along." I said, and then stuffed a corn-bread muffin into my mouth. Changed the subject. "Daddy, you and Poppa Joe been out on the course today?"

"First thing this morning." Daddy stuck his chest out, started cheesing. "Now ask him who won."

"Oh, here we go." Poppa Joe stood, threw his empty Budweiser bottle into the trash can and grabbed another one from the refrigerator. "I admit my game was a little off this morning."

"This morning?" my father asked.

"Nate, tell your daddy to go jump in a lake, would you?"

Laughter filled the kitchen.

"Speaking of a lake, can we go fishing in the morning?" I asked.

"Sure thang," Poppa Joe said.

"But early. Before the birds get to chirping," Daddy said, reminding me that he and Poppa Joe were usually up at the crack of dawn. "I'll wake you up."

"What about church?" Mama asked. "I've got to show Nate off at church in the morning, now. He don't come here that often and some of the old sisters at church sure would like to see him. They remember when he was knee-high to a chipmunk. And they just so proud of him, moving to Atlanta and all."

"We'll have the fish caught and cleaned by the time church starts, Savannah," Daddy said. "Besides, I don't think Nate is looking forward to seeing all those old sisters at church."

"Especially that skinny one who wears that big old hat and plops herself on the front row every Sunday," Poppa Joe added.

"And the big round one with the big knockers." Daddy made hand motions to describe Sister Allen's generous breasts.

"Behave, both of you," Mama told Daddy and Poppa Joe. "You both ought to be ashamed of yourselves."

Daddy's entire frame shook when he laughed, and tears were falling from Poppa Joe's eyes.

"I'll be back in time for church, Mama. I promise," I said, laughing and taking in a forkful of greens.

Just being in the room with my parents let me know just how much I'd missed adult conversation. It was lonely at home without Marva, which is why I'd found myself on the highway bound for Alabama in the first place.

When Daddy tapped on my door the next morning, I opened one eye just to make sure I wasn't dreaming. It was him all right, dressed in his fishing garb, baseball cap and those same black boots that he wore fishing when I was a child. I looked at the clock on the night table. Five o'clock, and the only thing moving was a cricket outside my bedroom window, chirping like he'd lost his mind.

"Get on up and wash your face, son," Daddy said. "Joe got the truck warming up."

Daddy was completely dressed and ready to go. Poppa Joe had the truck running, which meant he was also completely dressed. The two of them had drank Budweisers and argued until well past midnight. Al Green, BB King and James Brown had sung at least a dozen songs each. I'd pressed the pillow against my face just to drown them out, and here they were, both up at the crack of dawn, Poppa Joe's pickup blowing fumes down the block, fishing poles and live worms in the back of the truck.

I pulled myself out of bed, washed my face and made my way through the quiet house and into the kitchen.

"Mornin', son." Poppa Joe looked up from his plastic cup filled with Maxwell House, a tan fishing hat on his head with a catfish embroidered across the front of it.

"Mornin', Poppa Joe," I said, and poured myself a cup of coffee.

It was much too early for conversation and we were all quiet as we crept outside and piled into the cab of Poppa Joe's pickup.

Church wasn't as quiet as the choir sang about how Jesus will fix it. They swayed to the music in unison as the old wooden floor creaked with every movement. I slid into the pew with Mama on one side of me and Helen on the other. They took great pride in showing me off to their friends at church. They were proud that Marva and I had escaped Toulminville, a place that held no promise of a future for either of us. Proud that their children had gone to college and were now living in the big city—Atlanta. Educators. Successful, with a big beautiful house in a nice subdivision. Drove nice cars and successfully reared a child who was now in college. We were the epitome of success, while many of the other church members' daughters and sons had found meaningless lives of drugs and crime.

Just as I'd stopped at the gas station on the way into the city, Minnie Williams was the one who'd rang up my gas and bottle of Coke. She'd landed a job there right after our high school graduation, and I was shocked to discover that she still worked there.

"Hey, Nate," she'd said, and had picked up about twenty extra pounds since high school. "When did you get home?"

"Just got here," I'd told her. "Literally just got off the highway."

"How've you been?"

"Pretty good," I'd said. "You still work at the Chevron, huh?"

"I'm a manager now." She'd smiled, proud of her recent promotion.

"How've you been, Minnie?" I asked.

"Been all right. Just had surgery."

"Oh, really?" I'd asked in my concerned voice.

"Had them bunions removed off my feet," she'd said, and made a movement like she might show me. "They feel so much better now."

"O-oh, I'm glad," I'd said, referring to the fact that she didn't show me.

"How's Marva? I heard she ain't doing too well," she'd said. "Somebody said she in a deep sleep and can't get herself out."

"Something like that," I'd said, "but we're praying for her."

"Well I'm praying for her, too."

"You take care, Minnie. It was good seeing you," I'd said, and darted out the door.

I felt sorry for Minnie.

After the Jesus Will Fix It song, it was offering time. I peeled a twenty dollar bill out of my pocket and placed it in the offering tray. When my cell phone began to loudly play a little tune, every eye in the house stared my way. Mama frowned. I pulled it out of my pocket and silenced it. Checked the number. Lainey. I wondered if something was wrong. She'd been pretty distraught on Friday night when we had dinner. I found myself suddenly worried. Part of me wanted to rush into the basement of the church and call her back. I became fidgety.

"What's wrong with you?" Mama whispered.

"Nothing," I whispered back, and started tapping my size twelve Florsheim's against the wooden floor and clapping to the beat of the next song.

At my in-law's house, my brother Henry Junior had piled his plate with fresh-cut green beans and barbecue ribs that Poppa Joe had finished cooking on the old charcoal grill while Helen was at church. A baseball cap turned backward on his head, Junior was putting food away so fast, it seemed that he hadn't eaten in days.

"That my little knuckleheaded brother?" he asked as I walked through the door.

"In the flesh," I said, and gave him the handshake that's only shared among black men.

"When you get here?" he asked.

"Yesterday," I said.

"You mean you been in town two days and this the first I heard of it?" He kept putting food away. "Mama, why didn't you tell me that the star was in town?"

My mama looked at Junior, and then snatched his cap off of his head.

"How many times I gotta tell you to take your hat off in the house, Junior?" Mama asked.

"Sorry, Ma," he said and kissed her cheek.

"Where's Ebony?" I asked about the young lady he'd introduced to the family at Christmastime. Said they were thinking about getting married.

"History."

"You are pitiful," I said.

"I need to come down there to the ATL and find me one of them fine women they got. They say if I move there, I'd have about twelve women jocking me all at one time." He smiled and looked just like my mother. "That true, Nate?"

"I wouldn't know. I'm a married man," I said. "And if I wasn't, I wouldn't have twelve women at once. A brother would have to be out of his mind to do that."

"I wouldn't mind one bit." Junior stood and refreshed his plate.

He was my older brother, and you could tell by looking at us. But once he opened his mouth, you couldn't tell. When it came to maturity, I had him by a few years. I was the levelheaded one. Junior did what felt good at the moment, never planned anything, and didn't care about much. He changed women about as often as he changed underwear, and changed jobs just as often. He stopped caring about things after he injured his leg in college and ended his football career.

The whole time we were growing up and all through high school, everyone knew that Junior Sullivan would be the next O.J. Simpson. He had the size and the skills to go pro. Had scouts watching him in college. But when he injured his leg, and tore parts of it that would never heal, his career came to a screeching halt. He went into a depression so deep, my parents had to seek counseling for him. He gave up on everything. Dropped out of college and went to work at a local plant. That was the beginning of his downward plunge.

"How's my sister-in-law?" he asked.

"About the same," I said, and fixed a plate.

"You know I would've been there to see her, Nate, but you know...I got this new job and everything," he said.

"It's cool, man."

"Plus, I really don't wanna see my sister like that, you know?" He said, "That kinda stuff messes with my head."

"Don't even sweat it, Junior."

"Is that Nathan Earl Sullivan?" Someone tackled me from behind as if we were on the football field, slammed me into the kitchen counter.

I immediately put Marva's brother, Rick, in a headlock.

"What do you have to say now, Richard?" I asked, calling him by his birth name, which he hated.

"Watch it, boy. The name is Rick," he said, and we shook hands. "What's going on with you, man?"

"Same old, same old."

Rick was more of a brother to me than Junior had ever been. We were closer than brothers growing up; more like best friends. We played together, fought sometimes, and chased down some of the same girls back in the day. Went away to college around the same time. I went to

Alabama State, while he went away to Grambling on a full scholarship. He ended up moving back to Toulmanville and working for a local law firm. Married his high school sweetheart and they were living happily ever after. He was the spitting image of Poppa Joe. And he thought the world of my wife, his little sister, and was ready to kill anybody who looked like they might hurt her.

"If you ever cheat on my sister, I'll kill you, Nate," he told me once; serious, his face like stone. "I mean that."

Marva never revealed my affair to our families. It was a secret that we kept between each other, and never even talked about it again. After I'd confessed and begged for her forgiveness, it was long forgotten. I was grateful for that, as I didn't want her family or mine knowing that I had ever been unfaithful. Particularly Rick. I wasn't afraid of him, but didn't want anything to ever jeopardize our lifelong friendship. He might not have been as forgiving as my wife.

"How 'bout some one-on-one, man? Out back," Rick said as I dug into my plate. "Wrap your plate up and let's see what you got."

"Rick, fix you something to eat first," Helen said.

"I will, Mother. I just wanna take this old man outside and rough him up a bit," he said.

"Not right now," I said, and kept eating.

"What, you scared?"

"Not hardly," I said. "I'm trying to get my grub on right now."

"Food'll be here when you come back."

"You don't let up, do you?"

"Not usually," he said. "Let's see what you been teaching them students of yours about basketball. See what kinda game you got."

"Let's go," I said, wrapping my plate in aluminum foil and heading out the back door.

"Nate, you still have on your Sunday clothes," Mama said as the screen door slammed. "And it's cold out there."

"Plus you have to get on the road soon, baby," Helen added.

"That's okay, it won't take me long to whip this chump."

"Now see, there you go talking junk," Rick said, and followed me to the basketball goal in his parents' backyard; the one with no net, just a rusted rim. The same backyard court where we'd played a million basketball games over the years. The same goal where I'd dunked my first basket. The exact place where I broke my ankle and wore a cast for several months. The same place where I kissed Marva for the first time. That backyard held many memories for me.

"You take it out first," Rick said, throwing the ball straight at my chest.

I began to dribble the ball with my right hand, loosened my tie with my left hand, and prayed I didn't scuff my Florsheim's while trying to be seventeen again.

I popped the ball into the basket and then took it out again.

"Lucky shot," Rick mumbled.

"Don't hate, my brother." I smiled. "You asked for this spanking."

The ball popped into the basket again, and I roared with laughter. My brother-in-law didn't even crack a smile. Instead he stole the ball and took it to the basket; slammed it in. Did some sort of chicken-like dance around me.

"Take that!" he said.

"I'll give you that. But you won't be getting any more."

We talked junk, and wore each other out for at least thirty minutes on that old court. My shirt was soaked from the sweat that was also popping off of my forehead; the toes of my shoes were scuffed. But I had long stopped caring about the shoes. It had been a while since I just played a nice game of one-on-one. And it gave me great pleasure, putting a whipping on my junk-talking brother-in-law. Somebody had to shut him up.

We retired to the family room; caught the end of the Hawks game. It seemed like old times as Daddy and Poppa Joe's voices rang out from the kitchen. They laughed heartily, and every now and then Mama and Helen would giggle at their foolish talk. They were listening to some old Lou Rawls tune where he was telling a story in his baritone. I dreaded the drive back to Atlanta, but knew I needed to head home soon. I stole a quick snooze, until Mama shook me and told me it was getting late.

Headed down I-20 east toward home, I popped in Simply Red's newest CD. Simply Red had been one of my favorite groups since they'd released "Holding Back the Years" in the late eighties. What did a country boy from a small town in Alabama know or like about a red-headed British guy?

A lot.

"Holding Back the Years" had been a song I danced to with Marva. Senior prom. She wore lavender and lace, her head filled with curls. I think that was the night we'd both fallen in love with each other. It was the night we both fell in love with Simply Red, too. They'd become our favorite group, and we'd bought every album they ever made. I smiled about the time that we'd driven my dull green Buick Century all the way to Atlanta for the concert when they performed at the Civic Center.

The funny thing about the CD that I listened to now, was that Marva had given it to me for Christmas. But the truth of it is, it had spent more time in her car's CD player than it did mine. It was the CD that she'd played on her way home from Braselton that night of the accident. I'd heard it in the background as I talked to her on the phone. Simply Red's remake of Harold Melvin and the Bluenotes' "If You Don't Know Me By Now" blared through the phone right about the time she'd pulled off the highway bound for the Chevron to fill her tank.

"I'll call you back in a minute, Nate," she'd said. "I'm stopping for gas, and you know what they say about talking on a cell phone and pumping gas."

"You call me right back," I told her. "As soon as you get done."

"I will, baby." She laughed. "You worry too much."

"It's because I love you."

"How much?" she asked. Always asked that when I told her that I loved her.

"More than you know," was always my response.

Tears filled my eyes as I remembered that those were the last words we shared. The last time I heard my wife's voice.

CHAPTER 16

Lainey

My luggage stacked at the front door, I waited for my driver to arrive. I'd put the finishing touches on my eyes and lips and sprayed a little cologne behind my ear. I ran for the kitchen, grabbed my bagel from the toaster and smothered it in salmon-flavored cream cheese.

"Mmm." I hummed as I took a bite. "That's good."

When the doorbell chimed, I looked at my watch. The driver was early, but I rushed to the door. Swung it open.

"What are you doing here?" I asked my unwanted guest.

"Lainey, we have to talk."

"I don't have anything to talk to you about," I said. "I'm on my way out."

"I just need a few minutes," Glenda said, and stepped inside anyway.

"Make it quick. I have a flight to catch."

"I know I should've told you about Don and Ursula, but I didn't want to hurt you. I was protecting you. I thought that she was just another one of Don's flings, that is until he started bringing her to functions and flying her from country to country. He tried bringing her to my house once when Alvin and I were married, and I told him if he ever tried it again I'd blow his cover wide open. He knew she wasn't welcome in my space, not as long as he was married to you. I didn't know about the baby until after you'd miscarried the last time." She said, "I didn't know how to tell you that your husband had another woman pregnant at the same time that you were. And I couldn't tell you that she'd carried her baby to term while you'd lost yours."

"A true friend would've told me."

"I didn't want to hurt you, Lainey. You'd been through so much with him already, and I thought that was too much for you to handle," she said.

"Who were you to decide what I could handle?"

"Someone who cared," Glenda said. "I'm your friend, Lainey, and I love you. I'm sorry. I realize now that I should've told you. I thought it was over between those two because I never heard any more about her. Alvin kept it in such confidence, never breathing a word to me."

"You should've told me."

"I know now, honey. And I'm sorry." She said, "I pray that you'll forgive me, because I value your friendship so much."

"I'm on my way to find my own answers. I'm going to California."

"What's in California?"

"Ursula and Samantha," I said. "I wanna see this

seven hundred and fifty thousand dollar house Don bought for them in Westwood, California."

"Wow. I had no idea," she said. "Can you ever forgive me?"

"I don't know if I can," I told her. "I just don't know, Glenda. I just need some time, to sort things out. Think things through."

"Do you want me to go with you? I have a seminar this afternoon, but after that, I'm free."

"No."

"I'm sorry," she whispered, and moved toward the door. "I know you're hurting, but I'm here if you ever need me."

I never answered.

She left.

After receiving my boarding pass, I plopped down in the seat next to a guy who was chattering nonstop on a cell phone, barking orders at the person on the other end. Dressed in an Armani business suit, he told the caller on the other end of the phone to book him a hotel in downtown Los Angeles and set him up a dinner meeting with a client. He was talking so loud, I wondered if the person was hearing impaired. Wanted to tell him that he was interrupting me as I flipped through the *Atlanta Journal Constitution* and sipped on my Cinnamon Dolce Latte that I'd picked up at Starbucks on the way to my gate. When they began to board the first-class passengers, I prayed his seat was in coach and not next to mine.

"Lainey." Someone called my name, and I couldn't imagine who at Hartsfield-Jackson International Airport knew me on a first-name basis. I turned to find Nathan's handsome eyes staring into mine.

"Nathan."

"Hi."

"What are you doing here?"

"I have no idea." He smiled. "But I just bought a ticket to L.A. Cost me a bundle, too. This last-minute ticketing ain't no joke."

Armani Suit looked at us as if we were interrupting his phone call.

"What about your kids? Your Algebra class?"

"I got someone to cover both," he said. "You don't mind if I tag along, do you?"

"Not at all, but…"

"I really do need a vacation." He said, "Not to mention, I've just been worried about you. Don't want you to go this alone."

"That's sweet," I said, grabbing his boarding pass. "Are you in first class?"

"Coach." He laughed. "I tried to smooth-talk the sister behind the counter into upgrading me, but she wasn't hearing it."

"You're something."

"It's okay. I'm cool in coach. I'll grade some papers or something."

"Nate. Thank you for coming."

"Don't mention it."

I waited for Nathan to find his way off the plane, and together we headed for baggage claim, retrieved our bags and rented a Lincoln Town Car. Nathan threw our bags into the trunk of the car, removed his blazer, laid it on the back seat and then slid into the driver's seat. Driving down Wilshire Boulevard, palm trees swaying in the wind, I reclined in my leather seat. Los Angeles weather was a beautiful seventy-one degrees, with sunshine that you wanted to package up and take back home to Atlanta.

Nathan pulled the Lincoln in front of the W Hotel, a savvy and contemporary version of the Westin hotel line. The valet rushed to open my door, and I stepped out of the car. The concierge retrieved our bags from the trunk, placed them on his golden cart and we followed him inside. I checked into my reserved room as Nathan checked availability for a room of his own. Luckily they had a king available and were able to book us on the same floor.

"I'm gonna grab a shower and change." I tossed my leather bag across my shoulder. "Maybe we can go sight-seeing later."

"That sounds like fun," he said as we rode the elevator up.

We started off down Wilshire Boulevard, past the condos for the rich and famous, in the upscale area of Westwood. It was a high-dollar area; majestic. In fact, when you drove down Wilshire, you knew it was out of your league. Even the buildings mocked you, as if to say, "If you have to ask, you can't afford it." Making our way over to Hollywood Boulevard—Holly-weird as some folks called it—I sat straight up in my seat to get a good look at the weirdos. This was the part of California where a camera is a must. I pulled mine out of my leather bag.

"You're acting just like a tourist." Nathan laughed.

"I am a tourist."

"But you don't have to let the world know."

I didn't care; I snapped pictures of everything moving. From the prostitute standing on the corner flagging down every passerby that looked her way to the six foot five inch tall, deeply chocolate brother wearing a blond wig, a yellow spandex mini dress, fishnet stockings and fuchsia stilettos. His legs were muscular and toned as he strutted his stuff down Holly-weird.

"Would you like to get out and walk?" Nathan asked as he searched for a parking space on the street. Parking in L.A. was always a challenge. If you found a spot, it was as if you'd found a glass of water in the middle of the Sahara desert. We drove around the block, past the new Hollywood Highland complex with the huge flat-screen television reminiscent of the one in Times Square. I felt the onset of motion sickness as we passed it for the fifth time.

"I don't think we're gonna find a spot," I said.

"I think you might be right."

As two young teenage girls giggled and strolled past on the boulevard, I thought of Don's daughter, Samantha. If I'd seen her on the street, I wouldn't have known her. Wondered what she looked like, what she was like, if she'd spent much time with her father when he was alive, if he loved her. Wondered what my own child would've looked like; been like. Suddenly, I was reminded of why I was here, and it wasn't to drive down Hollywood Boulevard checking out the sights with Nathan Sullivan. I was here to confront Don's mistress and to find out what type of woman would build a secret life with a man she knew was married. I wanted to see this daughter of his; to see if she was pretty or awkward-looking. Would she have Don's eyes or his smile? To be honest, anger had given me the courage to travel to Westwood, California, looking to put my fears to rest and to just be plain nosy. But after I was there, in a new state of mind and in the presence of such wonderful company, I didn't really know why I'd bothered. But I'd come too far to turn back now. I had to follow through with my plan. I deserved every inch of the truth.

The restaurant that the concierge had recommended was everything he said it would be and more. Yamashiro, which means Mountain Palace, is a unique restaurant housed in a mansion that was built 250 feet above Hollywood Boulevard. So much history in this place: In the late 1920s Yamashiro served as headquarters for an elite club that was created for Hollywood's motion picture industry. Yamashiro served as Hollywood's first celebrity hangout. That was before the Great Depression, a time in which the country suffered but Yamashiro remained. There were even rumors that during those tragic years of depression, beautiful starving actresses made themselves available for hire at Yamashiro for an evening to those who could still afford such pleasures.

After Pearl Harbor, Yamashiro was mistaken to be a signal tower for the Japanese. However, for three decades after that it had been a restaurant with a succulent Japanese menu and wonderful Japanese ambience, serving what was called a CalAsian cuisine. Yamashiro was a beautiful, sexy and secluded little jewel that Nathan and I stumbled upon.

After dinner we partook of the breathtaking sunset view, an outrageous garden that overlooked the city of Los Angeles. I stood against the railing, my black after-five dress, in all of its splendor, clinging to my body. The neck of it low enough to say, *I'm sexy* without yelling *I'm available* to this man who was looking at me with wanting eyes. He tried to avoid staring, but it was difficult for him. I could tell. The dress was gorgeous; one that Don had brought back from one of his many adventures. Taiwan, I believe it was. I'd packed it for this trip, not really expecting the opportunity to actually wear it. But when the concierge described Yamashiro to us, I was glad I'd thrown it in my garment bag.

After our sightseeing tour through the streets of Los Angeles, we'd trekked back to the hotel, worn out, but starving. We'd both agreed to meet in the lobby at seven, dressed for the evening's nightlife.

"I don't wanna eat at the hotel's restaurant or spend the evening at the bar. I like to really experience a city when I visit," Nathan had said. "We can eat wherever you want."

"Let's try that place the concierge told us about…that Yama…what is it?" I'd asked.

"Yama something," he'd said. "I'm all for that. But I think you need to dress up. Are you prepared for that?"

"I brought a couple of dresses. What about you?"

"Got a suit."

With that, we were off to our respective quarters. I'd peeled my jeans and sneakers off, hopped in the shower and was in that dress so fast I had too much idle time left over. I brewed a pot of coffee and sipped on a cup as seven o'clock slowly approached.

Nathan had tapped on my door wearing a navy Italian suit, a colorful silk tie, and a pair of very nice shoes. I checked out the shoes first, because shoes told you a lot about a man. They were a dead giveaway to whether or not he could dress. There was nothing worse than a man dressed in an expensive suit, but had fallen short on the shoes. Shoes were just as important as fresh breath and good personal hygiene.

"You look gorgeous," he'd said.

"Thank you. So do you."

We looked like royalty as we strolled through the hotel lobby and then stood outside as the valet retrieved our rental car.

As I stood against that railing, breathing in the beauty of the sunset, the cool breeze from California's night air brushing lightly across my face, I couldn't think of any other place I'd rather be. I shivered as the night air brushed chill bumps across my arms. It was chilly, but I didn't want to leave; couldn't. It was too beautiful.

"You look cold," he said, peeling his jacket off. "Here, take my jacket."

He reached around me and placed it over my shoulders, his fingertips lingering around the collar and then brushing through my hair. Impulsively, my hands touched his chest; a chest that appeared to be chiseled from repetitions at the gym. As I caressed his broad chest, I never stopped to ask myself, "What are you doing?" I just continued. His eyes touched mine and sent electricity through my body. He drew closer. Close enough that the smell of his cologne teased my senses. His arms around my shoulders, he pulled me close. I wrapped my arms around his waist. I opened my mouth to ask what we were doing in this beautiful place, wrapped in each other's arms, but before the words tumbled out, his lips were on mine.

His pelvis pressed against my stomach, his strong hand palming the back of my head, his other hand pulling me closer. I knew I should've stopped, should've headed him off at the pass, but I couldn't. I couldn't stop him if I wanted to, and I didn't. But evidently the guilt of his lips against mine was too much for him. He pulled his lips away.

"I'm sorry…I just…you were just standing there looking so beautiful. I couldn't help myself."

Why did he have to be sorry?

I turned away, looked at the view of the city. His arms wrapped around me from behind, I could feel his breath in my ear.

"I'm very attracted to you, but I don't want to do anything that I'll regret later."

"I understand."

"We're both grieving right now, and I don't want to minimize that."

"Yes."

"You ready to go?" he asked. "You have a big day planned for tomorrow."

I'd planned a surprise visit to Ursula's seven hundred grand minimansion in Westwood. I thought I'd just show up on her doorstep and introduce myself, until Nathan suggested that we sit down over breakfast the next morning and prepare a strategy. I agreed.

"Yes, let's go."

As we strolled to the car, the night air breezing through my hair, not a word was spoken. I wanted him, and it had nothing to do with grief. I knew at the moment his lips touched mine that I wanted more than just his body, I wanted all of him. And he wanted me, too. But wanting each other was wrong, morally and spiritually. Wasn't it? Wasn't God disapproving of such a notion? Surely he was. I wasn't as committed a Christian as I should've been. In fact, many Sundays I spent reclined on my sofa in front of the television or curled up with a good book. I didn't give much of my time to God, but I knew right from wrong, and this had to be wrong.

CHAPTER 17

Nathan

Made-to-order omelet, wheat toast and orange juice: the breakfast of champions, and those who'd spent half the morning coming up with the perfect strategy.

"She's a real estate agent, so here's my idea…" I sweetened my coffee with two sugars and a ton of cream. I flipped through the *L.A. Times,* found the classifieds. "I say, let me go over to Ursula's office, pretend I'm interested in this quarter-of-a-million-dollar property. Ask her to show it to me. I'll feel her out a little bit, you know. Find out what type of person she is. You need to know if she's approachable, before you go trying to approach her."

"Nathan, I don't care if she's approachable." That sister-girl in Lainey drizzled out before she could control it. Her head and hand were moving at a rhythm of their own. "She need to be concerned about whether or not I'm approachable. She better hope I don't go ghetto on her."

"I was just saying…"

"And I don't need you to go over there to check things out for me, Nate. I can hold my own."

"I wasn't saying you can't hold your own, sweetheart, I..."

"You implied that I might be afraid of her."

"I didn't imply that. You interpreted it that way." I grabbed her hand. Tried to calm her. Get my point across.

"Well, I would like to just sashay on over to that funky minicastle that my husband purchased for her, and let her know exactly what I think of her. I want to let her know that I did not appreciate her sleeping with my husband..." She stopped in midsentence, as if the words were getting stuck in her throat. I wanted to correct her and say that her husband more than slept with this woman; he'd had a lifetime relationship with her. They had a child together, and a life, even if he wasn't physically there all the time. Wanted to tell her this, but opted for silence.

She struggled to convince me, as well as herself, that her coming here was not in vain. That she'd be justified in getting in Ursula's face. That a point needed to be made. Or closure. Or defeat. I wasn't sure what. I couldn't quite determine what was going on in her head. But I knew what was in her heart. She was hurt and as her voice began to crack, I knew it was much more than confrontation she was after. For that reason, I knew I couldn't let her walk blindly into an altercation with a woman of whom she knew nothing about.

I had to convince her of my strategy.

"Again, I strongly feel that I should meet her first. Just so you know what you're dealing with—good, bad or indifferent. I'm not comfortable with you going in blindly. I care about your well-being, Lainey."

That seemed to soften the tenseness in her face; the fact that I cared. Her eyebrows relaxed a bit. She let down her guard.

"Let me see this house." She grabbed the newspaper and scanned the homes-for-sale section. "She will never believe that a schoolteacher can afford a quarter-million-dollar property, Nate. Find something more affordable. Like this..." She pointed out a property in Hollywood.

I pulled my chair around the table, closer to her. Our shoulders nearly rubbing together. I could smell her Victoria's Secret shower gel and lotion. I recognized the fragrance, because Marva was the Victoria's Secret queen. That's all she wore. It reminded me of her. Guilt rushed through me; drifting by my heart and causing it to pound lightly.

I attempted to rid my mind of thoughts of my wife; her lying in a dark room; suffering. While I sat enjoying a made-to-order omelet and orange juice with a beautiful woman whose presence made me weak.

I read the ad.

"A condo in Santa Ana for two hundred, sixty-nine grand."

"That's more realistic." She smiled up at me; a smile that would light up a dark room. "Wouldn't you agree?"

"Not in Atlanta, but in L.A., yeah, I agree," I whispered, not quite sure what I'd just agreed to because I was suddenly distracted. From the moment I moved into her personal space, the connection between my mind and the newspaper was lost. Our faces were close enough to touch. Her breath smelled of bell peppers and tomatoes, the vegetables she'd loaded her omelet with. I wanted to kiss her. Again. What was wrong with me?

"Maybe we should talk about last night," I found myself saying.

"What is there to talk about? You said you were sorry, and I accept your apology. Let's not make it a big deal, Nate."

"So it didn't mean anything to you?"

"Nothing." She said it much too quickly.

"You're lying."

"You're calling me a liar?"

"I'm thinking that maybe you're not being honest." I laughed nervously. "I know you had to feel the electricity."

"Don't flatter yourself," she said confidently.

Was it my ego that was at stake, or did I really misinterpret that whole extraordinary, amazing moment last night? The one that had me tossing and turning through the night. Guilt filling my heart; lust filling my loins. The lack of a woman's touch had me thinking confusing thoughts. Thoughts of knocking on Lainey's door well into the midnight hour, to ask if she was having trouble sleeping, too.

My lips reached for hers again. She turned away.

"No," she whispered, placing her finger over my lips.

My eyes questioned her, but not for long. I'd crossed the line, and needed to get myself together. She wasn't interested in me.

"I think this is the perfect property." I cleared my

throat, and shifted my mind back to the subject at hand. "What will you do while I'm gone?"

"I'll get a massage or take a long walk." She said, "I'll be fine."

The atmosphere was normal again. No hormones flairing. No ungodly thoughts.

Meeting Ursula would be an adventure.

In the lobby of the building with a million windows, I pressed the up button and took the elevator to the sixteenth floor. Got off and looked for Suite 1622. Found it at the end of the hall. Pushed the door open and peeked inside.

"You must be Nathan."

Wow! That was all I could think of as the five-foot-three, wondrously fit, sexy creature with shiny caramel skin and hazel eyes, took my hand. Her handshake was firm, her light brown hair brushed her shoulders; the skirt of her soft gray business suit hugged her round hips.

"Yes, I'm Nathan," I said, and looked around her contemporary office. Oil paintings complemented her walls. "This is nice."

"Thank you." She smiled that gorgeous smile, where a cute little dimple played hide-and-seek across her face. "Don't tell anyone, but I'm an undercover interior designer."

"Wow, a woman who's multitalented."

"Let's get down to the business of why you're here." She moved her body across the room. Took a seat on a tasteful contemporary sofa and motioned for me to have a seat next to her.

"Well, I was interested in maybe taking a look at this condo here. This one, in Santa Ana. How far is that from the university...U.C.L.A., I mean...I'm a professor and will be teaching over there soon...I..."

"Nathan, let's cut through the crap."

"Excuse me."

"How's your wife doing, Mr. Sullivan?"

I stared at her. How did she know my last name? I never mentioned it when we spoke over the phone. And what did she know about Marva?

"I don't know what you mean," I said.

"Don't you?" she asked; eyebrows raised. "Aren't you Nathan Sullivan whose wife has been in a vegetative state for the past several months? The wife who was a victim of that dreadful accident that killed my Donnie?"

Her Donnie?

"Ursula, I..."

She put her hand in the air to interrupt whatever it was that was about to erupt from my mouth. Scooted her behind to the back of the sofa and crossed her long, toned legs.

"I knew who you were when you called this morning."

"How?"

"I've been expecting you. Well, maybe not you, but definitely Elaine. Or should I say, Lainey? That's what Don called her." She smiled a deceitful smile. "My cousin is a private detective, and I had him do some investigative work for me. I have some very interesting photographs of the two of you. Particularly the one at Yamashiro the other night."

"I don't know what to say."

"Oh, don't look surprised." She laughed. "You don't look anything like a Santa Ana condo man. You're a four-bedroom, suburban, wife and kids sort of guy. I would've figured it out."

"You would've, huh?"

"I must admit, you're much more handsome in person, than in your photo." She smiled.

I wasn't sure if I was supposed to thank her for the compliment or dismiss it as sarcasm.

"Tell Lainey to come see me. I'm sure she knows where I live. Let's get this over with." She made her way over to her desk, sat in the leather chair and began pecking on her computer's keyboard. "You can let yourself out, Mr. Sullivan."

I was dismissed. My ears knew it before my limbs did, because they wouldn't move. She was already engrossed in whatever was on her computer screen. She paused for a moment and looked up at me. Her body language said, "I asked you to leave, and I'm not playing."

I took the hint. Found my way back to the lobby.

CHAPTER 18

Lainey

Butterflies had buzzed around in my stomach since the moment Nate told me about his encounter with Ursula. Said she reminded him of the Catwoman from *Batman;* cunning and slick. She was very direct; and after twisting his arm, I finally got him to admit that she was even beautiful. Although I'd put on my tough girl act at breakfast, I knew I didn't want to face Ursula alone; knew that this would be more than I could handle. So when Nathan offered to come along, I was more than grateful. Just having him there would make it a little more bearable. He was becoming my security blanket; my partner in crime, my friend and confidant. I liked him, more than I cared to admit. I wanted him, but knew I had to keep my distance. He belonged to someone else. I couldn't chance falling in love with him today, and then his wife waking up tomorrow. I wasn't ready for that type of pain.

In fact, the moment we returned to Atlanta, I would cut all ties. It was unhealthy, the thoughts I had of him, and I needed to stop the madness before it was too late.

That was the wise thing to do, and that's what I intended on doing. But as for now, I needed him. Needed him to help me slay this dragon once and for all. I needed to see Ursula for myself. Wanted to size her up, ask her some questions, and tell her how she had made my life a living hell. Had she not filled the void in my husband's life, he would've been forced to make our marriage work. But instead, she'd given him a child. A child that I could never give him.

Nate pulled our Lincoln Town Car in front of the classic 1960's multilevel home with sweeping views. I stared in awe at its wonder, and sat paralyzed for several moments.

"Well, here we are," Nate proclaimed. "Are you okay?"

"I'm fine. Let's get this over with," I said, opening my door and stepping onto the brick sidewalk. I'd chosen a pair of Liz Claiborne heels; the sexy, strappy beige ones that accented my soft brown pantsuit. Earthy colors accented my skin; made it glow. A natural lip color and gloss, and eye shadow from the MAC counter at Macy's did wonders for my face. The American manicure and pedicure that Mia, my nail lady, gave me once every two weeks, accented my overall look.

I led the way up the walkway and to the door of the gorgeous home surrounded by alpine trees. A gardener worked in the flower beds as we passed. He looked up briefly, smiled, but kept working. I managed a smile back, and then found the doorbell. I pressed it once and then waited for footsteps to approach the door. I could feel Nate's breath on my neck and if I'd touched his chest, his heart was probably pounding as rapidly as mine. I heard rapid footsteps approach, and then a young boy, around ten years old, dressed in sweats and a T-shirt, swung the door open.

"Yes?" he asked.

"Hello, we're here to see Ursula," I said, and managed a smile.

"Mom!" he yelled at the top of his lungs. "Mommy!"

"I'm coming, sweetie. Stop yelling," I heard a woman say, but she was nowhere in sight.

"You can come inside," the boy offered, swinging the door wider, and Nate and I stepped into the foyer with the wood-beamed ceiling. The smell of garlic and onions filled the house; as if someone was smothering some potatoes. The sounds of hip-hop shook the walls; a tune that sounded like one of Beyonce's, assaulted our ears. I looked around, taking in the beauty of the place. The living room, which was off to the right, was decorated in very warm reds and yellows. The magnificent fireplace held a portrait of three graceful ladies dancing above it. There were family photos scattered about on the mantel, and I wanted so desperately to see them up close.

"I'm Ursula." The caramel woman with hazel colored eyes held her hand out to me. "You must be Lainey."

"I am."

"Nice to meet you," she said, as if this was a pleasant encounter. "And, Nate, it's good to see you again."

"Ursula." He smiled and took her hand.

"Come on in here." She gestured toward the living room. "Can I get you something to drink?"

"No thank you," I said quickly.

"I'm fine." Nate followed my lead.

"Mommy, can I go for a swim?" the boy, who was still lingering near his mother, asked. His eyes, hazel like Ursula's.

Please don't tell me that this mini-mansion has a pool out back, I thought.

"I need for you to finish your homework first, and then we'll think about it."

"Mommy, I just have a couple of chapters to read, and I can finish that in no time," he said. "Can I just read them before I go to bed tonight?"

"You will finish them before going for a swim, mister."

"Aw, Mom." He turned and headed for the stairwell.

"And, Donnie, please tell your sister to turn her music down."

Donnie?

"Did you say Donnie?" I had to ask.

"Donald Junior," she said boastfully. "You didn't know, did you? That Don and I have two children?"

"Ursula, I'm not here for a casual visit." I decided to cut to the chase. "I would like to know exactly what type of relationship you had with my husband. And why you would build a relationship with a man when you knew he was married. And give birth to his children, for God's sake!"

"Please have a seat, Lainey. I think you've misinterpreted this whole situation," she said, and seemed nothing like Nate had described. He'd described her as a barracuda, slithering across the floor, seeking whom she might devour. But she was normal; even nice. I was prepared to put her in her place, had she given me the lip action she'd given Nate earlier.

"I'd rather stand," I said. "We won't be staying long."

"Suit yourself, but I'm going to check on my dinner and fix myself a cranberry juice," she said, her Guess jeans hugging her round hips. She wore a top that I was sure I'd seen at Charlotte Russe. "You sure I can't get you anything?"

"I'll have one of those, um, cranberry juices," Nate said, and then took a seat on the plush sofa.

"Nothing for me," I said stubbornly, still standing.

She disappeared into the kitchen.

"What are you doing?" I whispered to Nate. "We're not here to visit. We're here for some answers."

"Well, I'm thirsty. We can have cranberry juice and answers, can't we?" He smiled, but I didn't. "Have a seat, Lainey."

My Liz Claiborne's *were* playing tug-of-war with my feet. I sat next to him.

"What does she mean, I've misinterpreted the whole situation?" I whispered again.

"I don't know." Nate's eyes roamed around the room, and mine followed.

On the mantel was a blown-up version of that same baby picture I'd seen of Don's daughter, Samantha, in his office. Then there were a couple of photos of her as a teenager. There were photos of Don Junior, too, but I couldn't make out the smaller ones.

"Now, in response to your question, or accusation, rather." Ursula appeared in the room and handed Nate a crystal glass filled with cranberry juice and crushed ice.

"Thank you," he said.

"Lainey, I met Don twenty years ago. He was a young attorney at the time, so full of life and fire." She smiled to herself as if remembering him. "He swept me off of my feet. He was so handsome and charming. He took me all over the world. Maui, Tokyo, Honduras. We had so much fun together. He became my whole world!"

I couldn't believe she was rubbing this in my face.

"I don't care to hear this."

"I think you should," she said, and continued. "Don swept me off of my feet, and when he asked me to marry him, I..."

"Marry him?"

"Yes, when he asked me to marry him, I jumped at the chance," she said, and that was the first time I'd noticed the rock on her finger. It was blinding. How did I miss it? "We were married in a little chapel right here in Los Angeles."

My mouth dropped, and I wanted to lift my finger to pick it back up, but I was frozen.

"You married him?" I asked. I needed to be sure I'd heard correctly.

"Yes, we were married just nine months after meeting." She walked over to the hidden coffee table, picked up a large framed photo and handed it to me. It was a wedding picture of her and, yes, Don. Garland in her hair and a smile as bright as the sunshine, she clung to Don who was wearing a white tuxedo and cheesing.

I felt sick. My head began to spin as I struggled to hold on to the photo.

"Just a few months later I was pregnant with Samantha, and I thought that was enough to keep my young husband close by. But I couldn't seem to pry him away from that Atlanta firm."

I literally was about to be sick.

"I need to use your bathroom," I mumbled, and followed Ursula to the guest bathroom.

My hands grasped the toilet bowl as I buried my head in it. I could hear the water running and after a few minutes Ursula was handing me wet cloth. She then left the room. A couple of minutes later someone's hand caressed my spine, and I assumed it was Nate's. I stood and caught a glimpse of my reflection and his in the mirror. I wiped my mouth with the wet cloth as Nate continued to caress my shoulders.

"You okay?" he asked.

I nodded a yes, but couldn't speak.

"I'll give you a minute," he said, and stepped out of the bathroom, shutting the door behind him.

I replayed Ursula's words in my head as I stood there in the mirror. Couldn't believe I'd heard what I heard. Was Don a bigamist? After regaining my composure, I found my way back to the living room. Ursula and Nate sat in silence.

"Are you feeling better?" Ursula asked.

"Yes," I said, and took my place back on the sofa next to Nate.

"I can see that this makes you very uncomfortable, so I won't talk about it anymore."

"No," I said. "I need to know. I need to know everything."

She glanced at Nate, as if to ask for his approval to continue. He nodded.

"Are you sure, Lainey?" she asked, and for the first time I saw empathy in her expression. "I know this is difficult for you. It was difficult for me when I found out Don was married to you."

"When did you find out?"

"After he died and our attorney proceeded to tell me that he left me nothing but our home here and trust funds for our children. I knew that Don had other money. I knew he'd invested well, and that he had property in Maui and a couple of apartment buildings in South Carolina. I wanted to know why I wasn't the beneficiary on the policy with the firm, as well as the private policy he had in addition." She was on the verge of tears. "After Donnie was born, I accused him of having an affair with someone in Atlanta. Wanted to know why he refused to find work here in L.A. or to move us to Atlanta. I only saw him twice a month, and I thought he needed to be more of a father to his son."

His son. Those words had me in a trance.

Why did Don stay with me when he clearly had a full-blown family in L.A.?

"He loved you," Ursula said through clinched teeth, answering my question as if I'd asked it out loud.

"He couldn't have loved me."

"He did love you. Spoke of you often, but referred to you as his ex-wife. I lived in your shadow. No matter what I did, I could never compare to you. Except have children. I knew that you were never able to have children, and that was the one thing I had on you."

"Mom, what's going on?" As Ursula wiped tears from her eyes, a younger version of her appeared in the doorway. She was tall and slender with long hair that brushed her shoulders. Her eyes were identical to Don's. "Are you okay?"

"I'm okay, baby."

"You don't look okay," she resolved, books pressed against her chest as her skeptical eyes moved from me to Nate and then back to her mother. "Are you thinking about Daddy again?"

"This is my daughter, Samantha." Ursula changed the subject. "Sam, say hello to Miss Lainey and Mr. Nate."

"Hello," Sam said, and when she smiled I saw Don's dimples dance across her face. I felt nauseated again.

"Hello," Nate and I sang in unison.

"Mom, I'm going over to the library on campus. If you need me, I have my cell, okay?"

"Okay, sweetie."

"Can I take your car, since my car is almost out of gas?"

"Keys are in my purse, Sam."

"Thanks, Mommy." She said it as if she was eight years old, and then bounced up the stairs again in her ripped blue jeans and a similar blouse that reminded me of a Charlotte Russe style.

"She's a freshmen at U.C.L.A. Journalism major." Ursula managed to pull herself together, and explained as if Nate and I had asked about Sam's major. "Don was a bastard!"

"Yes, he was," I agreed. "How could he do this to me...to us?"

"If he weren't dead, I'd have him arrested or taken out," she barked; serious, too. "I had my cousin, who's a private detective, find out all he could about you. That's when I discovered that he was still married to you, and had been for all these years."

"I have to go." I stood. "I have to think this through. This is a lot for one day."

"I understand," she said. "Imagine how I felt when I couldn't even partake in my own husband's funeral." She chuckled. "And my children...imagine trying to explain that to my children."

"I'm sorry for your pain, Ursula. I had no idea."

I was suffocating. I needed some fresh air to get my breathing back at a normal pace.

CHAPTER 19

Nathan

Billie Holiday's strong vocals had me thinking of a time when my grandparents were young and free. Had me reminiscing of a time of swinging and post–World War II as if I'd been there myself. A time when colored folk were mess attendants in the military, while white folk did all the fighting. That's the stuff they left out of the textbooks at the high school where I taught teenagers about their American history; a history that left out pertinent details about their heritage. I taught them a history that really didn't belong to them.

A shame.

Billie's voice cried out with such pain and heartache, and I wondered if she'd ever experienced happy times. I thought of Marva and wondered if she'd experienced more happy times than not. I wondered if the not-so-happy times were my fault. Wondered if there was something I could've done differently. Maybe I wasn't the best husband that I could've been. That was a thought that haunted me more and more lately; one that I couldn't shake. Sometimes it kept me up at night.

As Billie sang "Good Morning Heartache," I thought of Lainey and the tremendous heartache she must've been feeling. Again, I was helpless. There was nothing I could do to take the pain away. She wouldn't even talk to me. After we'd left Ursula's, we drove back to the hotel in silence. Her tear-filled eyes stared out of the passenger window the whole way. When I asked if she was hungry, she simply said no. When I asked if she wanted to go for a walk later, the answer was no. And finally I asked if she wanted to talk about it, her response was a resounding no. As we pulled up in front of the hotel, she rushed inside as I struggled to keep up.

"Nate, I just wanna be alone," she said. "Please understand."

I did, and walked her to her room. She stepped inside and shut the door, barely saying good-night. I wanted to hold her, but I couldn't. Wanted to make her pain go away, but she wouldn't let me. Instead I ended up at the hotel bar, a cognac in front of me. Although drinking wasn't a pastime I engaged in often, I found myself seeking it out tonight. It was the perfect cure for loneliness. Billie Holiday sang the blues to my soul as I watched an older couple slow dance on the marble floor across the room. I bet myself that they had probably set some rugs on fire back in their day.

I thought of my grandparents, full of their Canadian Mist and orange juice, doing a dance called the jitterbug in the middle of the floor in their shotgun house in Alabama. The thought of it brought a smile to my face. Thinking of home always made me smile. My days as a young boy growing up in that small Alabama town were happy and free. No troubles. No heartache. Just days and nights filled with kickball in the street, penny candy and capturing lightning bugs in a Mason jar. Times were so different then. Yanking on a girl's ponytail actually brought excitement to my young life. And if I made her cry, now that was best feeling in the world.

The thought of Lainey crying made my heart ache for her. Made me feel helpless and weak, and that's the last thing a man wanted to feel. What did I come all this way for? To leave her to suffer in her room all alone? "Lady Sings the Blues."

"You look as if you lost your best friend." The voice in my ear shook me out of my pity party. The arms that wrapped around me from behind and caressed my chest, felt warm and tender. That Victoria's Secret good-body-smelling-stuff-that-women-wear filled my nostrils. I grabbed the small, familiar hands into mine, kissed them. When I swung around on the bar stool, Lainey's puffy, bloodshot eyes met mine.

"You feeling better?" I asked, already knowing the answer. *No*.

"I am now that I've found you," she said, and I tried to interpret that statement. Now that she found me at the bar? Or now that she found me in her life?

"Now that you've found me, what will you do with me?" I asked teasingly, still holding on to her small hands.

"Let's dance," she said, ignoring my question and pulling me onto the dance floor next to the elderly couple, who were cheek to cheek now.

I pulled her small frame close to me, held on to her waist.

"Lady sings the blues, she's got them bad, she feels so sad…" Lainey sang the lyrics to Billie's song. Her deep voice shocked me.

"Girl, you can sing," I said to her after she'd finished the second verse.

"Used to sing in the choir."

"You don't anymore?"

"Now I just sing in the shower." She smiled, and I was happy to see it creep into the corner of her mouth.

"With a voice like that, you should be singing in somebody's choir."

She cocked her head to the side. "Nate, thank you for coming here, to California with me…and for just being there at Ursula's."

"No thanks needed," I said, pressing my forehead against hers. "That's what friends are for, right?"

"That's what friends are for," she agreed, and we held on to each other tighter.

In the doorway of her hotel room, I hugged her and then kissed her forehead. Planted a kiss on her nose and then her cheek. Finally my lips found their way to hers. I breathed her in.

"We got an early flight in the morning," I whispered. "You all right?"

"Stay the night with me, Nate," she whispered back.

Before I knew it, I was inside pushing the door shut behind me. My back against the door, our bodies pressed together, our lips touching again. I wanted her. Bad.

Inching closer to the bedroom of her suite, I couldn't let her go. Fully clothed, we collapsed onto the bed.

"I just want you to hold me," she said.

"I can handle that," I said, trying to get my hormones under control. The curve of her body pressed against mine, I reached over and turned on the radio. Tuned it to L.A.'s smooth jazz station, 94.7. Dave Koz serenaded us with the sounds of his saxophone.

"I always knew in my heart there was someone else. He never admitted to it, but I just knew. Intuition, I guess." Her words came softly, somewhere out of the blue.

"Did you ever confront him?"

"Many times," she said. "He always lied, and then always accused me of being insecure. Turned the tables. Said that maybe I was the one cheating."

"Why did you stay so long? He was a terrible husband. Not that I've been a perfect one, but…" I stared at the portrait on the wall. The colors matched the ones in the comforter that we lay on top of. "You're beautiful. Intelligent…"

"People always think that because you're beautiful, intelligent, and have all these things going for you, that you have confidence, too," she said. "Men have a way of absorbing themselves into you. They become your whole reason for living. Especially when you're young and impressionable."

"What about when you became older and wiser."

"You would laugh at the number of times I planned on leaving, but changed my mind. For many years I'd convinced myself that by some miracle, God would bless me with a child. I thought he'd speak to me from Heaven, just like he did Sara in the bible. He opened her womb, and she was an old woman!"

"Yeah, and Abraham was old, too." I laughed. "And the brother was still fertile."

"Yes he was." Lainey laughed, too. "What do you think about Sara giving her maidservant to Abraham to sleep with and bear children with?"

"I think she played herself. And afterward regretted it," I said. "But Abraham was a man, and wasn't turning down anything, especially when he had his wife's permission to partake."

"Would you partake if your wife gave you permission?"

I thought of Marva. Thought of what she might think of me being curled up in another woman's bed, holding her as if she belonged to me. Would she give me permission to partake? I think not. Guilt rushed over me, and I wanted to run as far away from Lainey as I could get. The curve of her body felt too comfortable; too familiar. Too good to be right.

"Any man would partake if given permission from his wife," I finally said. "Not saying that he should, but he certainly *would.*"

"I knew that something was up with Don, but I don't think I could've freely given him over to another woman. Especially not to bear him children, when I knew that not being able to bear children was my flaw."

"I don't think your inability to bear children is a flaw, Lainey. Maybe it just wasn't in God's plan for you to bear children with him."

"It was what Don wanted more than anything."

"*You* should've been what he wanted more than anything. Children or no children."

"Is your wife everything you wanted?"

"And more," I admitted.

"Then why did you cheat on her?"

"Stupid," I said, remembering that I'd told Lainey about my affair with Jackie. "The opportunity presented itself and I took it. But when it was all said and done, it was my wife who I loved and wanted to be with. I didn't want anyone else."

"You're a good man, Nate."

"A good man wouldn't be here with you right now," I confessed. "Not while his wife still has a heartbeat."

"Why are you then?"

I didn't have an answer. From the moment I'd laid eyes Lainey's cinnamon skin, I knew I wanted her. As wrong as it was, I did. I thought of Marva. What was I doing in California in the first place? Hadn't I given her my word...my bond of holy matrimony...in sickness and health? Yet here I was betraying her once again.

Dave Koz was hypnotizing me with the saxophone.

"I'm falling in love with you, Nate." She said it softly.

What did she say that for? Now the unspoken had been spoken; needing a response; needing to be dealt with. Her affirmation begged for a reciprocal response. To respond with my true feelings would've been a betrayal to my wife. To not respond would hurt Lainey's feelings. I shut my eyes lightly as I contemplated.

"Did you fall asleep on me?" she asked, and then her lips brushed against my cheek.

I didn't answer. Just let her think I was asleep.

"Sweet dreams," she whispered.

I kept my eyes shut until I felt her back to me again; the curve of her body against mine. She pulled my arms around her, my fingertips rested on the center of her belly. Before long, I could hear light snores escaping her mouth.

As she slept, I stayed awake, staring at the digital numbers on the clock resting on the nightstand. Watched as the numbers changed from 1:15 to 1:16 and finally, 1:17 before my eyes couldn't take it anymore. I joined Lainey in a place called slumber. Together we slept, wrapped in each other's arms, fully clothed.

CHAPTER 20

Lainey

"I feel bad that Don's children had to suffer because of his selfishness," I whispered as Nathan and I sat on the plane.

He just nodded and bounced his head against the back of the seat in first class. I'd upgraded his seat in coach to a first-class seat next to mine. Before long, light snores began to escape his mouth, and he slept the entire way from LAX to Atlanta's Hartsfield-Jackson airport. I stared out of the window and into the clouds, until the wheels of the airplane finally touched the runway's pavement.

At baggage claim, Nathan grabbed my luggage from the belt first and then his own.

"I rode the Marta over the other day," he proclaimed, explaining that he'd taken Atlanta's mass transit to the airport. "Didn't want to leave my car here."

"I'll just get a driver to take me home," I told him, and pulled out my cell phone to call one.

"You'll be okay?" he asked.

"I'll be fine." I smiled, and threw my overnight bag over my shoulder. "Thank you, Nate, for going with me."

"I had a good time," he said. "Despite the circumstances."

"A lot of drama, huh?"

"Yeah, but at least you got some answers, right?" he asked, and his smile lit up the entire airport. His fingers lightly brushed a strand of loose hair from my face. "I'm here if you need anything. Even if you just need to talk."

"You're a wonderful man, Nate."

We stared at each other in silence for a moment.

"I bet you miss your kids," I said, referring to his students and the basketball team.

"Surprisingly, yes." He laughed. "As much as they get on my nerves sometimes, I actually do miss their behinds."

"Well, you should get over to the school right away."

"Got practice this afternoon," he said; glanced at his watch. "Come here, you."

He pulled me into a strong embrace, my nose buried against his neck, his hands wrapped around my shoulders. He smelled so good, and I closed my eyes to inhale his scent. I was falling in love with him, but hoped he hadn't noticed. It was too soon; too awkward; too inappropriate to love him. Thankfully he'd fallen asleep and hadn't heard me spilling my guts the night before. The thought of him not returning the sentiment would've been too painful, so I was relieved.

"Call me the minute you get home. I want to make sure you made it safely," he said, and touched my face with his fingertips.

"I will. I promise."

"Good." He kissed my cheek and headed toward the airport's Marta station.

As the black Lincoln Town Car slowly pulled into my driveway, I noticed Alvin's silver Mercedes parked in front of the house. His tall, slender frame sat on my front steps, his chin resting in his hands. He stood when he saw the car pull up, placed his hands into his pockets. I stepped out of the back seat as the driver got out and pulled my luggage from the trunk.

"Lainey, hi," Alvin said as I approached the front door, key in hand.

"Hello, Alvin," I said as I turned the key in the lock. "Why are you here?"

The driver of the Town Car placed my bags inside the house and I handed him three twenty-dollar bills.

"Need change, ma'am?"

"No," I told him, and smiled. "Thank you."

"No, thank you," he said and then disappeared.

Alvin followed me inside and to the kitchen as I opened the blinds and let some sunshine in. I lit a candle to rid the house of the staleness that had been locked up for several days. I pulled my plant from the windowsill and gave it some water. Opened the window to let in some fresh air.

"Lainey, I'm sorry I didn't tell you about Don's child, Samantha," he said, rubbing his hand across his five o'clock shadow. "I kept thinking that Don would confess to you. And then after so long, I just forgot about it."

"It's okay, Alvin. I'm not mad at you."

"Really?"

"Really."

"Where've you been?" he asked.

"I went to California to meet Don's wife."

"Excuse me. Don's wife? What're you talking about? You are his wife."

"I mean his other wife."

"I don't understand." He frowned as if struggling to comprehend. I could tell that he didn't have a clue that Don was a bigamist.

"Sam's mother," I explained. "You know, Ursula? Don was married to her and me at the same time."

"I don't get it."

"What don't you get, Alvin?" I asked, becoming annoyed with having to express words that were so painful. Having to explain what was clearly elementary. "Don was married to me and Ursula...for years."

"No way."

"Yes, way," I said. "Ursula told me herself."

Alvin shook his head. "I had no idea, Lainey."

"It doesn't really matter now, Alvin. Don's gone, and I'll heal from this," I said, taking a piece of Tilapia out of the freezer and placing it on the counter to thaw. "You look terrible. Are you sleeping?"

"I guess you're not the only one hurting," he said, and dropped his head. "Breakups are so hard."

"The guy at your office?" I asked.

"He was much too young to handle a mature relationship."

"I had no idea you were gay, Alvin...all these years..."

"I'm not gay, Lainey. I love women. I just like to spend time with men every now and then. Doesn't mean I'm gay."

"If you sleep with men, you're gay."

"Well, I'm not going to argue with you about it." He chuckled.

In silence I began to unload dishes from the dishwasher. Alvin started rinsing the few that were in the sink.

"Have you talked to Glenda?" he asked.

"I'm not speaking to her."

"Lainey, she's your best friend." He said, "She just didn't want to hurt you."

"I would never have kept secrets from her."

"She loves you, Lainey. She was just trying to protect you."

"I can protect myself. She should've been my friend and told me the truth. Had I known the truth, I would've left Don long ago, rather than sticking around as long as I did."

"Would you have left?"

"Yes, I would have."

"You deserved better, Lainey," he said. "Don was my friend, but I hated the way he treated you. You were too good for him."

"Thank you, Alvin."

"I mean it, Lainey." He said, "You're beautiful, intelligent...I hope you find someone who treats you the way you deserve."

I thought of Nathan. Wondered what he was doing;

if he'd made it to basketball practice. Wondered if thoughts of me filled his head, like thoughts of him filled mine. "What are you thinking?" Alvin asked.

"Nothing," I said, and placed the last plate on the shelf. Alvin placed the few dishes from the sink into the dishwasher.

"Would you like for me to stay with you tonight? I'll run out and get some Thai, and we could grab a couple of movies from Blockbuster. What do you think?"

"No, I'm kinda tired. I just want to relax. Have some quiet time."

"You sure?"

"Yes, I just need to be alone."

"Okay, sweetheart." He kissed my forehead. "I'm gonna go, but if you change your mind, call me."

"I will Alvin." I smiled. "I hope things work out with you and your friend."

He shrugged his shoulders. "Who knows?"

He moved toward the front door.

I stood in the kitchen as I heard the front door shut. Staring out into my backyard, I wondered how different my life would've been without Don in it. Wondered if I'd have fallen love with someone else. Wondered if I'd ever find love again.

CHAPTER 21

Nathan

Talking to Marva's first-grade class was one of the hardest things I'd ever had to do in my life. Looking into the faces and bright eyes of fifteen six-year-olds, and telling them why their favorite teacher may or may not be returning to them, was pure torture.

"...and so, Mrs. Sullivan is very sick. Right now she's sleeping, but we're praying that she will wake up soon." I swallowed hard as the words spilled out of my mouth. "But if she doesn't...wake up...boys and girls...you must be very strong...and you must pray for her..."

Tears began to fill my eyes. I could feel them coming.

"Will Missus Sullivan go to Heaven?" The little redhead on the front row asked. "My mommy said that you have to be really good and say your prayers every night in order to get into Heaven."

"Your mommy is right," I said. "But let's hope that Mrs. Sullivan comes back to us for a little while longer before making her way into Heaven."

"Can we go see her?" the little dark boy with cornrows asked.

"We might be able to arrange for a visit," I said, and looked at the substitute teacher, Miss Adams, for her approval.

"I don't know if that's such a good idea," she said, smiling.

"Please," a little girl with two thick ponytails and teeth missing in the front her mouth whined. "We miss her."

"Yeah, and we want to see her."

"We'll be good."

"Is she like a vegetable?" the chubby girl asked. "My uncle was in a coma once and my mama said he would be a vegetable for the rest of his life."

"A vegetable? That's silly," Redhead said. "How can a person become a vegetable?"

"Not a real vegetable, stupid," Chubby Girl explained. "It means that their brain turns into a vegetable and they just stare into space for the rest of their life."

"That's enough, you guys. Let's thank Mr. Sullivan for coming by," Miss Adams said.

"Thank you, Mr. Sullivan," the children sang in unison.

"You're very welcome," I said. "I will tell Mrs. Sullivan that you all said hello."

"Tell her to hurry back please." The caramel-colored girl with braids spoke softly. "And tell her that we love her."

"And that we promise to be good if she comes back," Cornrows proclaimed.

"I promise. I will tell her."

"Can you give her this?" The Asian boy handed me a picture he'd drawn on construction paper in red, green and black Crayola. I took it.

"What is it?" I had to ask.

"It's an angel," he explained, his front teeth missing. "She can hang it over her hospital bed and the angel will watch over her as she sleeps."

Tears threatened my eyes again, and I knew I needed to escape. Miss Adams rescued me.

"Thank you for coming, Mr. Sullivan. It was very nice of you to take time out of your busy schedule to come and talk to the children, but I know you have other commitments."

"Yes, I do." My voice cracked a little.

I shook Miss Adams' hand, waved goodbye to the kids and was out of there in record time. My back against the other side of the door, I cried. Felt like my chest would cave in as I stared at the colorful angel that would watch over Marva. Relieved that no one was roaming the hallways and had witnessed my breakdown, I pulled myself together.

I passed Janice Ayers, the assistant principal, in the hallway.

"Mr. Sullivan, how are you?"

"Miss Ayers."

"How's Marva?"

"She's not doing well."

"I was so devastated when I heard the news," she said. "I'm so sorry."

"No apologies necessary."

"If you need anything, anything at all, you just call." Miss Ayers in her red business suit, her short sassy haircut, and mocha skin, smiled at me. "We're very fond of her here."

"I will keep you abreast of her progress," I said, hoping she hadn't noticed my bloodshot eyes.

"Please do, Mr. Sullivan."

"Call me Nate," I told her. I couldn't understand how we'd suddenly become so formal when I still had fond memories of her and her husband Clyde visiting our home, breaking bread with us, and whipping us in multiple games of Bid Whiz.

"It was tough talking to those kids, huh?" she asked.

"Very," I admitted.

"Thank you for taking time out of your schedule, Nate. I'm sure it meant a lot to them."

I just nodded. Needed to keep moving before the tears came back. I barely said goodbye, but made a beeline for my truck that was parked just outside.

I hopped inside and rested my head against the back of the seat. Tried to control my breathing, but it seemed almost impossible at the time.

Friday night and I was at home pacing the floor, wishing I had somewhere to go. Wishing I had something to take my mind off of Marva. The house was still, but reminded me of her; the delicate paint colors that she'd carefully chosen for every room, art that adorned our walls, the rugs that she'd caught on sale at Kohl's last spring, the lamp in our bedroom that she'd picked up at a yard sale in Buckhead. I stared at the eccentric lamp that sat on my nightstand, and knew it was more valuable to her than anything she would've purchased at Macy's or Rich's.

I picked up the AJC that I'd purchased at the gas station that morning, and started flipping through it until I found my favorite column. "The Vent" is a column where Metro Atlanta readers contributed their sarcastic and humorous remarks about politics, the happenings in Atlanta, traffic and other things that got under their skin and made them want to vent.

I started laughing at some of the comments that I'd read, then I checked out the sports page.

I decided that I needed to get out of the house. Remembered the little jazz spot that I had visited occasionally in downtown Atlanta. I didn't go out often, but when I did, I had remembered the place as being nice, with the best hot wings I'd had in my life. Didn't want to go alone, and contemplated calling Lainey. Picked up the phone to dial her number, but then wondered what I was thinking. Friday night was my night to sleep over at the hospital. I had slept in the uncomfortable orange chair in the corner of the room every Friday night since Marva's accident. My heart wanted me to continue the tradition, but another part of me wanted to get out and have some fun. In California, spending time with Lainey, I was reminded that I still had life in me.

I picked up the phone again. Dialed Lainey's number.

"Are you up for some jazz?" I asked when she answered.

"That would be nice," she said softly, and her voice smiled.

"I'll meet you about nine," I said after explaining to

her how to get there, and my heart throbbed at the thought of seeing her again.

In the mirror, I shaved away my five-o'clock shadow and brushed my teeth, splattered shaving lotion on my face and rubbed my bald head. The sounds of Norman Brown rang through the house as I broke in his newest CD; set the tone for my evening. The house felt so empty and the music seemed to echo and bounce against the walls. There was no life here; just loneliness and heart-ache. No laughter, no voices, no television tuned to the Home Shopping Network, as it often was. No smell of Chinese take-out that had been ordered because my wife wasn't the greatest cook.

No Marva.

I parked my truck at the Riverdale Marta station and hopped onto the train. An elderly woman with an armful of grocery bags and an unfriendly face stared at me. I smiled, but her face remained like stone.

"Hello," I said. "How you doing?"

"Evenin'," she said through tight lips.

At the next stop a gang of teenagers hopped on the train, their conversations filled with foul language and the word "nigga" more times than I could count. I wanted so badly to tell them how disrespectful they were being in front of the woman, who clutched her bags and purse tighter; wanted to tell them that their mothers wouldn't approve of such language, but the way they used the explicit terms so loosely, I couldn't be sure of what they were taught at home. I wanted to tell them that they should have more self-respect, not to mention respect for their elders. But I didn't. Instead I remained silent and just prayed that my ride would end soon. It could've been worse; I could've run into Leroy the Wino, wreaking of alcohol and begging for money to finance his next high or wanting to carry on a full-fledged conversation as if we were old buddies.

Those were the characters I usually ran into. The ones that preferred conversations with themselves, or who held conversations with imaginary people on the other end of a cell phone that didn't work. Then there were those who screamed that you were going to hell if you didn't confess your sins and turn from your wicked ways.

"Is Jesus Christ your personal savior?" a bald woman asked me once. "If he's not, you're headed for the pit of hell, you demon-child of satan. Look at you, in your polished suit and Flo-shime shoes. You a pimp, ain't you?"

"No, ma'am. I'm a schoolteacher." I'd tried to convince her, but there had been no hope of it as she continued to rebuke me.

I jumped off and then walked the block and a half to the jazz spot where I would meet Lainey. As I walked into the smoke-filled room, the bald brother on stage, wearing a black suit, was busy making love to his saxophone. I spotted Lainey when she raised her finger in the air from a corner booth. Her smile was wide and inviting, and she looked beautiful in her low-cut sexy black top.

Her hair was pulled back into an updo and her red lipstick was a change from her usual earth tones. A nice change.

"Hey." She stood and the black skirt she wore hugged her hips and revealed her smooth, sexy legs.

"You look beautiful," I said, and kissed her cheek.

"Thank you. And you look very handsome yourself." She smiled.

I'd chosen black jeans and a tangerine-colored silk shirt that buttoned down the front. Before I could sit good, a waitress appeared, pad in hand, to take my drink order.

"Bring me a Heineken," I told her, and she disappeared just as quickly.

"This is a nice place," Lainey said. "You come here often?"

"Every now and then," I told her. "I don't get out much."

"Well, I'm glad you invited me. I'm enjoying the band, and the ambience."

"I'm glad," I said. "How was your day?"

"Not bad, I just relaxed a bit. Had planned on just kicking back in front of the television all night...that is, until you called."

"I needed to get out," I said. "I visited Marva's first-grade class today to explain where she was and why she's not there with them anymore. They had so many questions, and...whew..."

"Tough, huh?"

"I cried like a baby when I left there. Had to be the hardest thing I've ever done in my life."

"Your wife would be so proud of you."

"I don't know. Not the way I was crying."

"She would still be proud." Lainey smiled.

"Those kids love her to death!" I said. "It was horrible to look into their little faces and know in my heart that she might not ever see them again. That tore me apart."

Lainey grabbed my hand and held on to it. She bounced her head to the music.

"You wanna dance?" I asked her.

"Yeah," she said, and stood. "Let's dance."

On the dance floor, I wrapped my arms around her waist as we moved to the rhythm of an old Luther tune that the jazz band played. She stared up into my eyes and momentarily our noses touched. I wanted to kiss those lips; the lips that I hadn't been able to get out of my head since our trip to California. The same lips that had proclaimed her love for me, and had me scared to return the sentiment. She moved in closer and I hugged tighter. Before long, we'd danced to three love songs.

We sat in the dark corner booth for hours laughing and talking like old friends. Being with her was so familiar, so comfortable. I shared my inner thoughts with her, and she didn't judge me.

"Nate!" I heard the familiar voice and flinched. "Nate is that you?"

My sister-in-law stumbled over to our table and pushed her way into the booth; forced me to slide over.

"Dar, what are you doing here?"

Lainey eyeballed Darlene and then me. With raised eyebrows, she wanted to say something, but remained silent.

"I think the question is, what are you doing here? And who's your little friend here?"

"Dar, this is Lainey. Lainey this is Darlene, Marva's sister."

"Nice to meet you, Darlene," Lainey said.

"She knows Marva?" Darlene asked me, her breath potent enough to light a candle.

"In a roundabout sort of way."

"Does she know that Marva's your wife?" Darlene shook her neck from side to side.

"She knows that, Dar."

"Then why is she all up in this dark corner with you, huh? All huddled up like y'all in love or something."

"Dar, we're just enjoying some music together. That's it."

"Okay, I guess that's cool." She pulled a Salem out of its package. Lit it and smiled. "I'm enjoying the music, too. Shoot, that's my song right there."

"Can you put that out, Dar? Neither one of us smokes."

"Whatever, Nate. Since when did you become all self-righteous and stuff?" She put the cigarette out in the ashtray on our table. "Hey, waitress! Get over here and take my drink order."

The waitress gave her a look that said, *I don't know who you think you talkin' to.*

"I know she ain't looking at me like I'm crazy. She better bring her fat tail over here and take my drink order!" she said, loud enough for the waitress to hear. "Nate, you'll buy me a drink?"

"Darlene, chill out. This is not the place for that ghetto-fabulous behavior." I ignored her drink request, thinking that she'd reached her limit already. "How did you get here anyway?"

"See that white dude over there?" She smiled and pointed toward the bar, at the only white guy in the place. "He picked me up just outside of Birmingham. I was walking because Sheryl had the nerve to put me out of her car. The stank heifer. Said I was flirting with her boyfriend. You know me, Nate. I flirt with everybody. It wasn't nothing serious. And if you saw Sheryl's boyfriend, man…"

"So you just got in the car with a total stranger?"

"He's not a stranger anymore." She laughed. "He's cool, Nate. Bought me something to eat and everything. He brought me to this club. I wouldn't of fell up in a place like this on my own."

"Dar, you can't just be hopping in the car with any Tom, Dick and Harry like that."

"His name is not Tom, Dick or Harry. It's Arnold, for your information." She grinned, thinking her little joke was funny.

"I don't care what his name is. You don't know him like that!"

"See how much my big brother loves me?" she asked Lainey, and placed her head on my shoulder; filled my nostrils with whatever alcohol she'd been drinking all night. Smiled at Lainey. "He loves my sister like that, too, you know? And she would not appreciate you all up in his face like this."

"That's enough, Dar," I said. "Come on, I'm taking you home."

"I don't need you to take me home, Nate. I have a ride."

"Not with that dude over there, you don't," I said, and pushed Darlene out of the booth.

She was barely able to stand on her own, and I stood and grabbed her waist to balance her.

"At least let me go tell him goodbye."

"You do that," I said, and she wobbled over to the bar. "I'm sorry to have to cut our evening short, Lainey, but I need to get her home," I explained. "I can't let her leave with that guy. I would never forgive myself if something happened to her."

"I understand," Lainey said. "I could drive you if you want. I know you took the Marta over here, and she's not in any shape to be on the train tonight. That would be an ordeal within itself."

"You're right about that. It would be nice if you could drive us, but then that would make your drive home that much longer."

"I don't mind, Nate."

"I would worry about you the whole time."

"You worry a lot, don't you?"

"Only about people I care about."

"You have this strong desire to take care of people. You're a nurturer." She smiled.

"Sorry, it's just my nature."

"Don't apologize. I think it's sweet." She smiled. "No need to worry about me, Nate. I'll be fine. Besides, I insist on driving you home."

"Well, if you insist, then I guess I have to accept."

"Yes, you do." Lainey stood and pulled her car keys out of her purse.

* * *

I helped Darlene into the back seat of Lainey's Suburban. She fell over after I was unsuccessful at snapping her seat belt; and she didn't offer much help. I hopped into the front passenger's seat as Lainey maneuvered out of the parking lot. As we slowed at the second light, snores from the back seat drowned the music. I glanced at my sister-in-law, her mouth wide open, her hair a thick mountain on her head.

"Does she always drink like that?"

"More often than not," I said, almost embarrassed.

As Lainey pulled into my driveway, I glanced into the back seat at Darlene who hadn't moved a muscle, mouth wide and still snoring.

"Dar?" I called, and she didn't budge. Her mascara ran down her cheeks.

I stepped out of the car and opened the back door. Called her again. Louder.

"Dar?"

I pulled Darlene out and swung her over my shoulder. Carried her into the house. Lainey followed behind me, carrying Darlene's purse. I carried her to our guest bedroom, slid her stilettos from her feet and spread a blanket over her fully-clothed, drunken body. I kissed her forehead and turned off the light as I left the room. Lainey was still standing in the foyer, Darlene's purse in her hand.

"Here, I'll take that," I said, grabbed the purse and placed it on the sofa in the living room. "Want some coffee?"

"Sounds good."

"Just one cup, and then I want you on the road before it gets too late."

"Protective, aren't you?" she asked, then followed me to the kitchen.

"I can be." I smiled. "You got a problem with that?"

"No. I think it's one of your best qualities."

"And what are my other qualities?"

"You're very handsome, thoughtful and kind."

"I'm handsome?" I asked teasingly, instinctively pressing my body against Lainey's.

"Very," she said, and placed her hands on my chest. "You have a beautiful home."

Changing the subject, she moved from my embrace.

"Thank you," I said, and started a pot of coffee. "Of course, I can't take any credit for the decorating."

I pulled two colorful mugs from the shelf, placed them on the countertop.

"Cream and sugar, right?"

"Yes," she said, and walked over to the back door. Glanced out at the deck, where my manly gas grill was stored. She looked around at our well-groomed backyard; manicured flower beds. "Nice yard."

"That, I can take credit for." I chuckled, pressed against her from behind. My lips brushed lightly across the back of her neck.

She seemed to relax from my touch, and then turned to face me.

I moved a loose strand of hair from her face. My lips found hers and I kissed her with the same passion that

I had kissed her with in my dreams. Her arms wrapped around my neck, I pushed her toward the kitchen counter; lifted her and placed on top. I positioned myself in between her legs and began to caress her breasts with the palms of my hands. I slid my hand beneath her skirt and rubbed her thigh. Made my way to the sweetness between her thighs and she moaned. My fingertips moved about in her wetness. She began to loosen my belt buckle and her hand toyed with the bulge in my pants.

"Nathan, I have to tell you…" Her breathing became rapid, and so did mine. "I'm falling in love with you."

"I'm falling in love with you, too," I said, unable to hold back.

"How long have you known this?" she asked, her eyes meeting mine.

"Since the moment I laid eyes on you."

She smiled. I lifted her blouse over her head and began to loosen the snaps on her bra. My fingertips danced up and down her spine, and she trembled. No words were spoken, just moans. My cell phone began to play a tune, but I ignored it. What I had going on was too good to end so abruptly. I continued to press my lips against Lainey's, but my cell phone wouldn't give. It rang again, begging for an answer.

"I have to get this," I whispered, pulling the phone out of my pocket and recognizing the number. "Excuse me."

I let go of Lainey, as she hopped down from the countertop. Guilt rushed through me as I looked at the half-nakedness of another woman in my wife's kitchen. What was I doing? Why hadn't I exercised control? Sex had never been a thing that moved me; even as a hormonal teenager, I knew how to exercise control. This isn't sexual, I thought as I fastened my belt buckle.

"Hello?"

"Mr. Sullivan, this is Amy, your wife's nurse." The soft voice said, "I think you should get over here as soon as possible. She's exhibiting signs of awareness. She's responding to movement, and actually tried to speak."

Joy flooded my soul. Amy's words rang in my head over and over again, *She's exhibiting signs of awareness...actually tried to speak*. Could it be that this nightmare was finally over?

"Thank you, Amy," I said, numb and staring into space. Barely hung up the phone, but wanted to go outside, wake up the entire neighborhood and dance in the street.

"What is it?" Lainey asked.

"That was Marva's nurse," I said. "She said that Marva's exhibiting signs of awareness. Said she even tried to speak."

"Wow. That's good news, Nate." She forced a smile. "It's what you've been waiting for."

"Yes, it is."

"You should get over there right away," she said. "I should be going anyway. It's getting late."

"Will you be okay driving home?" I didn't want to rush her, but knew I had to get to the hospital just to witness the events for myself.

"I'll be fine," she said.

"Can you leave me a message on my cell phone just to let me know that you made it home safely?"

"Absolutely," she said. "I had a good time tonight. And I'll see you later."

Lainey rushed toward the door and I struggled to keep up.

"You sure you're okay?"

"I'm fine." She said. "Go see your wife."

But the way she bolted out the door told me she wasn't okay.

I suddenly remembered that I'd left my car at the Marta station. I called a taxi, my heart pounding as I waited for it to arrive.

"She even tried to speak," I whispered to myself, and smiled.

CHAPTER 22

Lainey

I stood with my back against the outside of Nathan's front door for longer than I should have, as tears crept down my cheeks. How did I let myself get to this place of uncertainty? This place where I should've been happy for my friend, because I knew he'd prayed for his wife's recovery, but instead I felt uneasiness. Jealousy. I was happy for him, but something inside of me died the moment he had gotten off the phone and announced that Marva was aware...even tried to speak, he'd said. Selfishly, I wished she could've remained sleeping just a little while longer. And I hated myself for wishing that. Who had I become? Longing for another woman's husband? I knew my feelings for Nathan were unjust. It was downright wrong what I felt for him.

I finally regained my composure, secured my purse onto my shoulder and headed for my car. I had to get him out of my system, and the best way to do that was to go somewhere...somewhere far away, and clear my head. Get myself together, and fast, because I was tripping.

Don and I had owned a little two-bedroom villa at Hilton Head for years. We'd purchased it on a wing and a prayer when we were both young and broke. We'd vacationed there one summer; someone had given us a weekend getaway as a wedding gift. While aimlessly wandering around on the golf course, pretending we were wealthy, we bumped into Eddie Whitestone, the fast-talking Realtor who charmed us into taking out a mortgage on a vacation home that we knew we couldn't handle. Ironically, the villa turned out to be our best investment.

It was a perfect place for a getaway. As I pulled out of Nathan's driveway, I searched through my phone for the number of the management company that handled the rentals for our villa; dialed it. The answering service picked up, and I had Jessica, the young lady who managed our property, paged. She called back almost immediately.

"Elaine?"

"Jessica, how are you?"

"Mrs. Williams. It's so good to hear from you. Will you and Mr. Williams be coming for a visit soon?"

"Oh, Jessica, you must not know. Mr. Williams passed away recently."

"I'm so sorry to hear that. I didn't know." Jessica's upbeat tone turned solemn. "Mr. Williams was such a nice man."

"It's okay, sweetie," I told her.

"Was it sudden? Because I don't remember him being sick."

"He was in a car accident. Hit another car head-on."

"My God," she exclaimed. "Was the other driver hurt?"

"Yes, the other driver was injured badly. She's in a coma."

"My goodness, that traffic in Atlanta has got to be the worst in the country. Dangerous even," she said. "I'm going to pray for that woman's recovery. Her family must be devastated."

"They are."

"Mercy."

"Jessica, the reason I called was because I need to get away. I'm planning a visit and need to know if the villa is available. I would like to come as early as tomorrow morning."

"Can you come after noon tomorrow? I have a couple in there right now, a real nice husband and wife...they just got married. They're the cutest, sweetest little things I've seen in a long time," she said in her Southern drawl that was more South Georgia than South Carolina. "They should be checking out by noon tomorrow. But if you can't wait, I can put them in another unit tonight. I'm sure they won't mind, just as long as they can be together."

"No, no, don't go to any trouble. I can wait until they leave." I said, "I'll just drive down tomorrow afternoon sometime. That way I can catch an early dinner at Max's place."

"Oh, he'll be delighted to see you. I'll tell him you're coming and he'll fix you up somethin' real special."

"That sounds nice."

"And I'll have the place cleaned real nice for you," Jessica said. "How long will you be staying?"

"A week, maybe longer."

"That's fine. I'll find another unit for the folks I already have booked for the next couple of weeks," Jessica said. "Now you drive safe, honey, and I'll see you tomorrow."

"Okay, Jess. See you tomorrow."

Headed down 75 south, the sunlight beaming in my eyes, my Ray-Ban's at the tip of my nose, my bags loaded in the back of Don's Suburban, I opened the sunroof to let fresh air in. I pumped up the volume on Luther's "Dancing With My Father" CD. I thought of Luther and wondered how a man so young and talented could leave this earth so suddenly. Particularly when people, especially me, needed him to create more masterpieces; more ballads that would help us through times such as this one; times when we're heartbroken and lonely. How could he leave us like this?

I checked my cell phone again for the fourth time, just to see if I'd missed any calls from Nathan, but felt silly for even expecting such a call. What had I been to him besides a distraction? A means for killing time while his wife recovered. She was awake now and would take her rightful place in his life. After all they'd been through, it would take some time to repair the damage, but at least she was alive. God had given her a second chance. Unlike Don. He was gone forever.

Suddenly, I felt responsible for the damage. Couldn't I have insisted that Don let me drive us home that night? Couldn't I have pried the keys from his tight fist? Couldn't I have called us both a taxi or asked Alvin to drive us home that night? I wondered what I could've done differently, if anything.

Once I reached the island, I pulled into the parking lot of the local Piggly Wiggly supermarket. The coolness in the store had me thinking it was much too soon for air-conditioning; the island's temperature at a beautiful sixty-eight degrees. I grabbed a grocery cart, picked up a few steaks, chicken and fish. Grabbed some orange juice, milk, eggs and other items to stock the refrigerator for the next week or so. I grabbed a fragrant bouquet of spray roses and miniature carnations to garnish the dining room table with. I also picked up a few candles for the relaxing bubble bath I had planned for the evening.

When I reached the villa, I unloaded the groceries first. The smell of fresh gardenias met me at the front door as I swung it open. The sounds of light jazz played on the CD player in the living room. The sliding-glass door was open just enough to welcome in a light breeze, and I stepped out onto the patio to breathe in the fresh scent of the ocean air. Jess had made the place feel just like home. She even had a vase filled with fresh gardenias in the bathroom, along with a bottle of wine.

My cell phone rang, and when I recognized Glenda's number, I ignored it. She was the last person I wanted to hear from. In fact, I turned my cell phone completely off so that her calls wouldn't interrupt the peaceful and serene couple of weeks that I had planned for myself. I unloaded my luggage, hung my clothes in the closet, and thought I'd take a nice long bubble bath before heading over to Max's for dinner. After dinner I'd take a walk along the beach before retiring to my bedroom to curl up with one of the romance novels I'd packed for the trip.

Thoughts of Nathan began to fill my head again, and I pushed them away. I needed to get him out of my system, and that's what I planned to do. When I stepped back inside the villa, I placed my cell phone in a utility drawer in the kitchen, never to pull it out again until I was homeward bound. I was going to enjoy this peace if it was the last thing I did. I didn't want to confuse the issue more by speaking with Nathan on the phone, and didn't want him to feel any unnecessary pressure of having to call to check on me. He needed to focus on his family. I had to accept that I had been a mere pastime, count my losses and move forward. There had always been the possibility that Marva would recover. I'd even searched the Internet for statistics on the recovery of patients who'd been in a vegetative state. The statistics were positive, so what right did I have to be hurt? Nevertheless, I was. But not for long. Healing would begin today.

I started the water for a bath, lit a few candles and turned the music up a bit. The local jazz station had the nerve to play Billie Holiday's, "Lady Sings the Blues." How ironic and untimely. How tacky of them to remind me of what I was trying to forget. Billie's voice was so filled with pain, I couldn't take it. I rushed into the living room, changed the station to a hip hop one. Listened to some guy sing about being in love with a stripper, as if anyone cared. I popped in Luther's CD, and it was just what I needed.

The steamy hot water relaxed my limbs and I shut my eyes. Shut them so tight, that before long, my own snoring shook me. I had fallen asleep. I was exhausted, but my stomach's growling let me know that I was also hungry. I needed to get over to Max's and grab some dinner before it got too late.

CHAPTER 23

Nathan

Moving through the hospital at a pace much faster than a stroll, I finally made it to the Intensive Care Unit, breathing hard. Panting as if I'd just run a marathon. The drive over had been the longest ever, filled with anxiety and anticipation for what I'd find. I had tried waking my sister-in-law and giving her the good news; thought about asking if she wanted to ride over and share in the excitement with me, but she was still passed out in our guest room, with no hope of waking up anytime soon. So I left her a note. Rushed out of the house, barely remembering to lock the door as I hopped into the back seat of the taxi.

As I approached Marva's room, I slowed to an even pace, caught my breath and regained my composure. Loud voices from inside the room rang out. There was a team of hospital professionals in the room. Marva's doctor, a couple of nurses, the anesthesiologist were gathered around her bed, and seemed to be trying to revive her. Someone was performing CPR. I wanted to ask what they were doing, but I was paralyzed. I couldn't quite understand what I was witnessing.

Amy, Marva's nurse, spotted me, came out into the hallway, and pulled me into a corner, away from the chaos.

"What's going on in there?" I asked her.

"Marva went into cardiac arrest. She had a blood clot in her leg from lying still for so long—that blood clot moved rapidly to her brain and caused her to go into cardiac arrest. The doctor was called in almost immediately and began to resuscitate," she said.

"When? I mean how?"

"They're doing all they can to revive her, Mr. Sullivan. She's been placed on a respirator." She pulled me toward the family waiting area. "Why don't you have a seat in here, and I'll grab you a cup of coffee."

"I don't understand. You just called less than an hour ago and said she was doing well."

"She was responding earlier tonight. Her eyes were following me around the room, and she even attempted to say something to me. I was so excited, I couldn't help but call you. I've grown quite fond of both you and Marva, and wanted to share the news." She looked distraught. "But then, I don't know what happened. Everything happened so suddenly."

I barely heard anything else after she said resuscitate. I sat in one of the cushiony plaid chairs in the waiting area and stared into space for a few moments. Amy disappeared and was back with a Styrofoam cup filled with steamy hot coffee. I took it, but didn't drink right away. Couldn't. I sat there, anxiety overtaking my body. I wanted to get into that room and find out what was going on. Wanted to know what happened in just the short time it took me to drive over to the hospital. How could she have gone into cardiac arrest when she was responding to stimuli less than an hour ago? So many questions, but none of them were getting answered.

Before long, Dr. Garrett appeared in the doorway of the small waiting room. I stood.

"Mr. Sullivan, may I speak to you for a moment?"

He and I were the only two in the room and I invited him to say his peace right there.

"I'm listening," I told him.

"She's breathing right now, but only by way of a respirator. We performed CPR and have her stabilized as best we can. Because we don't have any preexisting agreements from her or your family, it's up to you whether or not we continue to sustain her breathing that way. But you must make a decision quickly—within the next twenty-four to forty-eight hours."

"A decision?"

"If you decide to leave her on the respirator long-term, we will need to perform a procedure called a tracheotomy. That's a surgical procedure in which an incision is made into her windpipe to form an opening. A tube is then inserted through the opening to allow the passage of air and removal of secretions. Instead of breathing through her nose and mouth, Marva would then breath through the tracheostomy tube."

"I don't know what to say. I can't make a decision like this on my own. She has family...she has parents, who..."

"We'll monitor her progress on the respirator for the next twenty-four hours, Mr. Sullivan." He swallowed hard. This was hard for him, too. "But I have to be honest with you. The blood clot was very large, and there's very little hope that she'll begin breathing on her own."

"But there is hope?"

"Very little."

I lost control of my legs. What exactly was he telling me? He held on to me; steadied me.

"I don't understand."

"It's a difficult situation when the patient doesn't have a living will, or hasn't taken measures to instruct us on what their desires are. It puts the family in a terrible position…having to make such the decision for them…"

I observed Dr. Garrett for the first time, with his jet-black wavy hair, perfectly trimmed mustache, a white medical jacket with his name embroidered on it. Underneath he wore khakis and a striped dress shirt. He was young; probably had just completed his residency. How many patients like Marva had he treated in his short career? I wondered.

"So what you're suggesting is that we pull the plug on her."

"What I'm suggesting is that Marva's unable to make her own decisions right now, and it's up to you and your family to decide what's in her best interests. And time is of the essence. You should decide quickly. At least within the next day or so."

"So let me make sure I understand you correctly. You need to know within the next twenty-four hours, if we're going to leave her on the respirator long-term. That way you can perform that surgical procedure…the trac…"

"Tracheotomy."

"Right. Tracheotomy." I was trying to rearrange the details in my head. "And because the blood clot is large, there's little hope that she will begin breathing on her own."

"That is correct. But we will monitor her progress for the next twenty-four hours, and that will give us some idea of how she will recover from this. My guess is that she won't ever be removed from the vent. There's very little hope that she will ever breathe on her own."

"But there is hope?"

"Yes. But very little," he said. "It's up to you and your family to decide if this is what you want for Marva long-term."

"Can I see her?"

"Sure."

I followed Dr. Garrett into Marva's room. As a machine pumped life into her, tears filled my eyes. I couldn't stand to see her suffer, but I knew it would be too difficult to let her go. I stood there for several minutes, staring; motionless. Then I stepped out into the hallway and called our parents. I knew it would be at least a couple of hours before they could get here, but I hoped they would put a rush on it. I paced the floor. I needed to think things through, find myself a clear and definite position before they got here. Needed to know where I stood in all of this.

I began to engage in self-talk. "Where do you stand on this, Nate? Would you want to be on a respirator, with no promises of recovery; no quality of life? What would Marva want? You know her better than anyone. Would she want this?"

* * *

My mother, Helen and Poppa Joe walked briskly toward me. Mama reached for me and pulled me into her bosom.

"How you holding up, baby?" she asked.

"Not so good." I broke down and cried into her chest like I did when I was ten and had fallen out of the tree in Miss Robinson's front yard. Had broken my arm that summer, and it had been Mama who'd rocked my tears away then, and she was still rocking my tears away, even now. I crumbled.

"It's gonna be alright, sweetheart."

Helen and Poppa Joe bolted for Marva's room. Helen stood over her bed, her face soaked from the tears. Poppa Joe stood in a corner, a frown on his face. It was the frown of a father who couldn't protect his baby girl any longer. A frown of defeat, and hurt, but he knew he had to remain strong for his wife. I wasn't as strong as Poppa Joe.

"Where's Daddy?" I asked my mother.

"He's parking the car. Be in here in a minute."

"I don't understand what happened," Helen said once she'd stopped crying long enough to talk. "You had just called us and said that she was responding. What happened, Nate?"

Her tone was accusing; sounded almost as if she was blaming me, or questioning whether or not I was responsible for the sudden change in Marva's condition.

Dr. Garrett walked into the room.

"Hello, I'm Dr. Garrett. The physician on duty tonight."

Helen pushed her way toward him. "I'm Helen, Marva's mother."

"Nice to meet you, ma'am." Tall and Curly shook my mother-in-law's hand. "It's not unusual for a patient to get a blood clot from lying still for so long. It moved to her brain so quickly..."

"Why didn't you revive her?" Helen spat the words like venom.

"Ma'am, we did all we could to resuscitate. We were able to stabilize her as best we could."

"So the machine is breathing for her?" Poppa Joe asked.

"Yes, sir," he said, his olive face showed true compassion. "However, I think you should decide quickly as a family if she should remain on the respirator long term, or if you wish to have her removed."

"Removing her is out of the question!" Helen said.

"Sweetie, let's go for a walk." Mama grabbed Helen's hand and ushered her out of the room.

Poppa Joe and I stood in silence as my father entered the room.

"Hey there, son." Daddy hugged me, and I hugged back.

He stole a glance at Marva, but avoided any conversation about the situation. Avoidance was his way of dealing with painful things. I'd received sensitivity from my mother; definitely not from him.

"How's it going, Daddy?"

"That Atlanta traffic is a bugga bear, I tell you. Folks here drive like they ain't got good sense."

"Traffic here never lets up."

"You right about that," he said, and inched toward the door. "I'm gonna just step out here into the hallway. You holler if you need me, son."

"I will."

"You all right, Joe?" he asked, grabbing Poppa Joe's shoulder on the way out.

"Fine, fine," Poppa said, and continued to stare at his daughter. "It's a painful thang for a father to see his child so helpless like this. A painful thang."

Daddy shook his head, but didn't stick around much longer. Poppa Joe and I stood staring at Marva as if by some miracle her state would suddenly change before our eyes.

My phone vibrated and I excused myself from the room. I'd left a message for Tracee to call me back immediately, and she was returning my call.

"Hi, Daddy. I got the message and called as soon as I could," she said. "What's going on?"

"Baby, your mother's not doing well. I think you should get a flight out tonight. I know you have classes, but this is important."

"Okay, Daddy. But what's wrong?"

"We'll talk about it when you get here," I told her. "Put the charges on your credit card, and call me back with your flight arrangements."

"Okay," she said. "But you're scaring me."

"I don't mean to scare you, sweetheart. But you need to be very brave right now. Braver than you've ever been in your life. You understand?"

"I understand, and I'll try my best. But I don't know how brave I can be. Especially when I don't know what's going on," she said.

"I think you're probably braver than you think."

"I hope so," she said softly. "I'll call the airline and get the first flight out."

"Good. Call me back." I hung up quickly and returned to Marva's side.

CHAPTER 24

Nathan

When Tracee arrived at Hartsfield-Jackson, I was there at the curb to pick her up. I hopped out of my truck and threw her bags into the back. I gave my daughter a tight squeeze and opened the passenger door for her. She hopped in.

"So what's up?" she asked as she snapped her seat belt around her.

"Your mother suddenly went into cardiac arrest. She's breathing, but only by a machine that's breathing for her."

"Oh my God!" She placed her hand over her mouth. "Is she gonna die, Daddy?"

"I don't know, sweetheart. The doctor said there's little hope that she'll ever breathe on her own," I said. "The family has to figure out if we will leave on her life support long-term or not."

"Is Granny and Nana at the hospital?"

"Yes."

"What are they saying?"

"Granny Helen does not want us to take her off. Nana isn't saying much at all."

"What about you, Daddy? What do you say?"

"I don't want to see her suffer, baby." I shook my head. "But selfishly, I don't want to let her go, either."

"Is she in pain?"

"I don't know. I think they have given her medicine and stuff for the pain. But it's got to be pretty exhausting to have a machine breathe for you."

"I don't want her to die, Daddy." She looked up at me as if she was three years old again. "Maybe things will turn around if we just be patient."

I didn't have the heart to tell her that we didn't have the luxury of being patient. A decision needed to be made quickly. But I knew then where she stood, and changed the subject.

"I noticed you're not messing with my radio station this morning. You mean, I can finally enjoy my oldies station without interruption?"

"I don't feel much like music," she said, and began to stare out of the passenger window.

"You hungry?" I asked. "Want some pancakes or something?"

"I don't feel much like eating, either."

Silently, she continued to stare out of the window. I felt as if she was a million miles away and I couldn't reach her.

I pulled into the McDonald's drive-thru. Ordered a cup of coffee and a McGriddle.

"Gimme an order of hot cakes and sausage, too," I told the young lady who'd taken my order. I glanced over at Tracee, her chin resting in the palm of her hand as she stared out the window. "Got you some pancakes, baby."

"I'm not hungry."

"You might change your mind," I said, and handed the woman at the window a ten-dollar bill.

"I doubt it," Tracee mumbled, and I knew I'd lost her.

After hours of just sitting around the waiting room, afraid to approach the subject, I decided that the subject needed to be approached. I stood.

"We have to decide what to do, as a family."

"You know my position, Nate," Helen said.

"But, Helen, the child is not breathing on her own," Mama said. "She has no quality of life this way."

"You're only saying this because it's not your child, Savannah. If it was one of your children, would you give up on them so easily?"

"Sweetie, Marva is very much my child. I love her just as much as you do," Mama said. "I may not have given birth to her, but..."

"I know, and I'm sorry, Savannah. I know you love Marva. But this is just so painful."

"I know, honey." My mother wrapped her arms around Helen.

"I don't like seeing her this way," Poppa Joe said. "She will never recover from this."

"What do you have to say about all of this, Nate?" my father asked. "She's your wife."

"I don't know what to say, Daddy."

"You have to have some opinion, son. Some say in it, right?" Poppa Joe eyeballed me.

All eyes landed on me, waiting for my response; my verdict, as if I was the judge and jury.

"What's going on up in here?" Darlene rushed into the waiting room like a thunderstorm, wearing the same clothes she'd had on the night before. Her face looking hungover as usual and her hair a wild mess on her head. "Why y'all looking all sad? According to Nate's note that he left for me at the house, Marva's out of the woods now, right? What? Did she suddenly take a turn for the worse or something?"

Everyone was silent as Darlene's eyes roamed from person to person.

Helen shook her head and rolled her eyes at her daughter.

"What did I say?" Darlene asked as she looked around at the solemn faces in the room.

"Darlene, honey. Marva went into cardiac arrest last night, and they weren't able to resuscitate. She's on a respirator that's breathing for her," Mama explained. "The family's trying to make a decision of whether or not she remains on that life support machine."

"Well that's a no-brainer. If she's breathing, what's the problem?"

"She will never breathe on her own," Poppa Joe explained. "And life support is no way to live the rest of your life."

"She hasn't made much progress since last night, and the doctor's don't think there's much hope," Mama explained.

"Nate was just about to tell us what he wants to do

about it." Poppa Joe stood and turned the channel on the television to ESPN.

"Well it should be a pretty easy decision for him." Darlene laughed. "Considering he already has a new girlfriend."

"What are you saying, Darlene?" Helen asked.

"Tell them, Nate."

"Daddy, what is Aunt Darlene talking about?" Tracee asked, looking at me square in the eyes from across the room. She wore tattered jeans and a sweater with MUDD embroidered across the front of it. Her long brown hair brushed her shoulders. She peered at me with her mother's eyes.

"She's just a friend, Dar. And you know it."

"I found them all huddled up in a corner booth last night at the jazz club," Darlene said and pulled a Salem out of its package. "It's a wonder he ain't pulled the plug on my sister already."

"That's enough, Darlene." Poppa Joe stepped in.

"You can't smoke in here, baby," Mama said right before Darlene lit her cigarette. "This is a hospital."

"What is she talking about, Daddy?" Tracee asked again. "What woman?"

"She's referring to Elaine Williams. She's the widow of the man who hit Marva. It's no secret that we've become friends. She's a very nice lady."

"Oh, I met her," Helen said. "She is a very nice lady. Darlene, you're always causing a commotion. You can't just come into a normal setting and behave in a normal way, can you?"

"Of course I can't. Not like Marva, right, Mama?" She began to force crocodile tears from her eyes. "I'm sorry I can't be more like her. She's so perfect and everything. You know what? I don't care if you pull the plug or not!"

Darlene took off toward the elevators, and I took off after her.

"Dar, wait!"

"What do you want, Nate?"

"What do you call yourself doing back there?" I asked once I caught up to her.

"Telling everybody about your little girlfriend." She was crying hard. "I'm not stupid, you know. That woman likes you, and you like her, too. And y'all not just friends."

I was speechless; I knew I couldn't deny what I felt for Lainey, and I didn't even try.

"I'm right," Darlene said with a look on her face that screamed, *Gotcha!* "I knew it."

"I didn't mean for this to happen. I wasn't trying to hurt Marva."

"You don't owe me an explanation," she said. "It's them who are always persecuting and judging people. As if they ain't never done nothing wrong."

"Your parents love you, Dar."

"They have a lovely way of showing it," she said. "Always comparing me to my sister."

"It's you who compares yourself to Marva. It's you who chooses to walk in her shadow instead of getting yourself together. If you stopped drinking and..."

"Who are you to judge me, Nathan?"

"I'm just telling you, from a big brother who loves you...you need to get it together, girl," I said. "You're getting too old for this disruptive behavior. I'm telling you, when people see you coming, they automatically assume that you're bringing drama with you. And guess what? Most of the time you are."

"So I'm the drama queen, huh?" she asked sarcastically.

"You *are* the drama queen." I smiled at my sister-in-law. "You're so beautiful, Dar. Look at those eyes, and that smile as bright as downtown Atlanta at nighttime. I've always thought you were attractive."

She smiled at my compliment.

"And you're smart, Dar. You're funny. You have so much character, and so much to offer." I touched her chin, and lifted her face so that her eyes met mine. "You could be anything you wanted to be. But, baby, the alcohol is destroying you. Don't let it."

The elevator doors swung open. Darlene's smile dropped. She pulled away and stepped inside.

"Later, Nate."

I stared into her eyes until the elevator doors completely shut. Prayed she'd heard me.

CHAPTER 25

Lainey

For as long as we'd owned the property on Hilton Head, Max's place had offered the finest dining on the entire island. Don and I had spent countless hours having dinner while enjoying the relaxing sound of jazz, and the ambience of this restaurant over the years. Max was like family, and took good care of us whenever we breezed through town for a weekend.

I followed the hostess to our favorite table near the baby grand piano. Wearing my sundress with a shawl wrapped around my shoulders, I took a seat and began looking at the menu. Although, I always ordered the broiled scallops on a bed of rice, I thought I'd see what other specials Max had to offer.

"Let me guess, you're having the scallops." I heard a familiar voice, and felt fingertips on my shoulders. "That's a shame, because I had the chef prepare a wonderful filet mignon just for you."

"Are you saying that my scallops are boring?" I smiled and stood to get a hug from Max, who was dressed in his usual black tuxedo.

"No, I'm saying you should broaden your horizons."
He laughed heartily. "How are you, sweetheart?"

"I'm fine."

"I heard about Don, and it broke my heart." He said,
"Are you holding up all right?"

"Doing my best."

"Well, you look fabulous. Lit the place up when you
walked in!"

Max was beginning to age. His old-school afro was
now salt and pepper, but his face was still the same;
handsome as always.

"Thank you," I said. "You look pretty good yourself."

"For an old man, huh?"

"Those are your words, not mine." I smiled. "How is
your family?"

"Lenny is graduating college this year. Wants to go to
law school, you know." He was proud; I could tell by
the way his chest stuck out when he mentioned his
youngest son. The one who'd given him the worst
trouble. "I can't believe he's actually doing something
with his life."

"I remember the time you and your wife had with him."
I smiled at my old friend. "You should be very proud."

"He's graduating at the top of his class, Lainey." His
laughter echoed through the room. "You and Don
remember what we went through with Lenny when he
was in high school. He was cutting school, getting sus-
pended, experimenting with drugs. And then that thing
that went on...you know, when he ended up in
Juvenile?"

"I remember," I said. "I kept him in my prayers."

"We didn't think he was gonna graduate high school, let alone college. And certainly not at the top of his class."

"And now he's considering law school."

"Considering?" Max said. "He's been accepted and ready to go next fall!"

"That's wonderful."

"I owe it all to your husband. He encouraged Lenny to go to law school. Had a nice long talk with him…" Max shook his head. "He helped me out a lot with that boy, and I'm grateful. It tears me apart that he's not here to see the results. He would be so proud."

"Don knew about Lenny going to college. And he was proud." I wasn't sure if Don really knew, but I needed to give Max some hope. "I'm sure he was so proud."

Max took a seat at my table.

"How you holding up, Lainey? You doing okay?"

"I'm fine."

"Be straight with me." He grabbed my hand. "I've known you and Don since you were first married. You're like family to me. If you need anything…anything at all, you let me know."

"I will, Max." I smiled at him. "And I'm fine."

"Good." He stood, just as the pianist began to play a familiar tune on the baby grand piano.

Went to show off his pearly whites and greet his other customers.

CHAPTER 26

Nathan

I stared at the television mounted in the corner of the wall; the Pacers putting a spanking on the 76ers. The game was a nice distraction as I got lost in the excitement of it. My mother's fingertips massaged my shoulders.

"You hungry, baby?" she asked. "You haven't had anything to eat. Why don't you go on down to the cafeteria and grab a bite."

"I'm fine, Ma. I really don't feel like eating."

"Son, you should put something on your stomach," Helen said.

"I will in a little bit." I said it just to get them off my back.

Poppa Joe and Daddy argued over the basketball game, while Tracee chattered with someone on the other end of her cell phone. All the while, my insides were in turmoil. I'd slipped away at least five times throughout the night to pray. Asked the Lord for direction; for some answers. Wondered what my test was in all of this. The clock was ticking fast. It had been more than twenty-four hours and the hospital staff needed for us to make a decision quickly.

"I think it's time we decide what we're going to do, baby," Helen said, and everyone froze at her announcement.

Everyone had dreaded this moment, and pretty much had avoided any conversation about why we were here. Helen was right; we needed to make a decision.

"Daddy, what's going on?" Tracee asked, hanging up with the person on the other end of her cell phone.

"We have to make a decision about your mother, sweetheart. Time is of the essence."

"We can't just let her die, Dad."

"Sweetheart, come with Nana." My mother grabbed Tracee around her shoulders. "Let's go downstairs and get something sweet. See if they got some sweet potato pie or some peach cobbler."

"No, ma'am, Nana. I don't wanna go, I wanna be right here," Tracee said. "I'm not a little girl anymore. I want to be a part of the decision."

My mother looked at me for approval or disapproval.

"Let her stay, Ma," I said. "She's old enough."

Poppa Joe and Daddy continued to watch the game, not offering any input one way or another. They avoided the subject like the plague.

"I've had time to think it over…" Helen began to speak, tears filling her brown eyes. She wiped them away. "I don't want to see her suffer long-term. The doctors have said that if they perform that procedure, that there's still no guarantees."

"What are you saying, Granny?" Tracee yelled, as if betrayed by the entire family.

"I'm saying, baby, that I don't want to see your mother suffer like that." Helen stood. "Sweetie, she will never recover from this. The machine is merely keeping her heart beating. That's no way for anyone to live. I wouldn't want to live that way."

"What about what she wants?" Tracee asked, to no one in particular. "Maybe she wants to stay alive."

"We don't know that, sweetheart, because we never talked about it." I explained. "She doesn't have a living will."

"Daddy, you said just the other day that she moved her eyes and stuff." She said, "Now you're just gonna give up on her?"

"I'm not giving up on her," I said, still in turmoil. Guilt had me arrested. "Tracee, I need for you to be a big girl."

"I'm not a kid anymore. You keep treating me like a kid!" she said. "Paw Paw...Gramps...what do you have to say? You're just sitting over there watching the game as if nothing's wrong. Paw Paw, this is your daughter they're talking about killing!"

Poppa Joe stood; grabbed Tracee's hand. "Come on, Poot Butt, let's take a walk."

Tracee went freely with her grandfather; leaving me with a decision to make; someone's destiny to decide. To allow Marva to remain on a respirator would be like prolonging her pain. It would be like taking away her dignity. But to remove her would mean goodbye to my wife forever. It would mean that I could never see her again, never hold her again, never have a conversation with her again. It would mean the end; death. No more would I feel her lips against mine; no more would she massage my shoulders after a bad day, or leave me sticky notes on the refrigerator.

Not to mention, I felt guilty. Guilt about loving someone else. That guilt would haunt me for the rest of my life. I would always wonder if my loving someone else weighed in on my decision to choose death for my wife. Just as the doctors say there's little hope, there's always that small chance for some hope. No man should ever have to travel this road. A road with no clear direction. Like a car with no windshield wipers and it's pouring rain.

"Nate, baby, I think it's time," Mama said, and I knew she was right. But for some reason, I couldn't move. I was paralyzed in my seat. "I'm gonna go get the doctor."

I watched as my mother walked down the hallway; watched her until I could no longer see her. Wanted to stop her, but my lips wouldn't move. Wanted to run after her, but my legs were stiff. Helen took the seat next to mine; grabbed my hand and held on to it. Sort of a peace offering.

After a brief conversation with the doctor, the decision was made.

We were each given a moment with Marva. Helen, Mama and Daddy went in together to say their goodbyes. Poppa Joe and Tracee wandered back to the waiting area and I searched for words to give my daughter.

"Where's Granny and Nana?" she asked. "And Gramps?"

"They're in with Mom, sweetie," I said. "Come here, baby. Have a seat."

She plopped down beside me, and Poppa Joe made the long journey toward his daughter's room. He knew the decision had been made.

"Baby, I really need for you to be strong right now," I said. "I need for you to be grown up."

"Daddy, this is so hard."

"I know it is, baby, but…"

"I'm so scared. If you take her off of that machine, she'll be gone for good."

"I'm scared, too. But the good thing about it is, we still have each other, you and me," I said. "We can help each other through this, and we have family who love us."

Tears began to fill her eyes.

"I know it's the right thing to do, Daddy. I guess I'm just being selfish. I already miss her so much, and now she'll be gone for good."

She stood and began to cry. Hard. I grabbed her from behind, and held her. Held her so tight, I wanted to squeeze the pain out of her.

"I hate this!" she yelled.

"I know, baby." I rocked my daughter. "I know this is hard."

"It's not fair." She cried harder.

"Shh-hh." I continued to rock her until she was finally calm.

"I hate this."

"I know." I kissed my daughter's forehead, and whispered, "Come on, let's go say goodbye."

We walked arm-in-arm toward my wife's room.

Goodbyes were so hard.

CHAPTER 27

Nathan

The sweet smell of roses had filled the air; hundreds of pink and white ones. And her hair had been graced with a million little curls. Her dress was the one she'd worn to Tracee's high school graduation; one that she'd spent hours in search of at Macy's just hours before the event. The one she'd initially planned on wearing made her look fat, she'd claimed, and when she'd tried it on, it just didn't work.

"I have to run over to the mall, Nate. Get something that won't put twenty pounds on me," she'd said. "We'll be taking pictures and stuff, and the last thing I need is to be looking like Miss Piggy at my daughter's graduation."

"Baby, you're not even fat." I was fighting a losing battle, trying to convince my wife of 143 pounds that she wasn't even close to being obese.

"You don't understand, Nate. It's a woman thing," she said, while making a mad dash for Southlake Mall.

She came back home with three dresses draped over her arm, one of which she'd settled on. The same one she'd worn today, pink and covered in lace. She wore a pink rose in her hair, and soft pink lipstick on her lips. A peaceful smile in the corner of her lips, and her eyes shut as if she was peacefully sleeping.

"You okay, sweetheart?" I asked Tracee, her eyes bloodshot and a Kleenex crumpled in her fist.

"Yes," she whispered, and then stared out of the smoke-colored tinted window of the limousine.

Across from us in the limo, Helen rested her head on Poppa Joe's shoulder.

"T'was a nice ceremony." She spoke softly, almost in a whisper. "She woulda liked it, Marva woulda."

Poppa Joe squeezed Helen's hand tighter and fought back tears of his own. His jaw tight, he stared straight ahead.

The ceremony had been nice, and I had managed to maintain control. That is until Marva's first-grade class began to recite a poem that they'd written for her. Watching their little faces, some of them with teeth missing in the front, some of them fidgeting and rocking from side to side, others just moving their mouths because they forgot the words. One little girl twirled her braid around with her finger, a thumb stuffed in her mouth, white stains from tears on her cheek. She'd been crying. She had been Marva's favorite. Asked a million questions, Shontay did. Those were Marva's words. She spoke of her often.

"Shontay's my favorite student, Nate," she'd said. "She's so helpful and smart. She's gonna grow up to be something special. You watch."

She must've been just as fond of Marva, I thought, as she read her little goodbye letter she'd written for my wife; a letter filled with words like, "You're the best teacher in the whole wide world" and "I hope you're going to Heaven to be with God, Mrs. Sullivan."

"I love you this much!" she exclaimed; her arms stretched out wide. "And don't worry, God will keep you safe from the spiders."

She was familiar with Marva's fear of spiders. As laughter rang throughout the sanctuary, tears crept down my cheek. It was just one more thing that I would miss.

The black limousine drove us from our little church in Riverdale, Georgia, to Marva's burial place in Toulmanville. The longest ride, it seemed, of my entire life. I shut my eyes and rested my head against the back of the seat. Wondered how we ended up here—in this place; this place where clocks couldn't be rewound. I wanted to cry, wanted to scream, wanted to ask God why. But I just rested my eyes instead. I closed them tightly and I thought of Marva.

As we drove past the little elementary school that we both attended when we were youngsters, I remembered her. Ponytails flying in opposite directions, big eyeglasses that were eventually replaced by contact lenses when she became a teenager, ashy knees and socks pushed down to her ankles. She hated me then; I was just little Nate from around the block, with a big head and Converse sneakers. In her parents' yard we caught lightning bugs back then; sealed them in a Mason jar with holes in the lid. I had no interest in her, either—not of the romantic type.

It wasn't until my junior year in high school—she was a sophomore—and my hormones were out of control. I remembered how she'd blossomed the summer before. She was different. She now had breasts, and curves in her hips. And she'd gotten contacts to replace those big goofy glasses. I saw her through different eyes, but to her I was still just Nate from around the block; her brother's best friend. Nobody spectacular, just another boy. And then she started dating Tyrone Johnson, linebacker for our school's football team. "What did he have that I didn't?" I asked myself this question every time I saw the two of them strolling down the hall, her books in his arms, his hand intertwined with hers. That was the first time I'd experienced any level of jealously.

"When you gon' drop that chump and give me a chance?" I asked her one day after school, as I trampled up the hill from the bus stop. She was giggling with a couple of her girlfriends. She looked at me as if I'd said something foreign.

"What are you talking about Nathan Earl Sullivan?" She pronounced every syllable of my name.

"I been checking you out, and I think you cute," I said.

That made her and her girlfriends giggle more. My ego was crushed because she hadn't taken me seriously. But I didn't give up. I knew that Tyrone Johnson was a playboy and it wouldn't be long before he slipped. And I would be there to pick up the pieces. By the end of the summer, he'd done just that. Got busted kissing another girl under the bleachers during summer football practice.

"Nathan, you're like my brother," she said when I'd tried to kiss her troubles away.

"I'm not your brother, though," I said matter-of-factly.

"Our families are so close, it just wouldn't feel right."

"You can't tell me that this doesn't feel right." My lips pressed against hers, my tongue probing the inside of her mouth, I drew her closer and caressed the small of her back. "This doesn't feel right to you?"

She didn't answer. But she didn't pull away, either. Instead, she moved closer in.

She was mine from that day forward.

As the minister said a final prayer, and they lowered her casket into the ground, that's when I cried the hardest. Dark shades camouflaged my tears. I wouldn't cry anymore, because I knew that all things happen according to God's will. For whatever reason, she was gone. But her life is what made the difference. The people she'd touched. The children she'd taught. Her service as a mother, wife and daughter. Her life as a Christian. Her task had been completed.

I glanced across the courtyard at Marva's friend Toni. Her friend of many years, of whom she'd had an argument with that night before the accident. Wanted to blame her; wanted to say it was her fault for arguing with Marva, making her insist on driving home in the middle of an ice storm. She stood there in her charcoal-gray suit, her hair pulled up into a bun on her head, dark shades covering her eyes. Chances are, she'd already blamed herself anyway. What good would it do for me to blame her, too? I let it go. Picked up a yellow rose that had fallen at my feet, grabbed my daughter's hand and strolled back to the limousine.

At Helen's and Poppa Joe's, the smell of collard greens filled the air. People had been bringing food over for days—fried chicken, vegetables, macaroni and cheese, and every kind of cake and pie you could think of. There was enough food to feed the neighborhood, and that's exactly what happened as people poured in and out of the house, paying their respects; people who had known Marva since she was in Pampers. Her classmates, people from church, just about everybody in Toulminville. The sounds of laughter and loud conversations bounced from the walls. There were so many people in the house, it was hard to move around. I decided to take refuge on the back stairs. Sat there in my Armani suit, my elbows resting upon my knees.

"Look like you need a game of one-on-one." Marva's brother, Rick, interrupted my thoughts as he handed me a bottle of Budweiser.

"Nah, I just wanna sit here awhile."

"You all right?"

"I'm cool," I said, and kept my responses brief. Preferred being alone, but knew that Rick would stay. He was worried; wanted to ease my pain, but didn't know how. He pulled up a lawn chair from the porch, and we sat there in silence for a while. His heart was just as heavy as mine. Marva was his little sister, and it had been his job to protect her. No matter how ridiculous it may have seemed, in his mind, he was supposed to somehow protect her from death, too. And he hadn't.

Darlene stuck her head out the door. "Nate, Mama said you need to come and eat."

"Not hungry," I said. "Tell her to put my plate up and I'll get it later."

She repeated what I said to her mother, and before long she was outside, too, lawn chair in tow.

"You all right, Nate?" she asked.

"I'm fine, Dar. What about you?" I asked, looking into her eyes and taking note that they were clear for the very first time in a long time. No bloodshot veins. Her hair was in a neat style, and she actually looked like a lady in her black skirt and white silk blouse.

"I'm cool," she said.

"I'm going to get some grub," Rick said, and slowly walked into the house. "Sure you don't wanna eat, man?"

"I'll be there in a minute," I said.

Rick disappeared.

"Nate, I been thinking about what you said." Darlene turned up a bottle of water. I was surprised that she didn't have a bottle of beer or a glass filled with Rémy Martin and Coke. "You know, that stuff you said about me causing drama all the time…and that I need to get myself together."

"Yeah?"

"I'm trying," she said. "I'm going to this little program next week, you know, this alcohol rehab thing…whatever you call it. S'pose to be a good program."

"That's good, Dar," I said, and smiled at my sister-in-law. "You serious?"

"I'm getting too old for this crap, Nate," she said. "And you know what? I spent my whole life hating my sister for having the life that I wanted for myself. I blamed her for all the wrong in my life. I blamed her instead of looking in the mirror at myself."

"She loved you."

"I never got a chance to make things right with her, Nate, and that's been killing me," she said. "What can I do? How do I make things right?"

"Just get yourself together. That's what she wanted for you more than anything."

"She said that?"

"She used to talk about the time when the two of y'all were close. When y'all got along—before the drinking."

"It was a hard thing losing Kevin like that," she said. "We were supposed to get married, you know."

"I know."

"I guess I just didn't care about life anymore, and it was easier to just drink my troubles away."

"I know you loved Kevin," I said, and remembered Darlene's fiancé who had been hit by a stray bullet during a robbery at the local grocery store. He'd just gone in there for a package of cigarettes that day and quickly became an innocent victim. I remembered Chester Reed running up the stairs of Poppa Joe and Helen's house, almost out of breath, sweat pouring from his ashy dark skin.

"Where Darlene?" he had asked, panting like a dog

in heat. "Kevin just got shot at the Piggly Wiggly. The police and everythang over there!"

As Marva and I rocked on the porch swing, Darlene's round belly was the first thing you saw as she came out of the house and onto the porch. She caught the end of Chester's words and began screaming and shaking her hands uncontrollably. She started down the street.

"Oh my God!" she yelled over and over again.

"Dar, come on, I'll take you over there. You can't walk to the Piggly Wiggly," I said, and coaxed her into my old Firebird with the T-top. At six months pregnant, she carefully eased into the passenger's seat. I eased out of the driveway; my foot like lead as I drove her to the Piggly Wiggly.

The sight of Kevin's body lying on the pavement made everything inside of me numb. It could've been any one of us lying there, as we all had visited that store at least half a dozen times a day. I remembered as a child, my mother had sent me there a million times in search of Jiffy cornbread mix, a dozen eggs or a block of lard to fry chicken with. And even as a young adult, I frequented there, just to pick up few items here and there.

I remembered the white maternity blouse that covered Darlene's belly was bloody as she kneeled and rocked him. Tears streaming from her eyes, she screamed, "No!"

After his funeral she stopped living; stopped eating; stopped sleeping. It wasn't long before her careless behavior claimed the life of the child that grew inside of her. She miscarried, and that was the straw that broke the camel's back. She became a full-fledged, card-carrying alcoholic. Lost sight of all her hopes and dreams. Resented her sister's life, because it was everything that she was supposed to have. Unfortunately her dreams ended back then.

But now, she sounded like the old Darlene again.

"Yeah, you're probably right, Nate." She leaned back in her lawn chair, drank from her bottle of water again. "I'm sorry about that thing with the lady the other night...you know, the lady from the car accident. I wasn't trying to bust you out or nothing."

"Don't sweat it."

"You love her, Nate?"

My silence was her answer.

"My sister's gone, and she ain't coming back." She said it in almost a whisper. "I know you're hurting right now because of Marva, but there will come a time when you will want love again. All I'm saying is, I wouldn't blame you."

I didn't respond, but her words soothed me.

"I know what it's like to lose someone. And it's a hard thing trying to fill that void. Some of us fill it the wrong way, like me. Don't travel the road that I chose." Tears began to fill her eyes.

I didn't know what direction I was headed in, but I was relieved to know that someone understood my inward turmoil.

"Anyway, I'm going inside to get some of that fried

chicken." She stood, fought the tears, and headed up the back stairs. "You coming?"

"In a minute," I said, and found peace in the breeze that blew across my face.

CHAPTER 28

Lainey

As I slowly opened one eye, I thought I was dreaming. That is until the loud banging on the door shook me from my sleep. I glanced over at the digital clock on the mahogany nightstand, turned it around so I could get a better look at the time. Six forty-five. Surely it had to be a.m., because at six forty-five the night before, I was busy enjoying fresh seafood at Max's restaurant.

I pulled myself out of bed as the knocking grew louder. Pulled a bathrobe around me and made my way to the door.

"I'm coming," I said to my early morning caller.

I looked out of the peephole and the back of the person's head looked familiar, but still I waited until they turned around. I swung the door open.

"What are you doing here?" I asked.

"Lainey. Don't shut the door on me," Glenda said. "Can I come in?"

I pulled the door wider and allowed her to enter. I strolled to the kitchen and started a pot of coffee.

"What are you doing here at this hour? And how did you even know I was here?"

"Somehow I knew you would be here, but I also talked to Alvin. He told me." She smiled, but I didn't return it. "I got up at the crack of dawn to drive down."

"No kidding," I said, placing a filter in the compartment of the coffee pot and dumping enough gourmet coffee in to make six cups. Glenda started pulling creamer and sugar from the shelves. She pulled down a couple of mugs.

"Lainey, please forgive me. I'm so sorry that I didn't tell you about Don's affair with that woman. I wanted to just forget about it, and pretty soon, I totally blocked it from my mind." She pleaded, "I need your friendship."

"It's okay. It doesn't even matter anymore," I told her. "And by the way, it wasn't just an affair. The two of them were married."

"Alvin told me that, and I didn't believe him. How could they be married when Don was married to you?"

"Believe it. He married both of us."

"Isn't that against the law?"

"In this part of the world, yes." I smiled.

"That lying, sleezy..." she said. "I never liked Don, you know."

"I know." It felt good to release my negative energy and have a conversation with my best friend again. I started to relax.

"I always thought you deserved better."

"I did. But I loved him," I admitted.

The aroma from the coffee floated through the house. Glenda found her way to the patio, and I followed.

"It's so beautiful here. I love it."

"Me, too," I agreed as I looked across the beautiful countryside. Birds chirped as the sun began to creep its way up into the sky. I breathed in the fresh smell of the morning air.

"So what will you do now, Lainey?" she asked.

"Make the best of my life, I guess." I walked back into the house and into the kitchen. Poured two cups of coffee.

I handed Glenda her cup, seasoned with two sugars and no cream; just the way she liked it.

"Thanks, sweetie," she said, and then plopped down in the lounger on the patio. "I'm sorry you had to find out things the way you did."

"I went there."

"Where?" she asked.

"California. To see her for myself."

"And?"

"She's pretty," I said, and sat in a lawn chair opposite hers. "They have two children. Samantha and, get this...Donnie Junior."

Glenda rolled her eyes and sipped her coffee.

"You went alone?"

"No." I couldn't help smiling.

"With who?" she asked, leaning forward to get a better look at my face. "A man?"

"Nathan."

"Nathan, the guy-whose-wife-was-in-the-accident Nathan?"

"Yes."

"Do tell," she said, a broad smile on her face.

"Nothing to tell."

"Come on now, tell me everything. How did this come about? What did you do while you were there?"

"I just casually mentioned that I wouldn't mind his company, and he just popped up at the airport." I sipped my coffee. "We were becoming good friends, and didn't see any harm in it."

"Did you share a hotel room?"

"Of course not." I said, and pulled my robe together. "He's a married man."

"You like him," she exclaimed, a wicked smile on her face. "You like him a lot."

"I admit that," I said. "But it doesn't matter because it seems that his wife is going to be all right."

"All right? I don't think so," she said.

"What do you mean?"

"I mean, she's gone."

"Gone?"

"Dead."

"What? No way," I said. "The last time I saw Nathan, he was rushing over to the hospital because she was being responsive."

"Well, I don't know when that was, but the woman died last week."

Something in my heart dropped to the floor. I was frozen stiff.

"Are you sure?" I asked, and immediately thought of Nathan and how devastated he must have been. My heart ached for him.

"It was in the AJC," she said.

"Are you kidding?"

"Of course not. I wouldn't joke about something like that. I remember the article, Lainey, and the headline 'Atlanta Woman Dies After Car Accident Left Her in Coma.'" She said, "It was a really sad article. Had her picture and everything. I thought you knew."

"I had no idea. Nate received this phone call one night from the hospital, saying that she was responding and everything. I just assumed she was out of the woods, and that she'd be coming home soon. That's when I bolted and hit the road for here."

"You bolted. That's clearly a sign that you think of him as more than a friend. Am I right?"

I didn't have an answer.

"What's really going on?" she asked, looking me square in the eyes. "It's me. Glenda."

"I think I'm in love with him." Hearing those words spill from my mouth sent chills down my spine.

"Does he love you?"

"I think I was just a distraction for him while he was grieving for his wife," I told her, and then remembered the last night we were together. "You should've seen his eyes light up when he thought she would be okay. I don't think he feels anything for me."

"Have you talked to him?"

"No." I leaned back and placed my feet in the chair, my knees pressed against my chest. "I'll probably send flowers to the family or a card."

"Why don't you call him?"

"Not until he's out of my system."

Glenda stood. "You want more coffee?"

I handed her my mug, and my mind drifted a thousand miles away as she strolled to the kitchen.

"Let's go to the beach!" she yelled, and snapped me out of my trance.

"Let's go eat breakfast!" I suggested. "I'm starving."

"That's fine, but please don't make me go to Max's place." She laughed, as she stood at the patio door. Handed my mug back to me, coffee seasoned with cream and an abundance of sugar. Just the way I liked it.

"He thinks you're cute."

"I know. That's why I prefer IHOP or somewhere else."

"Don't be that way."

"And I hate that salt-and-pepper fro that he wears," she said. "He's such a flirt. And ain't he married anyway?"

"Yes, he's married." I laughed and was so grateful that I had my friend back. "Let me find something to put on so we can find a pancake house."

CHAPTER 29

Nathan

Fred Hammond's voice bounced off the walls as I sprinkled cheese into the scrambled eggs. The bacon was a little more done than it should be, but it was tough trying to pull biscuits out of the oven, scramble eggs and flip bacon all at the same time. Made me wonder how my mother managed to prepare a meal of greater substance than this, and keep it from burning. There was an art to cooking, and I definitely was not an artist. I was a basketball coach, a teacher, a father, a son...everything but a husband. I wasn't a husband anymore, and that realization brought tears to my eyes...yet again. It seemed that every thought of Marva lately brought tears to my eyes. I kept hoping it was a phase that would soon pass. But it wasn't passing fast enough.

I could hear Tracee moving around upstairs; the light sound of her footsteps creeping across the bedroom floor and then into the bathroom. I heard the shower running for about thirty minutes—too long for a shower, in my opinion—and then the patter of her footsteps on the stairway.

"Good morning, sleepyhead," I said when she popped her head into the kitchen, grabbed a piece of my over-cooked bacon.

"Hey, Daddy." She kissed my rugged cheek. My five o'clock shadow was getting out of control and I reminded myself that I needed a shave...like yesterday. "Bacon's a little crispy."

"I know it's crispy. That's how I like my bacon, chump," I lied.

"Since when?" she asked with a broad smile. "Admit it, you burned the bacon again."

"Yes, I burned the bacon, the eggs and the biscuits. So shoot me." I pinched my daughter's nose, the way I used to when she was five. "Grab yourself a plate anyway and have a seat."

She grabbed a plate from the shelf and filled it with my so-called breakfast items. Poured a glass of orange juice and sat at the kitchen table.

"At least the orange juice is freshly squeezed," I boasted.

"Yeah, by Tropicana." She laughed.

"Oh, you got jokes," I said, taking a seat across from her. "I squeezed that orange juice myself, girl."

"Daddy, please."

We both laughed.

"Did you sleep well?"

"I slept really good. I've been exhausted from this whole ordeal...the hospital, funeral, the drive from Alabama." She said, "We've been through a lot."

"Yes, we have." I had to agree with her. "Have you decided when you're going back to school, though?"

"Soon, Daddy. I just need some time to think things through right now."

"I understand, but I don't want you to get too relaxed here. Need you to get back to school and back to your routine."

"I will, I promise," she said, and frowned as she bit into a biscuit. "Honestly Dad, I'm worried about you."

"Why are you worried about me?"

"I just am. I know that you don't do well alone. And I know you'll be lonely."

"I have plenty to keep me busy. Got my students to keep me company."

She cocked her head to the side...the way her mother used to do when she was contemplating something.

"I can transfer to a school closer to home, if you want me to...like Georgia Tech or something."

"Of course not. You have a full scholarship at Howard. Why would you throw that away?"

"To be closer to you."

"Not necessary. Your dad is fine."

She was silent for a few moments.

"Is it true about that woman? The one from the car accident. Do you like her or something?"

"We've always been straight-up with each other, right?"

"Always."

"I care for her."

She silently scooped eggs onto her fork, popped them into her mouth. Didn't say another word about it.

"Faye and Shenese will be here soon. We're going to the mall," she announced.

"What? I thought we'd hang out today. You and me," I said, disappointed. "I had the day all planned out." I had strategically planned our day, which began with breakfast, then a matinee at the movies, dinner at Mick's. Tracee loved Mick's fried green tomatoes.

"Sorry, Daddy. With the funeral and everything, I hadn't had much time to spend with my friends," she said, stuffing a piece of bacon into her mouth. "But if you want me to, I'll hang out with you."

"Nah, you go on with your friends."

"You sure?"

"Yeah. It's cool."

"What will you do?"

"I don't know. Maybe I'll go pick up a few of my students and watch a ball game or something."

"Maybe we can have dinner at Mick's or something. I love those fried green tomatoes."

"You must've read my mind."

She refilled her glass with orange juice as the sound of the doorbell echoed through the house.

"I'll get it." Tracee rushed to the door and before long I heard whispers and giggles. After a few minutes, Faye and Shenese appeared in the doorway of the kitchen.

"Hi, Mr. S." Shenese's bright smile and tight jeans breezed into the kitchen. She was not shy and immediately found her way to the stove and grabbed a piece of bacon. "Um. A little crispy, huh?"

"We like our bacon crispy around here," I said sarcastically, pulling my bathrobe tighter and flipping through the AJC.

Tracee and Shenese giggled.

"Hi, Mr. Sullivan," Faye said, and quietly stood in the doorway. She was a little more reserved than Shenese.

"Hello, Faye," I said. "Shouldn't you both be away at college?"

"I'm home for the weekend, Mr. S.," Shenese said. "My dad bought me a car for Christmas, and U.GA. is just a hop, skip and a jump away. So I drive home just about every weekend."

"I'm at Georgia Tech," Faye said. "I'm still at home with my parents. Thinking about getting an apartment next semester, though."

"Yeah, me, too," my daughter chimed in, and my eyes shot toward her in question.

"You're thinking about getting an apartment?" Faye asked, and took the words right out of my mouth.

"With Darren?" Shenese asked, and my eyebrows lifted so high, I thought they might bounce off my face.

"Who's Darren?" I had to ask, but calmly nonetheless.

"That's Tracee's..." Shenese almost spilled the beans until she received a look from Tracee that said, *Shut up, girl. We're talking to my dad.* The same Dad of whom she used to share everything with. We'd just had a conversation about being open with one another. Had she forgotten that quickly?

"Friend!" Tracee interjected.

"Darren's Tracee's friend, Mr. S.," Shenese said. "Real nerdy guy, about five feet tall."

The three of them burst into laughter, and I knew that

Darren was far from nerdy and had to be much taller than five feet. He was probably about six feet four, and drove a motorcycle.

"Is Darren in college?" I asked.

"Yes, Daddy. He goes to Howard."

"He's a senior," Shenese added proudly. "Tracee, didn't you say he was going to law school next year?"

"Something like that," Tracee said, and realized her friend would sell her out if she didn't do something soon. "We better get going."

"What's the hurry?" I asked my daughter.

"If I'm gonna have dinner with you later, Dad, we need to get to the mall and get our shop on. We don't have much time."

"Yeah, well we'll talk about Darren over dinner. How about that?"

"Daddy, there's nothing to talk about, really." Tracee kissed my cheek. "We're out of here. Going to the mall. I have my cell if you need me."

The three of them were gone so fast, I didn't have time to formulate into sentences the questions that were swimming around in my head. But by dinnertime, I'd promised myself, I'd have all my ducks in a row. And I needed some answers about this mystery dude they called Darren.

I started the shower, and then sat on the edge of the bed. Thoughts of Lainey filled my head and I picked up the phone. Dialed her number. By the third ring, I discovered that I hadn't thought about what I might say. By the fourth ring, my heart was pounding uncontrollably; I was actually nervous. After the fifth ring I contemplated hanging up. By the time someone answered, I realized I was dialing the wrong number.

"Thank you for calling Home Depot. How may I direct your call?"

"Sorry, wrong number," I rumbled, then hung up.

I invited the team over to watch the basketball playoffs. They were a good diversion and it was nice to hear their voices ringing through the house. Even though Marva was gone, I still felt uneasy about them being in her room, the one that was off limits to any human interaction. But I allowed it because it was the room where the big-screen television was housed. There was nothing like watching Lebron James and Gilbert Arenas, a couple of NBA's newbies, bounce up and down the court during the playoffs.

"Coach, can we order a pizza?" Collier asked.

"How much you got on it?" I asked.

"Couple of dollars," he said, and began to dig into his pocket.

"I have a few dollars." Freeman pulled his wallet out of his back pocket. Pulled out three singles.

"I got five on it." Jenkins began singing, but didn't bother to pull anything out.

I ran to the kitchen, grabbed a plastic cup and passed it around the room.

"Put your money where your mouth is." I smiled at my students, who were definitely what I considered to be cheapskates.

"Coach, we're teenagers. We're broke," Douglas said, a huge grin on his face. "Can you help a brother out?"

"I can help you make a peanut butter and jelly sandwich in my kitchen," I said.

"Aw, Coach!" Jenkins said. "Have a heart. You know you can spring for a pizza."

"I thought you had five on it, Jenkins," I said.

"I'm broke as a joke," Jenkins said, and the others laughed. "I got about twenty-five cent."

"Twenty-five *cents*," I said, correcting his English. "If it's more than one, it's plural. I know you learned that in your English class."

"It's called Ebonics, Coach," Nelson added.

"It's called illiteracy," I said. "You don't have to prove yourself ignorant. You're already prejudged for that. Prove yourselves to be the bright young men that you are. That's the tough part."

"It was just a figure of speech, Coach," Jenkins said.

"The next time you use a word incorrectly, that's twenty push-ups." I warned. "That goes for every one of you."

"Man, that's foul, Coach! You can't be serious." Collier grumbled. "Now we all have to suffer for Jenkins's ignorance."

"Try me," I said, and grabbed the cordless phone from its base. "Now what kind of pizza are we ordering?"

"Pepperoni and hamburger."

"Meatlovers, dog," Collier said.

"Whatever's cool with me," Nelson said.

"I think that the ones who contributed to the pizza

fund should decide on what we order." I smiled and shook the plastic cup in the air; the cup that held just over five dollars in it.

"Meatlovers." Freeman, the one who'd contributed the most money—a whole three dollars, stuck his chest out as if he'd contributed a solid twenty.

"And pepperoni," Jenkins said, and dug into his sagging jeans. "Here's seventy-five cent—I mean, cents."

"What's that supposed to buy?" Collier asked. "That won't even take care of the tip."

"Mind your business, bro," Jenkins said, "mind your business."

"You guys are sad," I said, and pulled out my wallet. I pulled out two twenty-dollar bills; laid them on the table. Dialed the number for Pizza Hut. Ordered one pepperoni pizza and one meatlovers.

CHAPTER 30

Lainey

It had been years since I'd been on an interview, and Glenda tried convincing me that it was like riding a bike—you never forget how to do it. I did forget how nervous interviews made me, as the palms of my hands began to sweat. I noticed it when I handed the gentleman behind the desk my résumé. As he eyeballed it, my heart thumped. Loud. I was afraid he might hear it.

"You've been out of work for a long time, Mrs. Williams. Why the huge gap?"

"My husband made a very good salary and didn't require me to work," I explained. "I became a homemaker for several years."

"And why do you want to return to work now?"

"My husband was killed in a car accident recently, and..."

"I'm sorry to hear that."

"Thank you," I said. "He left me pretty well off, and I don't need to work now. But I've always loved advertising. That's my field, and I want to come back into the industry. I realize that a lot has changed..."

"The industry's changed tremendously. How will you catch up?"

"I'm a quick study," I said. "Give me a chance, and I'll prove that I can do this job just as well if not better than some of your newbies."

"You do have some wonderful experience." He breezed over my résumé. "Your skills would be an asset to Nichols and Finch."

"You won't be disappointed." I smiled.

"When can you start?"

"Monday morning?"

"Get here around seven and I'll introduce you to some people. Start you out on one of our smaller accounts."

"Thank you, Mr. Finch."

"Call me Edward." He stood and I followed his lead. Buried my hand in his. "I'll see you on Monday, Elaine."

I wanted to do a Toyota jump in the parking lot. It was exciting, having a career again. At one time, advertising had been my life. But then Don became my life and everything else became second. But now I wanted to participate in everything that I'd missed out on, and achieve everything that I'd placed on hold for my marriage—a marriage that had been a farce anyway.

On Monday morning I would enter the corporate world again, and that shook me. I would be playing catch-up in an industry that had changed rapidly since I'd last pounded the pavement. Not to mention, I'd be competing with youngsters half my age, much smarter and way more savvy. But I was up for the challenge.

* * *

I stopped by the mall on my way home—Macy's.

Macy's was having one of their seasonal sales and I stocked up on pantsuits, dresses and fancy blouses. I bought shoes and jewelry to match every outfit. I needed to look the part of an executive again. I felt a little intimidated about making an entrance into the world of marketing, particularly since the advertising world was highly competitive. College students entered the workforce with a wide range of skills, to include strong communication skills, which is an area that I could run circles around them in. Strong computer skills, which hadn't been a skill that I'd exercised lately. Creativity, I had, as well as a wonderful ability to learn quickly. If I worked on my computer skills a bit, I could give those kids a run for their money. My degree in public relations would come in handy and marketing was something I could do in my sleep. I was ready!

The long hours would absorb some of the idle time that I had. And the opportunity to travel would keep me busy during those times when my mind began to wander. This was exactly what I needed—a career—that would demand every inch of my life. I looked forward to being drowned in my work.

I left Macy's and trekked over to Best Buy. I needed to upgrade my computer with the latest technology and convince one of the techie sales associates to give me a crash course in Microsoft. I marched into the store and found my victim. He introduced himself as Earnest, wore black-rimmed glasses and braces on his teeth. His hair stood straight up with the assistance of the mousse that he'd lathered onto his head that morning, and his canvas sneakers was a dead giveaway to his nerdiness. Before long, Earnest had sold me on the latest of technology, earned a hefty commission, and worked for it by giving me that crash course that I'd demanded. As the doors of Best Buy had been locked, half the lights had been turned off, and it was five minutes to closing, Earnest and I stared at my computer as he flipped from screen to screen with the click of the mouse. By the time I left, I knew everything from creating a PowerPoint presentation to designing a colorful newsletter, to making the columns add up in an Excel spreadsheet.

I wanted to package Earnest up in one of those boxes and take him home with me.

As I walked in, I turned on the lamp next to the door, slipped my shoes from my aching feet, and set my new laptop on the sofa. Made my way upstairs, a bubble bath on my evening's agenda, followed by skewers of grilled shrimp and Cajun rice—a recipe that Emeril himself had prepared for me on the food channel the night before. I thought about calling Nathan, wanted to share my good news with him, but I pushed past the urge. I'd sent flowers to the house after the funeral, but hadn't attempted to make any other contact. Neither had he. Everything in me wanted to call to see how he was holding up, but I didn't want to intrude. People grieved differently.

"But he flew all the way to California with you to help

find answers about your dead husband," I told myself. Didn't that mean I needed to at least reach out?

"No, you would be intruding," I answered, and blocked out the self-talk.

Candles burned at the edge of my garden tub, the flicker of one hypnotizing me as my head rested against the porcelain. The smell of juniper floated through the air, as the sound of jazz crept through the vents from Don's stereo downstairs in the family room. Norman Brown's soothing, smooth voice tickled my ears and relaxed every muscle in my body. It was a tune that Nathan and I had danced to at the jazz club in downtown Atlanta not so long ago. I could still smell his cologne as our bodies pressed together and swayed to the music. His strong arms had embraced me and made me feel safe. I always felt safe around him, perhaps because he seemed to make everyone in his world feel that way. Protected. It was his way. I missed him. Missed his voice in my ear, his laughter, his beautiful face…his scent, his overprotection. Why had he absorbed himself into me this way? And why hadn't he called?

There. Now I was at the root of the problem. I tried to be mature about it, not expect anything. Tried not to feel hurt, or neglect. But the truth was, I was hurt. He received a phone call that night, one of hope that his wife would recover. He breezed over to the hospital, and I never heard from him again. Hadn't we at least been friends? Didn't friends check up on each other…making certain that the other was okay?

* * *

I sat at the edge of my bed, towel wrapped around my wet body, cordless phone in hand. I dialed Nathan's home phone number. It rang twice before someone picked up.

"Hello?" The female voice on the other end demanded a response. "Hello? Is anybody there?"

"Hello?" I said. "I'm sorry, I've dialed the wrong number."

"It's okay." She hung up before I could say another word.

I contemplated calling his cell phone, but common sense ruled against it. Instead, I threw on my bathrobe, bounced downstairs to my kitchen, plugged in my grill and placed skewers of shrimp and vegetables onto it. The aroma filled my kitchen immediately.

My phone rang, and I thought it might be Nathan calling back. Surely he had Caller ID and knew I'd been trying to reach him. Maybe he'd invite me to his little jazz spot, or maybe he'd ask me to meet him at IHOP for dinner. Maybe he just needed to talk, or cry in my ear. Maybe he just wanted to hear my voice. I didn't know for sure, but I rushed to the phone, picked up the receiver.

"Hello?"

"Lainey, it's me, Alvin. You busy?"

Disappointment. Wasn't the voice I was expecting.

"Not really. Just winding down, about to have dinner."

"You alone?"

"Yes, why? What's up, Alvin?"

"I need to talk to you," he said. "Can I come over?"

"Yes."

"I'll be there in fifteen minutes."

The sound of Alvin's voice caused me to tremble as I placed the receiver back in its place. Every day since Don's death brought with it a new challenge.

CHAPTER 31

Nathan

As the referee's whistle echoed across the gymnasium, I rubbed my bald head. Frustration filled my heart, as another team ran circles around my boys. We were giving it our best shot, but we just couldn't seem to score the points. Collier was even exercising his interpretation of what a team player was, by passing the ball to his teammates, and actually running the plays that we'd practiced. His game tonight had been the best I'd seen it all season. He was the high scorer for the team and had more rebounds than any other player in the game. Had me feeling proud as I watched him run down court, tired and frustrated.

I folded my arms across my chest and watched as the other team took the final shot just as the clock buzzed. The swish into the basket put them ten points ahead of us, instead of the steady eight that they'd been all night. I grabbed my forehead for a moment, but then changed my posture as my team rushed toward me. Their heads hung low, they quietly strolled to the locker room.

"I know it's frustrating to lose, guys, but I have to tell

you that you played a good game out there tonight. I'm proud of every one of you."

"Thanks, Coach," they said dryly.

"We did everything we could out there, but sometimes there's just a better team."

"We lose to them every time," Nelson complained.

"It's okay, we just need a better strategy next time, that's all."

"I couldn't even get the ball down court, their defense was so tight," Freeman said.

"And their center was slapping down every shot." Mitchell shook his head. "What is he, like seven feet tall or something?"

"Nobody on the team was under six-four." Douglas groaned.

"A bunch of corn-fed boys from somewhere down in the country," Jenkins said. "I never played so hard in my life."

"We need to work on our defense." Edwards pulled his jersey over his head, used it to wipe sweat from his forehead. "That's what they had on us, their defense."

"That and their rebound ability."

"They beat the brakes off of us."

"They may have won the game, but you played a great game," I told them. "You can't win every game, but as long as you do your best, that's all that can be expected."

There was silence in the locker room as they took my words in.

"Get dressed and I'll see you all at practice tomorrow."

* * *

In my office, I packed up my briefcase, loosened my tie.

"Coach, can I talk to you for a minute?" Collier stood in the doorway of my office. His jersey swung over one shoulder, his gym bag swung across the other.

"What's up?"

"He's here."

I stared at him silently for a few seconds, trying to understand what he was talking about.

"Who's here?"

"My pops," he said, and frowned.

"Your father was in the stands tonight?" I asked.

"Yep, he was out there. Why couldn't we have won tonight?" he said, and turned to walk away. "The one night he shows up and we get spanked."

"Collier, wait," I called to him. "Let me tell you something, son. You played a good game tonight. You implemented all the plays we practiced, you had more points and rebounds than anyone on the team. You did everything you were supposed to do out there tonight. It's not about winning every game, but how you play."

"You think he was proud of me?"

"If not, he should be," I said, and grabbed his shoulder. "I certainly was."

"Really, Coach? You were proud of me?"

"The best game you ever played, in my opinion."

"Thanks," he said, and almost smiled. He wasn't completely convinced, but at least it sounded good.

I followed Collier out into the gymnasium where Mr. Collier, his father, pulled his trench coat tighter. His face like stone; thick eyebrows and a mustache that reminded me of what Collier might look like someday. His arms folded across his chest, he stood patiently waiting for his son.

"Mr. Collier. How are you?" I asked, and held my hand out to him. "I'm your son's coach…Coach Sullivan."

"Pleased to meet you, Coach." He took my hand in a strong handshake.

"Good game my boys played out there tonight. Particularly Collier here." I slapped Collier on the back. He grinned until his eyes met his father's.

"You lost."

"Yeah, we lost, but as I tell my kids…it's not about winning or losing, but how you play the game." I said, "And Collier here played a good game. He was my highest scorer tonight."

"His jump shot is sloppy. And he's too careless with the ball." His posture never changed, he just continued to stand with his arms folded across his chest.

"His game has improved quite a bit over the season."

"Can't get a scholarship like that," Mr. Collier barked. "Gotta be the best."

"Like your other son, right?" I asked.

"Dre is in a class all by himself." He stated proudly, and at that comment, he smiled, and loosened his stance. "He's running circles around them boys down there in Athens, Georgia. On a full scholarship. That boy got skills."

"Your son here has skills," I said, and was really getting perturbed with his attitude. "They just need to be developed."

"Skills are not something that can be developed at this point, Coach. He either has it or he doesn't. When I was his age, I was headed for the NBA. If it weren't for this injury to my knee—which never healed, by the way— I'd be retired pro right now."

"Collier, do me a favor." I turned to my student. "I left my yellow notepad on my desk. Can you run and get it for me? It's got some important notes on there that I need."

"Yeah, Coach." He looked at his father for approval, and Mr. Collier nodded his head. "Be right back."

As soon as he was out of earshot, I started into Mr. Collier.

"Are you trying to live out your aspirations of being in the NBA through your children, Mr. Collier?" I asked frankly.

"Excuse me?"

"Is that what this is all about? Are you hoping that one of them becomes the NBA star that you never were? And since you've pinpointed the one you want to carry it out, the other one is of no use to you?"

"I don't appreciate your tone, Coach Sullivan."

"That boy of yours is a fine ball player, regardless of what you might think. He works hard at every practice, and is very skilled in the game. The only problem is, he's so busy trying to vie for your attention, that he can't focus on his game. He resents you for not showing up at his games, and he resents his brother even more for capturing all of your attention."

"He told you this?"

"Doesn't have to. I spend enough time with these boys

to know exactly what they're thinking and feeling. I know them well."

"I'm a good father, Coach. I provide for my family and I've raised my sons to be good men."

"Your ability as a father and provider is not in question here."

"What is in question?"

"He needs your support. Needs to know that you value his skills as a ballplayer, just as much as you do your other son. That you might show up at a few of his games, regardless of whether or not he's NBA material," I said. "His future depends on it. His future in basketball and his future as a man, depends on your acceptance. He loves this sport and wants to excel in it."

"His future depends on whether or not he gets a scholarship, and I just don't see that happening in basketball," he said. "Maybe he can get an academic scholarship or one in music. He likes music. But basketball…he's just not good enough."

"I disagree."

"We can stand here all night and disagree with each other, Coach Sullivan. But the bottom line is, his game is not that good."

"You're right, Mr. Collier. He's not that good," I said. "It was nice meeting you. Glad you could make it out tonight. You have a good evening."

I turned to walk away from him. Went to say hello to another parent. I could feel his eyes burning into the back of my head as I walked away. My conversation with him was done. All I could do now was keep coaching Collier, be a positive influence for him, and at the end of the day, hope that I'd left him with something to motivate him. Whatever happened to parents supporting a child's dream, simply because that's what parents did? Everything in me wanted to grab Mr. Collier in a headlock and instill the answer to that question in him, but I knew I couldn't engage in physical contact with a parent. I'd be arrested. It was hard, but I restrained myself.

I took the long way home. Ended up in Alpharetta somehow, sitting outside of someone's house like a stalker. My dreams of her cinnamon-colored skin and light brown eyes, had me yearning to see her. Wanted to hear her laughter. Wanted to tell her that I'd missed her and that I needed her in my life. Needed her like the air I breathed. But I needed permission first. Permission to love her. How did I get that? I needed permission from Tracee, my daughter who felt as if her mother had been taken from her, and I was to blame for it. Needed permission from Helen and Poppa Joe, my in-laws who loved their daughter to death.

And from Mama. I could hear her now, "Baby, it's too soon to be taking up with another woman. You're still healing. You don't wanna be on the rebound, do you, son?"

Daddy would just shake his head and say, "I don't know, son. I just don't know. What ya mama say?"

Thoughts of my family had me wanting to sneak around; have a secret love affair until it was safe to tell them the truth. Wanted to see if our love for each other was true or if it was just based on our unfortunate circumstances. We'd both been hurt and devastated by all of this, and that was enough to make anyone seek refuge in another person. We were safe for each, had the accident in common. We were good support for each other, but could there really be more to what we felt for each other?

As I sat in my pickup truck and contemplated whether or not I should knock on Lainey's door, a silver Mercedes pulled into her circular drive. The windows were tinted and it wasn't until the person stepped out of the car, that I knew it was a man, wearing a very nice suit. A businessman, I thought. Insurance man, or someone there to discuss her estate. Common sense ruled that thought out; it was too late at night to be conducting business. He headed for her front door, rang the bell. There she was, in her bathrobe, beautiful as ever, as she swung the door open. The man hugged her waist and kissed her on the cheek. Definitely wasn't the insurance guy, I thought, as jealousy rushed through my veins. Had she started dating someone...so quickly?

Blue lights flickered in my rearview mirror.

"I'm just sitting here, man!" I shouted to nobody in particular. "What is it?"

The officer sat in his car for a few minutes, obviously calling in the tag on my truck. He stepped out of the car and walked up to my window. I let it down.

"Evening officer," I said.

"You live in this neighborhood?" he asked.

"Uh, no, sir. A friend of mine lives there." His eyes

followed my finger as I pointed toward Lainey's house. "I was about to go up and ring the bell."

"I need to see your driver's license, please." The white officer, with his Southern drawl, shined the light of his flashlight in my face.

I reached into my back pocket, grabbed my wallet. Slipped my driver's license out and handed it to the officer. He took it; studied it for a moment.

"This your correct address on ya license?"

"Yes," I said.

"Long way from home, ain't ya?" he asked.

"Just visiting a friend."

"I'll be right back," he said, then disappeared.

I could see him in my rearview mirror as he sank into the driver's seat of his patrol car, called in my license, making sure it was legit and that I didn't have any warrants. After what seemed like a lifetime, he returned to my car. Handed me my driver's license back.

"Look, Mr. Sullivan, this neighborhood is very serious about their Neighborhood Watch system. One of the neighbors thought you were a stalker," he said. "If your intent is to visit your friend, please don't sit in your car two houses away from the house. Go up and ring the bell. I don't know what's going—whether this friend is really an old girlfriend that you had a big fight with. Maybe you suspect her of cheating, and you're waiting for the guy to show up or something. I don't know. But it ain't a good idea to sit out here in your car like this. The neighbors are nosy and they call the police. Go knock on the door next time, ya hear?"

"I will," I said. "Thanks."

I waited for him to pull off, and then I pulled off, as well. Found my way back to the expressway—Riverdale bound. What was I doing on the other side of town anyway, looking for a woman who had obviously moved on?

CHAPTER 32

Lainey

Alvin was sweating and breathing hard. Had me nervous as he followed me to the kitchen.

"Thanks for letting me come by, Lainey," he said, and opened my refrigerator, pulled out the pitcher of iced tea. Reached for a glass from the shelf. He always made himself at home. He'd always been like family to Don and me.

"What's up, Alvin? You sounded funny on the phone." I fluffed my Cajun rice and sprinkled it onto my plate next to my skewers of shrimp.

"Lainey, you've known me for a long time." He poured tea into his glass. "Been just like family to me."

"True."

"I'm HIV positive." He just blurted it out, paralyzed me.

"Alvin, I don't know what to say."

"I've been having relationships with men for a very long time. Began before I met and married Glenda. I've been attracted to men since my junior year in high school. And when I went to college, I had my first relationship with a man." He sat at my kitchen table. "When I met Glenda, I was instantly attracted to her. Fell in love with her immediately. It confused me, because I'd never been attracted to women before her. Thought that I might be heterosexual after all. And thought that if I married her, that would prove that I was straight and not gay."

"Alvin, I had no idea."

"Three months after we were married, I was in an extramarital affair with a man who was an attorney for the firm." He sipped his tea slowly. "Don knew about Kevin and threatened to blow my cover with Glenda. Said that if I didn't end it, he would tell her everything. Well, that's when I turned the tables on him. Said that if he told Glenda about Kevin, I'd tell you about Ursula. He didn't want that."

"So he kept your secret and you kept his." I laughed sarcastically. "How convenient. Why are you telling me this now? Because you're sick?"

"Because I think that Glenda might be at risk," he said, almost in a whisper. "I can't say for certain when I contracted the disease, but after I found out, I tried contacting all of my previous lovers. When I called Kevin, I found out that he's dying of full-blown AIDS. He was diagnosed way back when we were together, but he didn't tell me."

"Oh my God." All I could do was place my hands over my mouth as I tried to absorb everything Alvin was saying. My heart ached for Glenda. "Have you told Glenda."

"I don't know how."

"You have to tell her, Alvin." I almost screamed at him. "She has a right to know!"

"I was hoping that you could...you know...tell her for me." He said, "It would be easier coming from you."

"Easier how?" I asked, furious. "How will it be easier coming from me?"

"You're her dearest friend, Lainey."

"Alvin, how could you let this happen?"

"My intention was never to hurt Glenda," he said. "The day she asked me for a divorce, I was relieved, because I'd been planning to leave her for months, but didn't know how to tell her."

"She said that you were having an affair with another woman."

"I was having an affair, but it wasn't with a woman."

I balanced myself as I almost lost control of my legs. Sat across from Alvin at the table. Looked into his beautiful hazel eyes and wondered how he'd managed to live such a troubled and confused life. Wondered how he slept at night, or looked at his reflection in the mirror each day.

"This is your fight, Alvin, not mine. You made this bed, and now you have to lie in it."

"Lainey, will you be able to look Glenda in the eye and not tell her the truth...after you practically crucified her for not telling you about Don."

"It's your place to tell her."

"I can't." Tears formed in his eyes. "I need you, Lainey. If it's left up to me, I'll take it to my grave."

"I don't believe you!"

"I'm a coward, Lainey. I know I am." He stood, tears running down his face like a waterfall. "I'm sorry about Don. I'm sorry about everything."

"How am I supposed to tell her something like this?"

"With love, Lainey. With the love that you have in your heart." Alvin kissed my forehead, then walked briskly toward my front door. Left me sitting at my kitchen table.

As I sat at the bar, waiting for Glenda's head to pop through the door, I suddenly regretted inviting her to a public place. Should've had her over for dinner, or showed up on her doorstep. A restaurant was a bad idea, and I didn't realize it until it was too late. Her text message said that she was in the parking lot, on her way in. Said to go ahead and get us a table and order her a Chablis.

Pappadeaux's was packed, as always. Atlantans' strong desire for seafood kept the place jumping on a regular basis. I followed the hostess to our table, my mouth already watered for their fried calamari appetizer and the lump crab cakes I'd have as an entrée. Glenda always started with the fried alligator or the boudin, which is Cajun sausage stuffed with dirty rice. It was her favorite appetizer, but she always complained about it adding pounds to her spreading hips.

She looked remarkable in her tan pantsuit and pink silk blouse. Her make-up was flawless, and her hair had been freshly relaxed and bouncing as she walked. I waved my hand to let her know that I was there. Her Chablis was chilled and waiting for her. The waitress was bringing our appetizers as Glenda approached the table.

"Hey, sweetie," she said, and sat down.

"I ordered you the boudin."

"Right, so my hips will spread."

"It'll take a lot more than that to move you up a dress size, girlfriend." I laughed. "I ordered the fried alligator, too."

"Thank you," she said, and sipped her wine. "How did your interview go?"

"I got the job!"

"I'm not surprised." She smiled. "Congratulations. This calls for a celebration."

Glenda motioned for the waitress.

"How can I help you?" the brown-faced woman with deep dimples asked.

"Bring her a Chablis," she said. "We're celebrating."

The waitress disappeared.

"I was so excited about the job, I stopped at the mall and charged up my Macy's card. Then went by Best Buy…bought a new laptop and made the nerdy sales guy give me a crash course in every Microsoft program there is."

"You a trip," she said as the waitress set a glass of wine in front of me. "Let's toast…to a new and exciting career."

"And friendship."

"And my new book that's scheduled for release next month."

"And friendship," I repeated.

"Why you keep toasting to friendship?" She asked, setting her glass down. "You got something you wanna tell me?"

"Matter of fact, I do, Glenda."

"Well, spit it out."

"Let's order first and have dinner."

"Let's not," Glenda said, and peered at me. "Let's clear the air instead. You know me, I like it straight-up. So give it to me that way."

"Glenda, Alvin came by the house last night...he..."

"Lainey, just say it."

"He told me that he's HIV positive."

Glenda sipped her wine, and looked at me as if I hadn't said anything.

"I'm sorry to hear that. But what's that got to do with me?"

"Alvin's gay, Glenda. And has been since before you and him were married. You divorced him thinking that he was cheating with another woman, when in fact he was cheating with another man."

Glenda stared at me in amazement.

"Wow," she said, with no excitement in her voice.

"The man he was seeing at the time was diagnosed with full-blown AIDS."

She continued to stare, into space mostly.

"Wow," she said again. "That's deep."

"Alvin forced me to tell you. Said he would take it to his grave if it were left up to him," I explained. "But that he never meant to hurt you."

"I think I'm gonna have the crab cakes as my entrée. What about you?"

"How can you think of food at a time like this?" I asked, almost in tears.

"What am I supposed to do, Lainey? Stop living because my ex-husband is gay? Because he's HIV positive?"

"Get tested and make sure you're okay, Glen." Tears were forming in my eyes. "You have to get tested."

"I've been tested every year since the year I left Alvin. I knew he was gay. Knew all about Kevin and the others."

"So you've known."

"Yes."

"So many secrets. So many lies." I sighed. "It seems that the people who are closest to me are the ones I know the least about."

"I'm sorry about Don, Lainey. I should've told you about that."

"I agree. But I'm not holding that against you anymore. I just want to heal from all of this. Move forward with my life."

"Will Nathan be a part of your future?"

"I don't think so." I held the menu up to my face, hid behind it.

"Lainey, I know you care about him, and he definitely cares for you. You're both available now. You both have gone through things, but nothing you can't heal from."

"He hasn't tried once to reach me since the night he rushed off to the hospital."

"Have you tried reaching him?"

"Once or twice," I admitted. "Once I think his daughter answered the phone and I lost my courage to ask for him. I didn't want to hurt her. She's been through enough with losing her mother. Besides, he's got his family, his wife's family…they're all intermingled into one. I could never be a part of that. Could never take her place. I'm gonna absorb myself into my new job, and live happily ever after."

Glenda shook her head as the waitress appeared.

"Are you ready to order, ladies?" she asked, pen and pad in hand.

"Give us a minute," Glenda said.

"Yes, ma'am." The waitress disappeared to wherever servers disappear to.

"So I guess the subject of Nathan is null and void."

"Null and void," I confirmed.

"Fine, I'll let it go. But he might not," she said, taking a sip of her wine. "He just walked in."

Dressed in a business suit and a tie that had been loosened, Nathan appeared in the doorway with a group of men. He looked so handsome, his bald head shining, his face clean-shaven, his smile hypnotizing as he argued with one of the men about sports or whatever men argued about. He said something funny, and the rest of the group laughed at his comment. He didn't even look my way, he was so caught up. As the hostess escorted them to a table, my heart pounded. I hid my face with the menu as he passed; never looking my way.

CHAPTER 33

Nathan

"Look man, Kobe is as cocky as they come. That's all I'm saying." I grabbed the menu and gave it a quick look-over. "I'm not saying he's not a good ballplayer."

"You act as if his being cocky affects his game in some way." My colleague and long-time friend, Stan, had been a Lakers' fan for life.

"You asked me what I had against Kobe Bryant," I said. "My response was, the negro is just too cocky for his own good. That's my opinion and I'm entitled to it."

"Next subject," Jerry said as he signaled for the waitress.

Once a month, the four of us got together and had dinner together. We'd been teaching at the same high school together for seven years and had become the best of friends over the years. Our families had barbequed together, worshipped at the same church, watched each other's children grow up and go away to college.

Mike insisted that we come to his part of town to check out the new pool table his wife had bought him for his birthday. So today, we ended up on Jimmy Carter

Boulevard, having dinner at one of the best seafood restaurants in town, and talking junk to each other as we always had.

"Bring us a couple dozen oysters, sweetheart," Tim told the waitress as she approached the table. "And four Heinekens."

"Three Heinekens and one water." I corrected the order.

"Water?" Tim asked. "You stopped drinking beer."

"Man, I live in Riverdale. That's a long drive from here, and I need to have all my faculties."

Their laughter rang through the restaurant.

"You think after one beer you couldn't drive to Riverdale, man?" Mike asked. "Then you could just crash at my place."

"You getting soft on me, Sullivan," Stan said. "What's up with that?"

"Just have a phobia about drinking and driving," I said, and the entire table fell silent as they all remembered my wife's accident.

"Hey, I'm sorry man. I forgot," Stan said. "Bring me water, too, sweetheart."

"Make that water for me," Mike said to the waitress.

"I definitely can't drink alone." Tim grabbed his menu, and began looking it over. "I'll have water, too."

"All righty then, four waters," the waitress said. "You still want the oysters?"

"Make it three dozen instead of two," Tim said. "Mike's paying, so let's make it worthwhile. The last time it was his turn to pay, he weaseled out of it."

We all laughed and agreed.

"I didn't weasel out of it," Mike said. "I just misplaced my debit card."

"Well, check your wallet, bro, and make sure you got it this time," Stan said.

As Mike pulled his wallet out, I stood.

"Be right back," I said. "Order me the fried seafood platter if I'm not back."

"Got you covered," Stan said, and I excused myself from the table and headed toward the restrooms.

I stopped momentarily at the bar to check out the score from the basketball game. The Lakers were down by six points and it was the fourth quarter. I gloated at the fact that they were losing and turned to get Stan's attention. He was too busy running his mouth to notice the wide smile on my face. Stan's salt-and-pepper hair in an old school afro, he was the oldest in our group and was more like a father or older brother to all of us. He'd taken me under his wing since the first day I'd walked into the school. Marva and I had just moved to the Atlanta area from Alabama and didn't know a soul. Stan and his wife invited us over for dinner for the first time, and that was the night we became family.

As my eyes swept across the restaurant, I caught a glimpse of Lainey's friend Glenda. Her eyes met mine and she smiled. I waved and she waved back. When the woman she was having dinner with removed the menu from her face, I realized it was Lainey, and my heart pounded rapidly. She looked at me, and my world stood still. Her beautiful smile let me know how much I missed her. I moved toward their table immediately.

"How you doing, Glenda?" I asked. "Lainey?"

"Doing fine, Nathan. Good to see you," Glenda said. "My sympathy to you and your family. I'm very sorry about your loss."

"Thank you," I said. "Lainey, can I talk to you for a minute? Outside?"

"Okay." She slid out of the booth.

"Glenda, please excuse us," I said.

"Take your time." Glenda smiled.

I led Lainey out to the brick patio and down a short flight of stairs to the wooded area behind the restaurant. There was a waterfall out here and the sound of it added to the ambience of the place. I stood face-to-face with the woman of my dreams.

"How are you?" she asked.

"I'm better," I told her.

"How's your family? Your parents and your daughter?"

"Everybody's doing okay."

"I'm so sorry, Nathan. About what Don did, and about everything that's happened," she said. "I often think about that terrible night and how it changed all of our lives. How we all lost so much. And now we're having to deal with the aftereffects of it. I mean, one day you're doing fine, and then the evening after this terrible nightmare, you wake up and realize *your* whole life has changed."

"It's bittersweet, really," I told her. "It's true, I lost Marva and you lost Don. But if it weren't for the accident, we wouldn't have found each other."

"Was it worth the cost, though?"

"I ask myself that every day. And I have to say that it

at least gives me hope of a better tomorrow. Well, it did until the other night."

"What happened the other night?"

"I saw you and your friend together."

"Excuse me?"

"The guy you're dating. He showed up at your house the other night, and you answered the door wearing practically nothing," I said, and couldn't believe she was playing the nut roll. "The dude in the silver Mercedes. I was sitting outside your house when he pulled up."

She looked as if she was thinking back to the night in question.

"Were you stalking me?" she asked with a sister-girl attitude.

"Is that your new man?"

"I asked you a question first."

"No, I wasn't stalking you. I was about to knock on your door when Mr. Mercedes beat me to it." I tried not to reveal the true depth of my jealously. "Now answer my question. Is that your new man?"

"You're jealous."

"I'm not jealous. I'm just concerned."

"That was Alvin, Glenda's ex-husband. He's an old friend of mine." She smiled. "You were jealous, weren't you?"

"Okay, I was a little jealous." I grabbed her hands in mine. "I haven't been able to get you out of my head since I last saw you. I miss you."

"I miss you, too."

"What do we do about it?"

"I don't know," she said. "You need time to heal."

"I need you."

"You're still grieving."

"I'm still in love with you."

"What about your family? Your daughter? Have you considered what they might think about you moving on so soon?"

"I have to believe that they love me enough to want me to be happy," I told her. "I'll deal with them."

"Are you ready to lose your daughter...maybe forever?"

"I'm willing to take my chances that she'll come to accept you."

"Let's just take it slow and see what happens," she said.

"I need to kiss you."

I brushed my hands across her hair and pulled her close to me. Her arms squeezed me and my lips found hers. Felt like I'd found the missing piece of a puzzle as she fit snuggly in my arms. I knew then that what I felt for Lainey, people are lucky if they find it once in a lifetime. I'd found it twice.

ONE YEAR LATER...

CHAPTER 34

Nathan

Smoke from the barbecue grill crept through the neighborhood, alerting the neighbors that somebody was cooking something good. I flipped chicken legs, wings and thighs with silver tongs. The sun beamed down on the back of my neck and I wiped sweat from my forehead with a terry-cloth hand towel. I trampled up the back steps and into the kitchen to grab the homemade barbecue sauce that Helen had concocted. She handed it to me, along with a brush, and then turned to finish stirring the ingredients of her homemade potato salad. I looked over her shoulder to see how it was coming along. She placed a spoonful of it in my mouth.

"What you think, baby?" she asked me.

"Little more mayo. And maybe just a dash more salt," I said proudly. Since I'd been watching Emeril, I thought I was a chef. Had been trying my hand in the kitchen.

I stepped into the living room as Poppa Joe was singing along with BB King, his artist of choice. His wifebeater barely covered his stomach as he sang, "You Done Lost Your Good Thing Now." When Daddy joined in, I thought the two of them would blow a gasket. Daddy's five o'clock shadow needed to be shaved.

"You wouldn't know nothing about that, would you, Poot Butt?" Poppa Joe asked Tracee, who sat on the edge of the sofa, praying that her grandfathers behaved themselves. "Come here and dance with Paw Paw."

"Leave the child alone, Joe, you embarrassing her," Daddy said, and sipped from his glass of Old Grand-Dad.

"Paw Paw, I thought you weren't gonna call me Poot Butt anymore," she said softly.

"Oh, you embarrassed about ya nickname now?" Poppa Joe asked. "I been callin' you Poot Butt since you was three years old."

"I know Paw Paw, but…"

"What, you embarrassed in front of ya little friend here?" he asked, apparent that the alcohol was beginning to set in. "Come here, son."

Tracee's friend, Darren, approached cautiously. He didn't know what to make of our family. Only a few hours before, I'd threatened to break his legs if he ever hurt my daughter. She'd finally admitted that they were dating, and I figured it was pretty serious when she asked if he could come to Toulminville for the Fourth of July barbecue. You didn't invite just anybody to Toulminville. It wasn't a glamorous place, and you only brought people here who you were serious about sharing your history with.

He seemed to be a decent young man; spoke intelligently when he opened his mouth. Was polite and mannerable, and careful to use *ma'am* and *sir* when addressing his elders. He'd passed my test, but he still had to get past Poppa Joe and Daddy, who weren't so quick to hand their little grandbaby over to just anyone.

"Yo daddy listen to BB King, boy?" Poppa Joe asked him.

"No, sir. He's a James Brown man."

"James Brown?" Poppa Joe frowned. "You can't even understand what that negro is saying. *He's a James Brown man*. You hear that Henry?"

"Yeah, I heard," Daddy said. "You go to that school there in Washington DC with my granddaughter? What is it, uh…Howard University?"

"Yes, sir."

"What's your major, son?"

"First year law student, sir."

"You hear that Joe, Derrick here is gonna be a lawyer."

"It's Darren, Grandpa." Tracee rolled her eyes as she corrected her grandfather. Embarrassment had new meaning in her life.

"Darren. Derrick. What's the difference?" Daddy said, and tipped his glass filled with Old Grand-Dad.

"So you gon' be a lawyer?" Poppa Joe asked. "You ain't gon' be a crooked lawyer, are you, son?"

"No, sir."

"We're gonna go sit on the front porch, Paw Paw." Tracee interrupted their interrogation and she thought of an escape plan.

"Joe and Henry, leave that young man alone. He

didn't come here to be interrogated by a couple of old farts. He came here to meet Tracee's family." Mama came to her rescue. "Tracee, why don't you and your friend run on down to the corner store and get Granny some cornmeal for the cornbread." She reached into her bosom and pulled out a wrinkled, old handkerchief filled with cash. It was moist from her sweat.

"It's okay, Granny. I got some money," Tracee said, her face flustered as she and Darren rushed out the door like two runaway slaves.

"Who's that little honey Tracee got with her?" Darlene asked as she breezed in, her thick mane pulled back into a neat ponytail, her stomach the size of a watermelon.

"That's her little boyfriend," Helen said, as if the two were twelve years old. *Her little boyfriend.* You never really grew up in the eyes of your grandparents.

"Aw, that's cute," Darlene said, her makeup was beautiful. "What's going on, Nate?"

"Hey, Dar," I said, and took in the beauty of my sober and pregnant sister-in-law.

"Guess what?"

"What's that?"

"Today's my sobriety anniversary. One year clean, man," she announced.

"That is all right, Darlene," I said, and had to kiss her round, chubby cheek. She'd gained at least fifty pounds.

"I'm real proud of you, baby," Poppa Joe said, and I could see every muscle in her face relax at her father's compliment. It made all the difference in the world that he was proud. All she ever wanted was positive attention from her parents; unfortunately her behavior had warranted the opposite.

"When's that baby due, Dar?" Mama asked. "Looks like you 'bout to pop at any moment."

"Any day now, Mother Savannah." She laughed.

"You planning on marrying that young man?" Helen asked, referring to the baby's father, the man Darlene met her first week in rehab. "Or y'all planning on shacking up forever."

"We're talking about marriage, Mama. It's just that marriage is a subject that scares me a little bit," she said. Noticing that I had tongs in my hand, she changed the subject. "I know Nate is not trying to cook on the grill."

"Yes, I am, girl. I can burn." I smiled.

"Yeah, burn up some stuff." She laughed. "Where's my sister-in-law?"

"She was changing the baby," I told her. "I don't know where she is now."

"I'm right here." Lainey smiled and pulled Darlene into a strong embrace. She rubbed Dar's growing stomach. "We're gonna have a baby soon, aren't we?"

"Hopefully tonight! Within the next hour or two would be fine," Dar said, and reached for Nate Junior. "Come here, auntie's little rug rat."

"I tried getting him to sleep. But he wasn't having it," Lainey said.

"Too much excitement going on around here," Mama said. "Who can sleep with BB King singin' the blues?"

"I can sleep just fine when BB King is singing," Poppa Joe said.

"Joe you can sleep through anything," Helen said. "Turn the music down a bit so the baby can get to sleep."

"He's not interested in sleeping, Ma." I looked at Darlene as she smothered my son with kisses. "See, that's why he's rotten."

"No, he was rotten the minute the two of you brought him home from the hospital," she said, and rested little Nate on her stomach. "I'm sure the boy can't get a bit of peace with his overprotective parents around."

"Whatever, Dar. We'll see how spoiled your baby is when he gets here."

"He? You mean her." She rolled her eyes. "This is a little girl in here, and I'm gonna spoil the mess out of her! She won't know what hit her. She don't even know how long I've waited to love her. You know what I mean?"

"I know what you mean, Dar," Lainey said. "I have so much love in my heart for Little Nate, that I can't even give it all to him. I've waited so long for a child of my own. And it doesn't even matter that I didn't give birth to him myself. He's still mine and Nate's. At least he has Nate's blood in him."

"I feel you," Darlene said, and Little Nate became fussy.

"Give him a Popsicle," Daddy said.

"He's too little for a Popsicle, Henry." Mama tasted her greens to make sure they were tender. "He's only a baby. Barely even teething."

"A Popsicle might actually do his sore gums some good," Helen said, and opened the freezer. Pulled a Popsicle out and took Little Nate from Darlene. Commenced to rubbing his little gums.

"Daddy, how did Nate get to be in charge of the grill?" Darlene asked, surprised by the sight of me wearing an apron and holding tongs in the air.

"I'm teaching Nathan how to barbecue. It's a family tradition," Poppa Joe said. "He's gon' have a son-in-law soon, and will need to pass on the tradition to him, too."

"Wait a minute now," I said to Poppa Joe, not wanting to rush my daughter into something she wasn't ready for. "They're just dating. I give the brother six good months."

"No, I think he's a keeper." Darlene laughed. "With his fine self. My niece has done good for herself."

"Don't tease Nate like that, Dar. He's already walking on eggshells," Helen said, still rubbing a Popsicle across my son's aching gums.

"I'm not teasing. And Nate needs to just get over it. Tracee is not a little girl anymore. She's a young woman."

"And she's grown up to be a fine young woman, in spite of what she's been through."

"Yeah, she's been through a lot," Helen agreed.

"I just wish I could reach her. Wish we were closer," Lainey said.

"You will, honey," Mama assured her. "You just keep being the sweet lady that you are, keep showing her love. She can't help but love you in return."

"She's stubborn like her mama," Helen said, rocking Little Nate who was crying now. "She'll come around."

"Lainey, can I get you a glass of lemonade, honey?" Mama asked.

"No, I can get it. I know where the kitchen is, Mother," Lainey said. "But first I wanna go out here and show my husband how to work this barbecue grill."

"Why is everybody sweating me and this barbecue grill?" I pulled my wife into my arms. Kissed her forehead. "I know how to work the grill, baby."

"All right, I confess. I asked her to keep an eye on you and the grill." Poppa Joe laughed. "Now go on out there, before you burn up the chicken, boy."

Lainey pushed me out the back door, her arms wrapped around my waist.

She had become a real part of the family. She even knew her way around my mother's kitchen, could even cook, and wasn't shy about showing off her skills. All four of my parents had accepted her, and she fit right in with them. Even Darlene had not only accepted Lainey, but they'd become good friends.

Darlene had lived in Marva's shadow and had spent a lifetime resenting her sister. Now she regretted the time she'd lost, but felt as if God had given her a second chance with Lainey. She embraced her as her sister. Every time I turned around Darlene was popping up at our condo in downtown Atlanta, whisking Lainey off to some shopping mall or flea market. Sometimes they had lunch together or spent the day getting manicures and pedicures. Lainey had even gone to a few of Darlene's AA meetings to support her.

Tracee, however, was still a work in progress. She hadn't yet accepted my marriage to Lainey. Not completely. She was cordial when she saw Lainey, but she didn't try to build a relationship. She was terribly disturbed when I put our house on the market, and even more so when I packed up Marva's things in cardboard boxes and sent them to a homeless shelter. After Lainey and I were married, we purchased a condo downtown. It was close enough that Lainey could walk to work if she wanted to. Her job with the advertising firm was a position that gave her great pride. I took care of Little Nate most of the time because she worked long hours and traveled more than I liked. But I knew she was happy there, so I supported her dream.

Tracee was still grieving for her mother and for a moment I thought she might drop out of school or require therapy. But instead she latched onto Darren. He had been her security blanket in all of this; I'd lost my place as the man in her life. It hurt, but there came a time in every girl's life when she became a woman, and her father had to let her go. I guess it was that time.

I had a son to raise, Little League baseball games to attend, haircuts to jack up. I was so grateful to the surrogate who had selflessly agreed to bless Lainey with the child she was never able to carry to term. Through her, I was able to give Lainey the greatest gift she'd ever known, and for that I was proud.

As I flipped the meat on the grill, I could hear Poppa Joe's voice drowning out BB King's. Someone must've told him that he could sing, because he tried it every chance he got. I thought of the years I'd known him and Helen, how they'd practically shared in the responsibility of rearing me. Thought of me as their own son, and treated me that way, too. How did they find it in their hearts to love Lainey just as much?

As Helen stood in the doorway with Little Nate, his lips purple from the grape Popsicle he'd been sucking on. He giggled and tried to jump out of her arms when he saw me.

"How's that chicken coming, baby?" she asked.

"Coming along pretty good."

"You want me to take him?" I asked her.

"If you ever take him or Lainey away from me I'll never forgive you, Nathan Earl," she said. "Promise me you never will."

I climbed the few steps as quickly as I could to reach her.

"I promise," I told her. Wrapped my arms around her and Little Nate. "You're stuck with me and them for life. We're family...forever."

I kissed her cheek. She touched my face with her palm.

"We're family...forever, baby," she said. "Now please go in there and tell Poppa Joe that BB King don't need his help."

"Yes, ma'am," I said, but didn't have the heart when I saw him and Daddy arm-in-arm, a drink in each of their hands, rocking from side to side.

They were serious about the blues.

GET THE GENUINE LOVE
YOU DESERVE...

NATIONAL BESTSELLING AUTHOR

Vikki Johnson

Addicted to COUNTERFEIT LOVE

Many people in today's world are unable to recognize
what a genuine loving partnership should be and
often sabotage one when it does come along. In this
moving volume, Vikki Johnson offers memorable
words that will help readers identify destructive love
patterns and encourage them to demand the love
that they are entitled to.

Available the first week of October wherever books are sold.

Forgiveness takes courage...

A MEASURE OF
Faith

MAXINE BILLINGS

With her loving husband, a beautiful home and two wonderful children, Lynnette Montgomery feels very blessed. But a sudden car accident starts a chain of events that tests her faith, and pulls to the forefront memories of a very painful childhood. At forty years of age, Lynnette comes to see that it takes a measure of faith to help one through the pains of life.

"An enlightening read with an endearing family theme."
—*Romantic Times BOOKreviews*
on *The Breaking Point*

Available the first week of July
wherever books are sold.

A soul-stirring, compelling
journey of self-discovery...

journey
into My Brother's Soul

Maria D. Dowd

Bestselling author of
Journey to Empowerment

A memorable collection of essays, prose and poetry,
reflecting the varied experiences that men of color face
throughout life. Touching on every facet of living—love,
marriage, fatherhood, family—these candid personal
contributions explore the essence of what it means to
be a man today.

**"*Journey to Empowerment* will lead you on a
healing journey and will lead to a great love of self,
and a deeper understanding of the many roles we
all must play in life."—*Rawsistaz Reviewers***

Coming the first week of May
wherever books are sold.

www.kimanipress.com